Dirk

Mimmi

Wolfgang

The Maui Quest

By D.W.M. Beck

Customer reviews welcomed at:
http://www.amazon.com/books

Like us on Facebook at The Maui Quest.

For Tutu and Grandpa,
who made us part of Maui

Kai's Maui

Prologue
THE MESSENGER DELIVERS

November 30, 1778
Hana, Maui
As Captain Cook sails several leagues offshore

A messenger hurried through the rainforest. He wore a loincloth, and he carried a small bundle wrapped in red tapa cloth. He moved quickly. His crew and canoe waited anxiously at shore for him to return so they could leave the war zone.

On the forest floor it was dark as twilight. Giant Halulu trees, prized for canoe making, reached to the canopy. The messenger saw only the path. He ran past hibiscus the color of blood. He was breathing hard. He thought only of his mission. As he neared the clearing, he heard the unmistakable cries.

            *   *   *

Chief Kamehameha studied his opponent. His opponent was growing tired. Kamehameha roared, raised his club, and charged.

Around him, hundreds of men grappled in the clearing. They wore helmets, capes, and loincloths, and were drenched in sweat. Their feathered helmets were shaped like crescents of the moon. Their feathered capes flowed, gleaming red, yellow, and green. They sidestepped the bodies of the fallen. Their weapons were stone spears, pikes, and throwing axes. Some used plant-fiber strangulation cords, battle clubs, slingshots, rocks, and bare hands. Screams pierced the growls and thuds.

Kamehameha was young, at his physical peak -- slim, strong, muscular, and quick. Military training had prepared him well. Although illiterate, he was educated. He could recite long oral chants. He knew astronomy, navigation, religion, and genealogy, including his own bloodlines as well as those of other persons of significance.

None of that mattered now. Only his training and experience in the arts of war would help him live to see the end of the day.

Tonight, if I live, he promised himself, I will feast on pig, coconut, and poi-fed dog. And drink narcotic Awa.

Had he been gifted with sight into the future, he might have seen that in seventeen years he would be the greatest leader Hawaii had ever known. He would become the first warrior king to unite all the islands in one kingdom. But Kamehameha lacked clairvoyance. His gift was killing.

Kamehameha stared into his opponent's eyes, mesmerizing him. In his stare, he focused his desire to kill. The other man was tall, with a foreboding scowl. Kamehameha drew close. He thought of the hundreds of men from his company of warriors who had so recently been killed in a humiliating defeat. He wanted revenge.

In one swift motion, Kamehameha brought the club down hard on the other man's forehead.

The skull cracked. Blood and brains oozed like egg from a shell. The man fell to the ground. With swift certainty, Kamehameha stabbed the back of his neck. A dark pool grew.

Kamehameha breathed. The man was another corpse added to the thirty Kamehameha had already killed today. He wiped his hands in the grass. If the others performed well, they might end four years of battles and skirmishes.

In his peripheral vision, he glimpsed an incongruous sight. At the outside edge of the battlefield, a prone man was creeping towards Kamehameha, face down in the dirt.

The groveling man did not wear the dress of a warrior. His status dictated his method of approach: he was a messenger. Why was he risking his life to interrupt a battle? Who would need to send Kamehameha a message so urgently?

"Be quick!" Kamehameha demanded.

"Lono, the god of fertility, has returned from the sea," the messenger reported. "He and his god-men are off the coast in their giant canoe, heading this way. It is just as those from the island of Kauai told. He has iron to trade, and weapons that kill

6

from a distance. His men want food and women, and he wants to meet our leaders."

Kamehameha paused, stunned. So the rumors from Kauai were true? Certainly, months ago powerful strangers had come and brought a foul sickness, which had spread from the foreigners to the women of Kauai who had given themselves to the foreigners. The sickness had spread, plaguing and killing men and women on every island. Also, Kamehameha had seen certain small objects, very strong and sharp, fashioned from a strange material not found in Hawaii except in certain pieces of wood which washed ashore infrequently. The people of Kauai had used the hard shiny material to produce fine fishhooks and cutting tools.

Kamehameha was most interested in weapons. From what he had heard, the weapons of the strangers were all-powerful. Someday, he would acquire those weapons and master his enemies entirely. As he thought about superior weapons, he felt intense desire to meet the Lono strangers and see their weapons for himself.

"How do you know it's Lono?" he demanded.

"The shape of his boat matches a religious icon, its sails are like tapa cloths, he comes from foreign parts like Lono, and he comes now, just when Lono's festival will begin…"

The evidence was convincing, yet Kamehameha doubted the fertility god would bring sickness. God or not, the strangers had new weapon technology that Kamehameha coveted. "Are you sure?" he demanded. If he was going to petition to halt the fighting, he must be certain.

The messenger shook. He was exhausted, not only from his trek through the forest, but from paddling and sailing hard without rest to reach Kamehameha before Lono passed this part of the island. He had to be careful in the presence of such a great man.

"What if your information is false?" Kamehameha demanded.

"I myself have gone by canoe right to the ship! I saw Lono with my own eyes," said the messenger desperately. "And

I brought you something from his ship." Carefully, he brought forward a red cloth bundle held close to his body. He unwrapped and held out the protected object.

Kamehameha stared at the strange item. It was unlike anything he had ever seen or imagined, made of materials unknown to the islands. Without thinking, he reached out to stroke it. The object was indisputable proof: the visitor who came by sea was truly Lono.

Kamehameha turned away. He needed to report the information so he could call a conference of warriors. They must stop the battle, and prepare.

"Keep it safe for me!" he commanded over his shoulder. He strode back toward the heart of the battle. The leaders must paddle out by canoe and visit Lono on his ship before the god-form disappeared again.

The messenger nodded. He re-wrapped the object in its red cloth. Quickly, he crawled away backwards the way he had come, mouth in the dirt as required by law. But even as the dirt met his lips, he was careful to keep the priceless object safe. As he slipped silently back into the rainforest, his ears rang with the cries of the wounded and dying.

Chapter 1
MAUI, THE PLACE OF DAD'S STORIES

The present
Kahului, Maui

Kai entered the ocean. Clear seawater washed his body clean. He felt new and buoyant. He stretched his stiff limbs and floated in the shallows, letting the water take him. The water was a blessing, a baptism. The first sensation of coldness wore off and it began to seem neither warm nor cold, like air. He was floating on a cloud. He was an ancient creature, meant for this element of water. The water cradled him. His hair billowed in the faint current of tiny shore waves.

The sea floor was a three-dimensional maze of corals. Coral shaped like brains and cauliflower and six-foot-tall mushrooms sprouted from the sand. Some seemed to cling to rocks. Kai wound his way between coral antlers and coral leaves. He was in a green tunnel, swerving between coral walls. Teal-and-purple parrotfish brushed against him. Striped fish swam nearby. Long yellow fins waved like ribbons in the current.

A beautiful girl swam close to him, her hair undulating like the fins of the fish. A swish of water brushed against him from the nearness of the girl, like an underwater wind.

On the ocean floor, a large dark shadow loomed. The dark shape swam closer.

Suddenly, a loud voice interrupted Kai's dream: "Fasten your seatbelts for landing."

The dream! Hadn't he had that same dream before?

Kai blinked and rubbed his eyes. Now, finally, at eighteen years old, he was about to see Maui for himself, after so many years of merely dreaming based on the stories Dad had told.

As soon as he stepped off the plane, Kai could smell the flowers. A delicate sweetness rode the warm wind --- something like rose, gardenia, and jasmine. A young woman stood nearby, selling leis: fresh orchids, tuberose, rosebuds, and white ginger. Her abundance of dark, glossy hair fell to her hips and rippled like a horse's tail. Her simple dress was bright red and patterned with flowers. Beneath her luxurious mane, her waist was delicate. The girl met Kai's eyes, and smiled.

Kai took a deep breath of the fresh moving air. He could smell the Pacific Ocean. Maui smelled earthy, and alive, like plant happiness. He had landed in a magical garden, windswept and clean. He was 2,400 miles from San Francisco, and 4,000 miles from Asia, as far as he could be from the rest of the world's pollution.

"You local?" the stranger beside him asked. He looked scruffy and friendly. His shirtless chest was like tanned leather. His swimming shorts were faded and shredded. A gold earring twinkled in one ear. He wore plastic flip-flops. Kai sized him up: a middle-aged, contented, penniless hippie-surfer.

Kai's own clothes weren't much different: baggy basketball shorts, faded t-shirt, and sandals. His backpack was old. His eyes and skin were brown, like his Hawaiian dad's. Clearly, Kai wasn't headed to the luxury resorts with the blond woman beside them in her spotless white linen and designer high heels.

"Need a ride?"

"I'm good," Kai said. "But thanks. My family's coming. My dad was from here." *Dad...*

Kai thought back over the last year. Dad's death had come too soon. The truth was, after the divorce, Dad hadn't kept Kai in his life. When he got cancer, Dad had tried to make up for it by moving nearby, but there hadn't been much time.

Kai had been so young when Dad left that sometimes, Kai felt the good times he remembered were a dream, or maybe a story he had made up from things Mom said. For a long time now, Dad was a person who showed up at odd times, every few years, said a few nice things to Kai about how proud he was and spent the night on the couch until he found somewhere else to stay. Sometimes he needed a few meals when he was between jobs. Dad's visits were fun, full of stories and laughter. But Dad always came when he needed something, not when they needed him. Then he would disappear again.

Last spring, Kai's high school graduation had come and gone. Just like at every other major event in Kai's life, he had secretly hoped Dad would show. Like always, he had been disappointed. His frustration boiled into anger. Kai promised himself he would never wait again.

His mom, as always, had tried to help him understand. She knocked on his door, softly, a few hours after he'd slammed it. Sitting on the edge of his bed, she'd looked at him with her steady eyes.

"It has nothing to do with you," she said, reading his mind. "It's not that Dad doesn't love you, or isn't proud of you. It's just that he can't be tied down ---"

"You've been telling me that since I was small!" Kai burst out. "But it's not true! He doesn't care!"

Mom sighed. Her hair was beginning to gray, and there were wrinkles around her eyes that Kai usually didn't notice. But in the warmth of her brown eyes Kai could see that she loved him and that she was proud of him. "He's not like other people, Kai. He just can't stay in one place, pinned down. He feels suffocated. He's like...a stray that can't come indoors. He tried hard to stay with us. It almost broke his heart to leave you..."

"Why are you always defending him?" Kai demanded. "He doesn't deserve it!"

"We can't control him, Kai. You just have to take what he can give. Let him go. I learned a long, long time ago that I would only be happy when I let him go. I went on with my life. I didn't try to make him change, because he can't."

"So I'm supposed to just forget about it? Forget my dad doesn't give a damn?" Why did Mom put up with him?

Why did she so obviously still love him?

"You won't be happy until you do," she said.

Kai studied her. Was that really Mom's view? Had she really totally forgiven Dad for everything? "How many years of therapy did that take you?" Kai asked slowly.

Mom laughed, as she often did at Kai's jokes. There had never been time or money for therapists, and Mom preferred to find her own answers. Mom's laugh was a comfortable sound that filled the room with warmth and suddenly, Kai felt the tension inside him lessen.

"Do you remember when Dad taught you to swim?" Mom asked.

Of course, Kai remembered. It was one of his first memories. For some reason, he'd been terrified of the water, but he had wanted to learn so he could go to a pool party with his friends. Mom didn't know how to swim. He'd begged Dad. Dad had taken the next day off work to teach him. Dad had been patient, starting with getting Kai to put his head under. They'd spent the afternoon together, with Kai riding Dad like a dolphin, swimming between his legs, and learning to use his arms. By the end of the day, Kai could swim half the length of the pool, and he'd never been afraid of water again. Mom was right --- Dad had loved him, at least then.

"I never told you this," she said, "but he got chewed out really badly at work for not showing up that day."

"Really?" Kai asked, surprised.

Mom nodded. Her eyes shone. "But he told me it was worth it, having that day to with you."

Kai wasn't quite convinced. "He hated his job," he said.

Mom laughed. "You're right," she said. "But he loved you."

She stayed on the edge of his bed, waiting. Like always, Mom had managed to make him feel better. Maybe she was right. Maybe Dad did care.

A few weeks later, his mom had given him the news.

"Dad's sick. Throat cancer." Mom paused, letting him process the information. "It's bad."

"He didn't tell us until now?" Kai asked. So maybe that's why he missed my graduation?

"He didn't know," said Mom.

"So, where is he?" Kai asked. Suddenly, being upset over graduation seemed so silly. Was Dad dying?

"He's moving back," said Mom. "He wants to spend time with you while he can."

Kai set his backpack on the curb to wait. The sunlight warmed his skin. Fast-moving clouds slid across the sky, glowing bright white. The palm trees rustled and waved. Kai let the tropical trade winds wash over him. Soon, he would meet the extended family he had never known.

The Maui surfer standing beside him smiled.

"No worries, man," said the man. "You'll like it here! Hey, my ride's here." As he moved away, his goodbye wave was the hang-loose sign: thumb and pinkie up, wrist tilted side to side.

Kai returned the gesture. But somehow the sadness of the last few months was suddenly back.

When Dad finally moved to the nearby hospice house, Kai was ready to see him. Didn't Dad know he'd been waiting his whole life to be asked to come close?

Dad looked so different. Smaller. Diminished. He had been a huge man in his prime. Yet his face was gentle. His dark eyes smiled as he greeted Kai with a wave. He had lost his hair due to the chemotherapy, and Kai was surprised to find that he missed Dad's ponytail. Watching the nurses inject pain meds into the port in his chest, the whole scene had felt wrong. Yet it was so good to know that Dad had moved here just to be close to Kai.

"Tell me what you've been up to," Dad said. And Kai began.

That's how their visits started. Then Dad would lay back in bed and rest while Kai talked. At first, Kai told him sports news. They watched games together on TV. Then, gradually, Kai found himself telling Dad about friends from his job at the restaurant. One day, he told Dad about his girlfriend. He told him about going to the park with Mom, and about what they were having for dinner. He told Dad what he thought about music. He found himself talking about things he hadn't thought about for years: things he'd done in the past that he wished Dad had seen, like when he pitched a no-hitter in seventh grade. It was hard at first to get used to talking so much without much input from Dad. But soon, Kai found himself saving things during his day --- ideas he wanted to share with Dad, stories he wanted to tell. Once, he told Dad how he thought life on earth would be in the future. Another day, he told Dad about a movie he'd seen. As long as Kai talked, Dad listened. Dad nodded and smiled, did the thumbs up sign and shook his head. Sometimes, Dad fell asleep despite struggling to focus and Kai felt disappointed. But usually, Dad was waiting for him and ready. Kai went when he could, usually on Sunday afternoons.

Although he'd hated Dad's weakness and the smell and the sadness of the place, it had been satisfying to tell Dad everything. The only thing Kai never talked about was why Dad ever left and the hole it had made in Kai's heart.

If only Dad had come back earlier!

Dad had been strong. He should be alive.

Kai had thought so many times in the last few weeks about the moment Dad died. It was a movie he couldn't stop replaying. It was hard to fall asleep because the movie was always there in all its detail. He wanted to forget.

Kai took out his cell phone and called his mom.

"I'm here," he said.

"Kai!" she said. He could tell from her voice that she already missed him. She had never been to Maui herself, and he knew she would have liked to come with him. Kai pictured his mom at home in the apartment. He hoped she would be okay without him. "I've got to get to work, but will you call when you've delivered the ashes? And Kai...I'm really glad you're doing this."

Kai waited beside the curb.

They were in the hospice room. Dad looked so weak. Every word was an effort.

"I wasn't a good father," he said. "I'm sorry."

Kai looked away. "You were okay," he lied. He'd spent so many visits telling Dad things, cheering him up. Kai had almost forgotten his own anger, and buried the pain. Did Dad really want to get into this now? Did they really have to talk about this?

"I loved you, always," Dad said. "Your mom...She was better for you. Good to be with her. But I never forgot you, you know? I was always thinking about you." He closed his eyes to rest.

Kai waited. There was so much he could say, now that Dad had opened this up. Harsh words. You messed up my childhood pretty good

*by running away! You screwed up! But the words stuck in his mouth.
Dad had listened so much...Kai thought of Dad moving here to be near
him. His heart sank. How could he ever explain?*

*"I am so proud of you," Dad said. "If there's one thing I'm
proud of in my whole life, it's you. I know I didn't make you who you
are...but I'm just so proud of you. Everything your mom has told me.
Everything you've told me, everything I've seen." Dad was working so
hard to make himself heard. He was fading.*

"I'm so glad you're my son."

Kai said nothing.

*"You forgive me?" his dad asked. His eyes were closed, as if he
could not look.*

*"Yes." The word came immediately, without thought. It suddenly
hit him that this was all he would ever get from his dad. His dad was
leaving. There would never be another interaction. The love between
them was so raw it hurt.*

Kai made himself still, holding the tears inside. As
suddenly as it had come, the sadness receded. He focused on
the warmth of the sunlight on his arm. He felt the wind washing
over him, and focused on the sweetness in it, and the smell of the
sea. *Soon, he would really snorkel in the ocean. A man on the plane
had said they might see humpback whales this time of year...*

An old green car pulled to the curb. A waving hand
stuck out the window, followed by the grinning face of a middle-
aged woman with shoulder-length hair and crooked teeth.

Kai smiled back. She looked like Dad.

"You sure are Nahoa's son!" Aunt Hepaula'ole said.
"Come on! Let's go home."

Chapter 2
THE STOLEN CAR

unt Hepaula'ole was a large, comfortable woman, with a deep, throaty voice. She reached through the open car window and squeezed his arm with a strong hand. Kai had a sudden hunch that his aunt used to wrestle his dad and win. Her brown eyes sparkled. "He looked just like you when he was young. I'm Hepaula'ole, but you call me Auntie H. Come here! Let's go home and get some food. We'll talk-story there with your Uncle Mano. Come on!" She had a faint accent, a lilt to her speech. Everything she said sounded slightly musical, unlike the flat mainland speech patterns at home. Was it that her voice rose in pitch at the end of each sentence? It was beautiful.

Kai put his backpack in the back seat and hopped in. His aunt pressed the gas and the car accelerated away from the curb, driving faster than the speed signs allowed.

A warm wind rippled the tall sugarcane in fields along the road and brushed Kai's face through the open window, washing away his worry and the tightness of the last few days. They passed an old sugar mill spouting dark smoke, and a strange earthy stench, the smell of rotting and burning, filled the car. Then the fresh wind was in their faces again with the scent of the ocean and the faint sweetness of flowers. His aunt herself was warm and welcoming, like the perfect day and the sea breeze. Kai felt a sense of excitement growing inside him. Finally, he was here! He could hardly wait to meet everyone, to explore, and to run and jump in the ocean.

"What you like to do in California? You surf? You're a big kid. What are you, six foot two? Got a girlfriend? You like school, sad to graduate last year?"

Kai laughed. "No girlfriend right now," he said. "No surfing. Not yet. We live too far inland."

"You live in an apartment? Got your own car?"

"Not my own," Kai said. "I'm saving up."

"You going to work here? Or you just want to hang with your Auntie H? Too bad we don't have anyone your age at home. Our babies are all grown up. Live in Oahu now. Maybe you'll visit them, too?"

"I'm only here for two weeks," said Kai. "I got a job as a dishwasher at home. I've been saving up for community college. I start in the fall. The restaurant gave me a couple of weeks off because of Dad." All that Kai had written in his letter to his aunt and uncle was that his dad wanted Kai to deliver his ashes.

"Dishwasher, that's good," said Aunty H. "Your dad, he did that once." She chuckled. "At a really nice restaurant. So much good food came through the kitchen, he got fat...Still was fat, last time I saw him. That was, mmm... twenty years ago. Just before he married your mom. He was in love! I never met your mom. Bet she's pretty. Long eyelashes, like you? I always thought he'd marry a local girl, stay here, you know. He had plenty of local girls to choose from. Girls, they loved him! But he wanted your mom. That's how I know she must be special. We were good friends, your dad and me. I always kept him out of trouble. But he was always in trouble anyway!" She laughed.

"What kind of trouble?" Kai asked.

"All kinds," said Aunty H. "Any kind there was. One time, you know, he stole a car. Drove it all over the island with some friends. Had themselves a party. Must have been about 13 years old. But you know what? There aren't that many roads on Maui. Not many places to keep a car secret." She laughed. "You know how I found out?" She glanced at Kai. "I was driving down the road and there he comes, a car full of local boys, they were all yelling out the windows. I thought: those boys are trouble. And then I saw my little brother driving!"

"What happened?" Kai asked.

"I helped him," said Aunty H. "I always did."

They were driving along the ocean now. The wind was strong and the ocean glittered with choppy, white-capped waves.

She was quiet for a moment, remembering. "We ditched the car on a sugar cane work road. Way back, hidden. Then I

17

drove them home. Next day, police found the car. They never found the boys."

"You were a good sister," Kai said.

"More like good mother," Aunty H said. "He kept me on my toes, little Nahoa. But you know what? I never could be mad at your dad. He was so full of jokes. So playful. We always had fun. I never could stay mad."

Kai understood exactly what she meant. He always had fun with his dad, too, when dad showed up, and Kai never could stay mad about the times Dad was absent.

A fleet of windsurfers, like brightly colored butterflies, skimmed the water far from shore. Closer to shore, a man waded out to his waist in the surf. He had a harness attached to his chest with cables that led to a kite. He held controls in his hands. The kite billowed in the wind. Suddenly, he leaped on a small surfboard and the kite pulled him away.

"You want to try kite sailing?" said Aunty H. "Harder than it looks. Hey, you tell me now about your Dad. How was he, before he died? You know, Uncle Mano, he and your dad had a fight. Long time ago. After that, I never heard from your dad much. I miss him. All these years, I've missed him. And now..." She shook her head.

Kai swallowed. He understood how Aunty H felt.

Chapter 3
THE COLLECTOR'S DREAM

The collector carefully unlocked the safe and peered into its depths. Here lay the collector's most beloved possessions. Nervously, the collector glanced around. Of course, no one was there.

Gently, almost like a parent stroking a sleeping newborn, the collector touched each one with the tip of a forefinger, taking in the pleasing smoothness of polished wood, stone, and shells worked to perfection by the artisans of long ago.

Soon, this collection might be complete: the world's premier private collection of ancient Hawaiian artifacts. With the addition of the right piece, the whole set would greatly increase in value. The collector was willing to do whatever was necessary.

"It won't be long," the collector told the beautiful, ancient objects, in a voice as soft and soothing as a mother's whispered lullaby.

Chapter 4
THE MYSTERY OF THE HAWAIIAN CHANT

The two-lane road led Aunty H and Kai home along the windswept Pacific.

"You got your dad's ashes with us right now?" Aunty H asked. Kai had just explained the procedure required by the airlines. "In your backpack?" she seemed surprised.

As Kai gazed out the window at the choppy sea, he remembered Dad's last words.

His dad met his eyes steadily. "I want you to do something. For me. For my memory…"

Kai waited, bracing himself. It was so like his dad: Dad had asked Kai to come because Dad needed something.

"I got a little money, not much, but enough…I want my ashes…Back home, to Maui." His dad's face collapsed with pain.

"Go to my sister. Bring my ashes. To the family heiau."

Kai's dad had always been into his Hawaiian ancestry. The Hawaiian Renaissance, his mom called it. Hawaiian pride. Resurgence of the old ways. Modern part-Hawaiians doing things their ancestors had done. Kai was part Hawaiian, of course, but that didn't mean much here in California. He didn't know anything about it. He had never been to Maui where his dad grew up. He'd never met any of his dad's people.

"You do it?" his dad asked, studying him. "For me?"

"Hey-ow?" Kai tried the strange word. "What's that?"

"Heiau. The old place. The temple. Rocks. Place for prayers. It's got to be the old one. Got to be the right one. Chant will help you find it. It's there." He pointed to the table beside his bed. On the table was a large envelope with Kai's name on it.

"Take it to your Aunt. She'll know what to do."

His breathing became labored.

20

"Promise me," he said. Suddenly, he was still.

"Dad?" Kai asked. "Dad!"

Just like that, he had gone. Kai heard the nurses rushing into the room. He touched his dad's hand.

He reached for the envelope. A piece of tattered paper fell to the floor. He recognized Dad's handwriting. Kai reached for it. Here was his message, his gift. Here was what Kai had left. There would be a lifetime of events he wished his dad could see. His dad would never see him go to college. He would never spend a single day just with Kai…Kai retrieved the paper with a start. He fought back tears. He could hardly see. He felt lost.

The chant was written entirely in another language. It was all meaningless. His dad had left him nothing but this?

It was written in Hawaiian.

Kai thought of the small wooden box full of ashes in his backpack, and beside it, the folded paper covered in scribbled words as strange as the twists and turns of his life.

Chapter 5
OLD SECRETS

"Almost home," said Aunty H.
Kai gathered himself.
She reached over and patted Kai's leg. "It will get better," she said. "You will always miss him, but it will get better."

They drove in silence.

"Where you going to put the ashes?" she asked.

"I...I don't know," Kai admitted. "He left me this chant. In Hawaiian. He wanted to be put in the family heiau."

"Heiau?" Aunty H paused. "Your Dad always had to do things differently. You know what his name means? Rebel! That's what he was. Always had to do it his own way."

Kai nodded. Dad had certainly been a free spirit. He had never let responsibilities bog him down. He'd always done things the way he felt. Came and went when it struck him as the right time. Did what he pleased, and asked others to work around it...Even in death.

"He liked the old ways," said Aunty H. "He teach you any of that stuff? No? He started to learn when he was a kid. Went to the kapuna, hung out, listened. I never had the patience, but he learned everything."

"Kapuna?" Kai asked.

"Wise woman. Your great-grandma, Meli, was one. She was Grandma Lokelani's mother. Meli knew all about the old ways." Aunty H winked at Kai. "In old Hawaii, the women were the ones who knew. Not the men. Matriarchal. Your great-grandma, she knew everything. Spoke Hawaiian. Knew about the old gods. How to respect yourself and the ancestors. She taught your dad. And he needed it! Kept him a little bit out of trouble. You want to know anything about the old ways, you could go to a kapuna, too."

"Oh," said Kai. "Can I see Great-Grandma Meli?"

"That one, she's dead."

"My dad said you would take me to the old heiau."

"He did?" Aunty H paused. "Maybe he meant Leilani? Our older sister, Leilani, she knew that stuff, too. She's the one that took your dad to the kapuna."

"Can we ask her?"

"She's in Afghanistan. We pray for her, every day."

They were in a crowded place now, where condos and apartment complexes lined the busy, dusty street. Grocery stores and little tourist shops were crammed together with box-shaped buildings. The buildings looked slightly old, and slightly out of style. In the few undeveloped lots along the road, the ground was parched. In the distance, the brown desert of the mountainside towered up to the sky: Haleakala. Would they go there? Would he get to see the view from the top? Maybe they would hike. Kai could hardly wait to see everything. He wondered if they would go to the beach tonight, or maybe tomorrow morning after he met the family he'd never known...

A fence covered in brilliant bougainvillea leaves glowed pink in the sunlight. Plumeria trees bloomed along the sidewalks. A white egret rose from a ditch and flew gracefully into a small swamp. Beyond the swamp, Kai glimpsed a sandy beach and the blue shimmering sea. The beauty, even here along the highway, was incredible.

"It's so beautiful here," he said.

Aunty H smiled. "We pau --- we're home! This is Kihei town."

Home.

Kai thought again of the chant. If the aunt who knew about the heiau was gone, he was going to need Aunty H's help. "Can you speak Hawaiian?" Kai asked.

"Nobody speaks Hawaiian," said Aunty H.

Kai stared at her. His dad had given him a chant in a lost language?

"Oh, I guess we'll find somebody to read your chant," Aunty H said. She explained the effort to keep the old language alive. Kids could learn Hawaiian in special public schools, learning all subjects in Hawaiian through elementary school. The State had two official languages, English and Hawaiian. "But if they didn't teach a few kids now, the language would die. Not even kapunas speak Hawaiian anymore. Just songs. Words. Blessings. Names..."

Where am I supposed to leave the ashes? You didn't tell me enough about the place!

He could hear his dad's voice. *Promise. You promised.*

Aunty H seemed to sense Kai's frustration.

"People use Hawaiian chants," she said. "But not very many know exactly what they mean." She considered. "Like when they're doing construction. New school or something. They bless the new place with a chant. Make it safe. Thank the old spirits, show respect...I have to think about who to ask. There must be someone, maybe at U of Hawaii or Bishop Museum? Somebody who studies and can read it. Or a kapuna who knows chants real well."

They stopped at a streetlight, and Aunty H looked at him. "I could tell a kapuna you're Hawaiian and that would help. Usually, they don't want to do it if you just show up from the mainland. You got to understand, and prove you believe before a kapuna will work with you. You got to have the right attitude."

"Attitude?" Kai asked.

"You know, respect the old ways. That you're going to use what they show you the right way."

"I just need to find the place for Dad's ashes," said Kai.

She turned down a quiet street. The houses along this street had yards with trees. The grass was rough, and some of the yards looked overgrown, but it was peaceful. Kai could feel again their proximity to the ocean. Between the yards were patches of sand.

"I guess I know a little Hawaiian," Aunty H mused. "My name, Hepaula'ole, is flower. You know what your name means?

No?" She shook her head in disapproval. "Your dad gave you a Hawaiian name and then he didn't tell you what it meant?"

They turned and passed a beautiful wrought iron gate with a dolphin on it. Coconut fronds rustled in the wind. On the grass, brown furry coconuts and green unripe ones lay here and there. Ahead stretched a large vacant lot covered in dry trees and underbrush. Wild chickens scurried here and there and pecking in the dust. A rooster crowed.

"Your whole name, I'm talking about. You call yourself Kai. That's a good Hawaiian name, too. It's your nickname? The real one's too long?" Kai nodded. Kai was the only thing he'd ever been called.

"What I'm talking about is your full name, your real name, Kaimi." The way she said it, it sounded like "*kye-EE-mee.*"

"You know what it means, your whole name?" Aunty H asked.

Of course, he had to write his legal name sometimes. But he never thought about its meaning.

"Kaimi is 'seeker,'" said Aunty H.

Seeker? Why had no one ever told him what his name meant? He knew it was a Hawaiian name, of course. But he didn't know it meant anything special. His dad must have chosen it. His dad had hoped that Kai would seek...What?

"You got an important name. You're meant to find something. You're meant to look, and figure things out." Aunty H said it with confidence, like a horoscope. She smiled at him. "Your Dad, he had plenty of secrets. Maybe he wanted you to figure out some."

I just want to find the heiau.

Aunty H pulled into a dirt driveway beside the vacant lot. At the end was a tiny one-story house with an orange tree and a lemon tree growing close beside it. Both trees were loaded with ripe fruit. Near the cracked concrete patio, several chickens from the forest were gathered.

"Why do you think...?" Kai started.

"Your dad, he always thought differently than most people." She turned off the car. It was so calm here. There was only the sound of the breeze. "Why did Nahoa make it so hard, huh? He was always making things hard!" She shook her head again and clucked. "Your chant, I bet he got that from your Great-Grandma Meli, the kapuna. When he learned the old things. Or maybe somebody gave it to our sister Leilani. She's the oldest, and she gave it to him. I'll ask her when I can. But it might be a while. She's not allowed to contact us all the time. Anyway, it was probably Meli. Maybe your dad was the only one in the family who was interested in it."

"He should have told me what it meant," Kai said.

Aunty H looked at him. "Maybe he didn't know," she said. "Maybe he just knew it has power, and wanted to give it to you."

Or maybe he ran out of time, Kai thought.

"Hey, you cheer up! We'll try to find somebody to tell us what it means. We'll find out. I'll help. You're a good son, to care. Your Dad was lucky. I got an idea. I'll bet you Mom --- your Grandma Lokelani --- will know what to do. She's got a heiau up at Iao she goes to sometimes. I've been there with her. I'll tell her you want to go."

She thought for a moment.

"Maybe your dad's priest will understand the chant. It's possible. He taught your dad when he was a boy. Knew Nahoa well. Saved his life, even. He knows Nahoa's secrets. We'll go there tomorrow."

Uncle Mano stepped from the screen door, shooing the chickens. He wore low hanging shorts and flip-flops. His smile was big and powerful. In an instant, a dark purple tattooed arm wrapped Kai in a hug. "Kai," he said. "Glad you came."

Chapter 6
DAD'S PARTY

"We told them to come now to meet you," said Aunty H. "I don't know how many will come. This won't be family because they couldn't come tonight. Just some people who knew him." Uncle Mano set a cooler full of beer on the picnic table under the orange tree. Aunty H carried out a platter of fried Spam slices, a tray of Portuguese sweet bread, and a stir fry dish.

A car-load of elderly guests arrived, giving hugs to Aunty H, Mano, and Kai. As they chatted with Mano by the cooler, Kai followed his aunt back to the kitchen to carry out the last load, a beautiful guava cake and paper plates.

"That looks so good," said Kai. His mouth was watering. He was suddenly ravenous.

"Your dad, he loved this cake," said Aunty H. "I haven't made it in years. He used to help me when he was a little boy." Suddenly, tears began to roll down her face. Aunty H shook herself, and tried to swallow them. She blew her nose. "He ever make this one for you?"

"I didn't know he could cook," said Kai.

"He helped me all the time, until I got married. He was about fourteen when I left..."

Kai set the cake in the center of the table. He liked being here, but he wasn't sure who to talk to or what to say. The first guests were visiting among themselves, having a good time.

An old man drove up in a dented Pontiac. He carried a large, heavy pot to the table. His hair was white, and his face was deeply wrinkled. He seemed to have a joke inside him that couldn't wait to burst from his lips.

"Oh, Uncle, I'm so glad you came!" said Aunty H.

"Uncle?" said Kai.

Aunty H laughed. "No, no, not your real uncle! That's just what we say, when we love someone. Uncle, auntie…He was our neighbor. He knew Nahoa when we were kids."

"Nahoa used to steal from my guava tree," said the old man, with a smile.

Aunty H poked him in the ribs. "You never told me that!" she said. "So that's where we got all those guavas. I made some good guava cake today."

The man winked and pointed to his pot. "I brought dog," he said. "Marinated. Special family recipe."

Dog? Kai had heard that some Filipino men ate dog meat but wasn't that illegal in the US?

"Thanks for the hot dogs, you old devil," said Aunty H. She led the old man to a folding chair near the cooler.

A skinny middle-aged woman with a warm smile came up and hugged Kai. She wore a floral shirt, pearl earrings, and makeup. She looked like a pretty schoolteacher. She introduced herself. "I was Nahoa's friend," she said. "When we were kids." There was something so genuine about her, Kai trusted her immediately.

She loved Dad, so much she loves me, too.

"We hung out together from middle school on. Until he got into trouble," she added. Just then, a friend arrived and she excused herself. There were many cars now. People were parking along the street and walking to the house, carrying platters.

What kind of trouble? Kai wondered.

A small, wiry man with muscular arms approached him. He looked about Dad's age. His eyes were very dark, almost black. As he drew close, Kai wondered how many beers he had already had. The party had just started, but he seemed like he'd had a few, maybe before he'd arrived.

He slapped Kai on the back. "Hey, bro! I was a friend of your dad's when we were young."

Kai noticed the hibiscus flower tattooed on the man's arm, and another symbol he recognized.

"Where'd you get that? My dad had that, too," said Kai.

28

The man smiled. "He never told you?" he asked.

What more didn't you tell me, Dad? "He just said he got it here on Maui," said Kai.

Dad's friend seemed to size up Kai. He dropped his voice. "It was a long time ago...We were in this...club."

You mean gang?

"Nahoa, me, some others. We were just kids, you know. Looking for something to do. Didn't know what we were doing."

What'd you do, Dad?

"We did different stuff. Pranks, mostly. Sometimes we'd camp. We had this place on the North Shore we took over...We'd go looking for lava tubes and crap like that. Like we were explorers. I mean, we were just boys, really. And we stole some stuff. From tourists, mostly. Like they'd leave a bag on the beach and we'd collect it while they were swimming. Just easy stuff like that." He looked thoughtful. "The thing about Nahoa was, he was never afraid. I mean, never. No matter what happened or who he was dealing with. He was absolutely fearless." To Kai's surprise, the man's eyes filled with tears. "Man, you look so much like him," he said. "It's freaky."

Dad's friend took a sip of his beer, shook his head, and wiped his eyes roughly with his tattooed wrist.

"He was so tough, but he was a deep thinker. Sometimes you couldn't tell what he was thinking...He had all this weird spiritual stuff going on. Dreams, visions. I mean, I know a lot of people who see that crap, but Nahoa, that stuff happened even when he was straight. I mean, he wasn't always on anything and he'd still have all this stuff happen to him. This one time, we were camping and he woke me up in the middle of the night. He'd seen something. He was totally wired. Wide awake. It was some kind of sign. Something big." He struggled to remember, and then shook his head. "I forget. Me, I don't go in for all that old Hawaiian stuff. But Nahoa sure did."

Kai waited.

"So anyway, we were pretty tight for a long time and then Nahoa he got in with the priest. He didn't hang with me much after that. Then he left for the mainland. He asked me to come with him, but I didn't want to leave." He paused. "Hey, Kai, you need anything, you come to me with that face like Nahoa and I won't say no." He went to get another beer.

Kai got himself a piece of cake. The frosting was pink and thick, rich with guava jelly. An old woman, bent but bright-eyed, smiled at him. She wore a faded dress and smelled sweet, like plumeria flowers. She beckoned him aside, away from the noise of those near the table.

"I'm a friend of your grandma's," she said. "I loved Nahoa. So much spirit! But difficult. One time, he gave your grandma such a scare. We were having a picnic down Makena side. A whole bunch of us."

Kai listened. The Nahoa she knew was a little boy, nothing like the one Kai knew as Dad. So which one was more real, the one these people knew, or the one he knew? How could one person be so different to each person who knew him? Now that he was gone, could Kai stick all the stories together to understand?

"We were sitting up in the shade and Nahoa and another boy disappeared. There were a few out surfing, so we were afraid they'd been washed out to sea. Nahoa was four. He could swim, of course, but the surf was up...We looked all over and finally found them about a mile away. In a little cave, hiding. They had walked all the way there. We'd almost given up hope. And Nahoa wasn't a bit glad to see us. He ran away! He always knew what he wanted. He always did what he wanted. I used to come over and he'd be..." The old woman looked at Kai. "Oh, honey, I'm sorry!" she said. "It's still hard, isn't it? I didn't mean to..."

"It's okay," Kai said.

"You know, I loved him, too," she said.

Kai nodded. He felt suddenly alone in the crowded party. All these people had gathered for Dad, and Dad belonged to them as much as to him. Yet they were all strangers.

He felt empty. A bubble of raw loneliness expanded inside his chest. *Why didn't I ask you to talk to me about your life, when I visited you all those times at hospice? All I did was tell you about what I was doing...I never asked about you! And now I know so little about you, Dad, and you're not here to tell me. Who will tell me now that you're gone?*

A loud burst of laughter erupted near the cooler. A group with beers was having a good time.

Kai turned away. The old woman saw his sadness. She reached out and took his hand.

Inexplicably, at the touch of her hand, Kai's eyes fill with tears.

Chapter 7
PLANNING A NEW RESORT

Wailea, Maui

Just a few miles south of Kihei, two businessmen met at the Grand Wailea, one of the largest—and most expensive—resorts on Maui.

The Grand Wailea attracted visitors from around the world. The resort's pool included slides, rapids, and a freshwater baby pool with a sand beach and a view of the nearby ocean. Guests dropped into the pool from a rope swing, or crossed on a wobbling bridge to a tunnel with the feel of Disneyland. A restaurant built on a pier floated in a pond stocked with colorful tropical fish, a stone's throw from the waves of the Pacific.

The lobby, like the sidewalk running between the resort and the beach itself, was of course open to the public. Like most of the major resort lobbies, it seemed built on a scale for giants, and contained art and collectibles, including large gilded statues of decadent chubby beauties reclining nude. As is common throughout Maui, the lobby was open to the fresh air of the Pacific without walls or even screens: because the weather is perfect at all times of year, no temperature control was ever needed.

The landscaped grounds were lavish. In the midst of groomed lawns, the Chapel, a popular place for weddings, was surrounded by its own small koi-stocked moat. Each of the Chapel's windows depicted stories from Hawaiian mythology. Where the lawns met the beach, a paved sidewalk followed the shore leading along Maui's most luxurious strip of resorts, past the Four Seasons with its Dolphin fountains, and the Freemont Kealani with its ocean-side units each with their own private dipping pools. Walkers and joggers glimpsed flowers, paths lit by torches, sweeping lawns, and avenues of royal palms, as well as a rugged natural cove of sharp lava rock between crescent beaches of golden sand.

On this particular night, on the sand in front of the Grand Wailea, a group of vacationers dressed for dinner sipped their drinks on chaise lounges and waited for sky and ocean to turn sunset colors. Some local boys ran and jumped their skim boards over the faces of the waves breaking near shore, doing tricks in the air as if they were skateboarders on ramps of water. A newlywed couple lay tangled in a hammock at the sand's edge, oblivious to the world. Their designer shoes lay askew, kicked off in the grass. The hammock swayed gently between the palm trees.

In the most exclusive area of the hotel, the private club-owned Tower, the two businessmen sat on an outdoor lanai, looking down at everything and watching the sea.

The developer was a giant man, six foot four and husky, with an unusually deep voice.

There was a faint knock at the door to their private suite.

"Not now!" the developer yelled.

"Service," said a faint voice behind the door.

"I said, not now," barked the developer. He rolled his eyes. "Some private butler!" he snapped. "Can't they give us a little peace!"

The investor was a Chinese businessman. He nodded in agreement, amused by the developer's strong reaction. Such hot-headed people as this were easy to manipulate. His obvious temper would make him easier to manage. The investor would remember the weakness.

The investor was good at reading people. He'd worked with many throughout his long and varied career as developer, factory owner, and CEO of several corporations. In recent times, foreign investors like himself had been behind most of the new projects on Maui.

"Next time I bring my personal assistant with me from China," he suggested. He spoke in broken English. "He do everything, just how you want. Everything."

In silence, the two men gazed across the water. The sun, a red blob on top of a yellow backdrop, gradually sunk in the sky, edging closer to the shadowed ocean. Below them, tiki torches around the resort gradually lit, small yellow lights from their height. Down by the water, a flame danced in the darkness, part of the fire-breathing ceremony. The developer eyed his freshly seared ahi with macadamia nut butter, but he wasn't hungry. He turned to the investor.

"I've found several possible locations for the new resort," he said quietly in his deep voice. "One is just south of here. Above a lava field. We can tour the site tomorrow."

"Good," the investor said. "Just make it best resort in Hawaii."

"Yes. My team will help you design the most spectacular resort the islands of Hawaii have ever seen. The private chefs, the spa, the lava rock-climbing wall, the outdoor dance club, exotic breed stables, the invitation-only private game room for selected guests…and for a nice little eco touch, Hawaiian archeology and mythology lectures. All of it will attract the world's most privileged travelers."

The two men envisioned the future and its profits with satisfaction.

"Of course," the developer went on, "such a large venture will have extra costs. Water, for example. The only site large enough will require extra infrastructure. A long extension of the existing systems. We'll have to pump water in, and that will cost more, but if you want a project of this size…"

"Yes," the investor said, deliberately. "Whatever it takes. We need more land. Our clientele, they like only the best. Dubai, Lebanon, they've experienced the best everywhere. Needs to be big to compete."

"Of course," said the developer. "We can't do anything as large as you're thinking right on the beach. There aren't any undeveloped areas with water access like you envisioned. We'll have to run a shuttle from your resort to a few different beaches. You can make it high end. A fleet of limos, maybe? With free drinks. Running every fifteen minutes to Makena's Big Beach."

"A good beach?" asked the investor.

"World class," assured the developer. "A mile long stretch. State Park all around it, with a small cinder cone to hike at one end. Undeveloped so it looks like Africa with cactus forest behind the sand. Or maybe the edge of the world. No sign of modern development. Actually, visually it is pure wilderness…Lots of whale action, and big waves for boogie boarding." He paused, and smiled. "It used to be a nude beach with a large hippie encampment. Some of your clients from the Middle East will enjoy that bit of kitsch. Nude blond youngsters frolicking in the sand. You might even decorate the limo interiors to reflect that."

The investor nodded.

"You might even run limos to a few different beaches in the area. They're all State-owned, public access. Every damn beach on the island is open to everyone, by law. So that's no problem. I imagine your guests will be drawn by the amenities and the reputation. The allure of staying at one of the world's most exclusive resorts. Anyone can go to the beach, after all…"

"Yes," said the investor.

"I'll get to work on arranging the land purchases, then. Permits. I know a good consulting firm to do the archeological survey. These places are always packed with archeological problems, even when they're not documented ahead of time. But I've worked with this firm before. They'll get us the permits. Without complications. We should begin construction as soon as possible, correct?"

"Yes. As soon as possible. I've heard rumors. Zoning changes coming very soon."

"Okay. I'll get right on the permitting. ASAP. Speaking of the project, could you send us preliminary payment so we can get started?"

"No problem," said the investor. "I set up access to account. You send me detailed cost accounting. I put money in account. But no fee until you finish. Must be done quickly. I hire you because you work fast. Otherwise, no."

The giant man nodded. Of course he'd do the job fast for the investor. That's what his reputation was built upon. It was clear what he needed to do.

Silence hung over the lanai. In the distance, the giant red sun sunk below the horizon. The beat of drums from a dinner show near the beach drifted up to them, mixing with the sounds of the waves.

Chapter 8
OWL

As Kai lay in bed at Aunty H's house, motionless air surrounded him. He heard the ticking of the alarm clock on his nightstand. He stared at the ceiling with eyes wide open.

Voices echoed though his head. The nurse: *You look like your dad...* His dad before his death, mouthing the words *promise me, promise me*, over and over... *Bring my ashes. To the family heiau.* Aunty H, in her throaty voice, saying *You got an important name. You're meant to find something. You're meant to look.* Uncle Mano saying *Kai...Glad you came.* Again, his dad. *Promise me...*

A shadow moved outside his room. Kai sat up.

He slid open his door. He moved silently. Suddenly he heard something in the hallway. He tensed for a second. He looked around. It was only the cat.

He slipped out the screen door and felt the cool coarse concrete beneath his bare feet. His aunt had warned about centipedes. He put on the flip-flops waiting outside, the ones his aunt called slippers.

It was about ten degrees cooler out here. The air remained warm and stagnant. The withered gray blades of the lawn brushed the sides of his feet as he walked away from the house.

Suddenly he stopped. A night sky full of stars stared at him. He stood paralyzed by their beauty. He'd never seen anything like this in California. The sky was deep purple and the stars gleamed like thickly scattered sand.

A large gecko clung to the wall under a round yellow light. Behind him, giant toads croaked. A block away, a car sped down South Kihei road. In the sky, millions of small specks of light greeted him. *Could Dad be up there?* he wondered. *If he is, what does he want?*

What do you want me to do? he asked the stars. He hesitated for a second, and the stars seemed to burn brighter. A low, rumbling voice inside his head.

Promise me...

A warm presence. Light. A figure in the trees. A shape. *What?* He squinted in the darkness. *Am I dreaming? I can't move.*

An owl! Snowy wings, talons of light. Eyes. Beak of piercing blackness. Body of white fire. *I can't get away.*

Kai's heart pounded. *I am seeing through. Beyond. Into what?*

Too close! Piercing gaze. *I am the prey.* An eyeball. Blood vessels. Shards of glass. His father's glazed eyes. Cold fingers. Underwater. Water around him. Pushing down! A wet blanket over his mouth. Air! He needed air! What do you see when you die? Terror inside. *Why am I seeing this?*

Suddenly, he could move again. *Free!* He spun around. No one was there.

The owl was gone. Through the trees where the owl had been, he glimpsed a small sliver of moon.

He was very much alone. His heart was beating fast.

"Kai," Dad's voice came from long ago, when Kai was a little boy sitting on his lap. "I will always be there for you. You are my little owl..."

Why had he been so afraid? *If it was you visiting me, Dad, I wouldn't be afraid, would I? Was it you?*

He remembered what Dad has said once. "You know, Hawaiians, they know owls are lucky. They're the ancestors, the protectors. They guide you, keep you safe. Some people think it's angels. But it's owls. You see one, you're lucky. Me, I been looking my whole life and I never see an owl...You are my little owl. Promise."

Kai shivered.

As suddenly as it had started, it ended, and he was alone with the beating of his heart.

Chapter 9
CLUES FROM THE PAST

At dawn, Aunty H woke Kai.
"Grandma can't wait to meet you. I'll take you on my way to work." Kai woke quickly. He couldn't wait to meet her, either. What would Dad's mom be like?

His father had been with him in a dream, showing him how to throw a baseball. Had he really done that once? Kai did know how to pitch a ball, and he certainly hadn't learned it from his mom. He struggled to remember. But when? When did Dad do that? Wasn't it just some boyfriend of mom's trying to impress her? No, it had been Dad. Dad had held his arm and moved it through the right positions, guiding him. Just like in the dream.

"Aunty H?" Kai asked, coming into the kitchen. "Did Dad know how to play baseball?"

"He played baseball," she said. "Why? You never saw him play? Didn't he play with you?" She was stirring a pan of eggs cooked in bacon grease. The warm smell filled the little kitchen. Kai hoped they would take it outside and eat on the picnic table under the orange tree.

"It's weird," Kai said. "I had forgotten. But then I dreamed it," he said.

Aunty H stopped stirring and stared at him. "Your dad, he wanted you to remember he loved you," she said. "So he came in a dream."

Kai wished he could believe her.

Aunty H led him outside. A tiny brown gecko scurried off the picnic table. She brushed a crumb of Spam from last night's party off the table with a leaf before she put a plate down in front of him. It looked greasy but good. A group of chickens smelled the food and came cautiously closer, watching from the sides of their heads.

"Nahoa, he loved a different way," she said slowly. "He loved me, too, you know. I was his closest friend, before your mom." She held up two fingers, tightly together. "Like this. Together. Same friends. Same schools. He could have gone off island to get a better education through the Kamehameha Schools. But he stayed with his friends, and me. He didn't want to leave us."

Aunty H's eyes grew misty.

"But sometimes, Nahoa just had to go alone. He needed to. Didn't listen, just went. Like when he finally left Maui. But that didn't mean he stopped loving."

It was dim and cool in the yard. Roosters were crowing in the forest beside the house. One crowed nearby, and another answered farther away. Sometime in the early hours it had turned cool enough that he was glad to have packed a sweatshirt. In the distance, Haleakala was a dark looming shape against the early morning sky, like a giant's shoulder. The yard smelled like damp earth, chickens, and rot, and sweet ripe citrus. Kai watched as a single sunbeam peeked over the summit: dawn.

Aunty H walked the yard slowly, picking up the scattered litter from yesterday's gathering. She looked older when she had to bend. Kai noticed how stiff she was. Aunty H piled the beer cans on the table, a testament to those who had come to remember Nahoa.

Kai grabbed his backpack with the ashes and chant and hopped in the car.

Now I can do what I came for.

They sped along the ocean, away from Kihei, along the coast. The beach ran for miles along the highway. Couples were strolling along the beach in the perfect brisk morning weather, with long empty stretches between them. Kai could hardly wait to get moving, and to explore.

"I want to walk here tomorrow," he said.

"Best beaches are a little south. Better for swimming. More sand. See those trees?" Kai noticed the long line of twisted, spiky looking trees along the shore. "Those trees, they drop thorns. In the sand. You walk there, you wear your slippers. Don't go barefoot. Missionaries planted those trees to make people wear shoes." She laughed. "That's what people say. Maybe it's not true, I don't know."

"Missionaries?" Kai asked.

Aunty H sighed. "So many missionaries have come to Maui. People got a lot of jokes about the missionaries. They were really powerful, once. Changed the whole culture, set rules for everybody, even the rulers had to listen to them. All gone now but we still got the thorns."

The colors were soft now, the land still shadowed and sleepy. Near the horizon, a pale sliver of moon hung over the West Maui Mountains. Their slopes, like Haleakala's, looked like dry, steep deserts. Kai noticed the white spinning shapes of a wind farm perched near the sky. They passed a wetlands park with a boardwalk.

"It looks so different from yesterday," said Kai. Yesterday afternoon, the ocean had been a rough, glittering green surface. This morning, it looked calm and blue, a giant's swimming pool.

"Morning is calm," said Aunty H. "Afternoon, trade winds. Then you get blowing sand."

They entered a vast field of tall green cane, a flat inland part of the island. Kai thought about the chant and the family heiau. Would it be around here? "Did our family always live in Kihei?" Kai asked.

"No!" said Aunty H. "Kihei is new. We're all scattered around, and family lived in different parts a long time ago." Kai hoped that wouldn't make it harder to find the heiau. "All around Maui. For more than a thousand years," Aunty H added.

Dad hadn't said exactly how old the heiau was.

"It's good you're interested in old stuff," said Aunty H. "Just like your dad. I guess our family lived just like everybody, moving around Maui to where the work was."

"I feel so stupid. I don't know anything," Kai said.

Aunty H studied him. "They don't teach anything about Hawaiian history in California?" She seemed to be deciding if he was serious.

If I'm going to find the right place, I need to know. My family's history will lead me to the heiau Dad wanted.

She looked thoughtful. "You know everybody raised taro? Sweet potatoes, fish. Fish farms. Reef fish. The old kings, they ordered the fish ponds. Back then, there were lots of Hawaiians. Just as many people here back then as today. But they were farmers, and fishermen."

"Then haoles --- white people --- came," said Aunty H, "and every last thing was changed."

The way she said it, it sounded distasteful, like "how-lees." Kai knew without asking, by the tone of her voice, exactly what she meant.

Chapter 10
PROTECTING THE SACRED OBJECT

Year 1790
Olowalu, Maui

U nknown to the crowd, today would be remembered. Hundreds of Hawaiians waited restlessly on shore to launch their canoes.

Off shore, the strangers' big ship rocked in the waves.

The strangers had come here to collect their stolen rowboat. A week ago, a Hawaiian from this village had killed the strangers' night watchman and taken the rowboat. The strangers were angry. They wanted revenge. They wanted their boat. An informant led them here. Even without a shared language, everyone understood. But the boat had already been disassembled for its iron nails. The rowboat could not be returned.

The Hawaiians on the beach had been waiting three days. Their Chiefess, Kalola, was cautious. The Chiefess could sense the anger of the strangers. She had prevented immediate interaction. Now, hopefully, the strangers' anger would have cooled. This morning she had sent her husband in a canoe to deliver what she could: the stolen boat's keel and the stripped thighbones of the murdered man.   Would the strangers be satisfied?

Halulu the guardian was impatient. Although he had nothing to trade with the strangers, he wanted to paddle out to see them. Since Cook's arrival, this was only the second ship to come to Maui. Everyone was talking about the foreigners, their weapons, their iron, and their strangeness. Halulu was an honored man, yet he had never met foreigners. In the past few years, many less important people had seen ships and foreigners.

Halulu should see for himself, too. Who could tell when another ship might come? It might be a lifetime! He wanted to go now, while he had a chance.

Suddenly, a commotion swept through the crowd on shore.

"What is it?" Halulu asked the man near him.

"The strangers gave the signal! We can go out!" the man said. "They are directing us to the side of the ship."

Halulu's heart leapt. They had decided to be reasonable! The crowd swirled with excitement. Everyone started moving at once. Families climbed hurriedly into the canoes. All must hurry, before the strangers changed their minds! The opportunity might disappear. A rush of people hurried into the surf. Children squealed. Women chattered. A man was pushed by the throng into the sea and came up laughing, wiping his face.

Halulu must hurry. He thought of his job: to protect the chief's object. Wrapped in red cloth, it was immensely powerful and valuable. Halulu guarded it. When they traveled, he carried it. Yet he had never seen beneath the cloth. He had been warned. He must never look. It was too powerful for his eyes.

He considered quickly. The object was near the altar, where no one but a priest could go. No Hawaiian would touch it. But these were uncertain times. When strangers came to shore, they sometimes took things, even sacred things. If they needed wood, they sometimes grabbed the wooden gods without asking permission. If the strangers came to shore, Halulu would be quick. He would carry the bundle into the forest and hide it. Now, he would leave it on shore where it would be safest.

Halulu ran to the canoes. There was one spot left. He climbed in and they began rowing swiftly to the ship. The water churned with canoes loaded with villagers. The first canoes had already reached the ship. More and more were arriving. The strangers were directing them. They wanted all the Hawaiians on one side of the boat. Halulu hoped there would be a narrow space where they could get a good view.

The men on the ship stood still, in formation. What were they doing? They raised their guns. Was this a ceremony? A command rang out through the air. The Hawaiians froze.

Suddenly, the sailors fired their cannons and muskets at close range into the crowd.

Shot and ball filled the air. Screams exploded. Bloody bodies fell in the waves. Children screeched. Dead and dying covered the water. Men were paddling, trying to back away. The water churned pink. A man's head splattered open like a ripe fruit. Bits of the head rained on Halulu. Halulu vomited into the sea.

The strangers stood perfectly straight on their ship. Their leader shook his fist and shouted angry, incomprehensible words.

Halulu realized their boat had not been hit. "Paddle!" Halulu yelled. He could no longer hear. He glanced back once to see if they would shoot again. The distant form of the strangers' leader was like a small evil stick. His voice was drowned out by nearby wailing. A woman in Halulu's canoe held her child. The child's eyes were wide with shock. Blood ran from the place that had been the child's hand. The child would die soon. The sea was red.

They reached the shore.

He knew what he had to do. He could not help the dying or the dead.

He ran to the object. He did not know what it was, but he knew it was from the strangers. Was this the source of their terrible power? If the strangers massacred over a lost rowboat, what would they do for this?

Without waiting, Halulu grabbed the object and ran. He ran out of the clearing, through the farms, and into the forest. He did not stop, even long after he left behind the cries of those who were dying and of those who survived.

Chapter 11
BLACK SNOW

The present
On the way to Iao

They whizzed along the highway with their windows open. "Tell me more," Kai said quietly.

Aunty H told him about Captain Cook, La Perouse, Chinese traders. "The Maui chiefs, they liked to trade. They were always fighting the other chiefs, keeping the others down. They wanted guns, so they logged. They logged the whole island. Kihei town is desert now, but it was all forest."

She described the trees --- sandalwood, ebony, and other hardwoods. Sandalwood was pretty, bright yellow for incense and fishhooks. Chinese wanted it. But sandalwood grew back too slowly. "20 years to grow one inch," said Aunty H. "Hardly any left at all now." Once the trees were gone, the soil washed away. She pointed at the dry hillside. "Logging made that desert."

"That's awful," said Kai.

Aunty H agreed. "Most things that happened after Cook were awful," she said.

Somewhere in this history is Dad's heiau.

"After logging, came whaling," said Aunty H. "Bad time. Especially for women. Ships would stop and dump sailors."

Kai put his fingers out the window and played with the warm wind. In the beauty of this magical place, on his way to meet Grandma, he felt very far from the dark time his family had once survived.

"Then nobody wanted whale oil anymore," Aunty H went on. "The family went back to farming. Sugar and pineapple. Big farms, owned by haoles. Haoles brought in all kinds of workers: Portuguese, Chinese, Japanese, and Filipinos. That's how you got Portuguese in you, did you know that?"

Kai shook his head, and laughed. "I'm part Portuguese?"

"Of course," Aunty H said. "How else you get those freckles?"

They drove for a while in silence. But Kai was still curious. *I want to know everything you can teach me about this place and how my family lived. I can't find a place from the past if I don't know the past.*

Aunty H told him about the growth of tourism. "First, rich people came by boat. Then airplanes brought all kinds of people. Now, there's plenty of work at the resorts. And it's crowded at the beach," she finished.

His family's way of life for the past two centuries seemed jumbled, full of drastic and unpredictable changes, as if Maui had been battered by a series of violent storms.

A strange, dark snow began to fall. It was black and curly. It hit the windshield. Kai stared at it in disbelief. The sky was cloudless.

"Ugh," said Aunty H. "I hate this stuff! Ash. So dirty! From burning the cane. Big mess. Falls here all the time. Sometimes the wind takes it to our house, too. Before they harvest, they burn the leaves off the cane. Makes it less work to harvest. Lots of people want Maui to stop with sugar. No money left in it anyway. Government pays to keep the price up. Only one sugar mill left on Maui. A few hundred people work there. They got to have jobs. So I don't know."

Along the road, a break in the green wall of sugarcane revealed a dark black field of burned stubble. Behind it, flames engulfed another field where they were harvesting. Tractors worked near the fire. Along the wall of flames, a giant flock of white egrets stood snow-white.

"They're waiting for cooked gecko," Aunty H said, looking at the egrets. "Fire's a good thing for the egret."

Kai thought about the history of Maui. Every era seemed to be a trade-off, a switching of power from one group to another. Good for some, bad for others.

"I'm glad you want to know about our family, and its history," Aunty H said. "So many people, they come here from off-island, and they just pass through. They don't want to know anything about what happened here, about the people who have been here all along. Just want to have some fun and then leave. They don't care enough to find out. I'm glad you're interested. You, you want to find out how we lived, what it was like."

They drove past developments of fancy view homes and into old Wailuku: a broad straight street, a church, and an old school. They turned uphill.

Aunty H smiled. "Kai," she said, "the way you care, you really are a local boy inside your heart."

Chapter 12
IAO VALLEY AND GRANDMA'S SECRET

"We're almost there," said Aunty H. Kai felt a sense of nervous anticipation. What would Grandma be like? Hopefully, she would be like Aunty H. Would they have a good time together? Would she be able to help him?

The road led into the mountains. On either side of the car, steep black and mossy-green cliffs climbed up into the gray wall of clouds. A river ran on the left side of the road, water flowing and pooling around smooth gray stones and small boulders. In the valley, trees with thick canopies and rough bark wound into a dense shady jungle mass. Kai looked off into the distance. The mountain tops looked so temptingly close. He could almost make out individual trees. Was it an illusion?

The car jerked. His aunt swerved from the main road into a short gravel driveway. Ahead was a small isolated cluster of bungalows, a neighborhood from Wailuku thrown into the rainforest. They parked in front of a moldy white house standing amid a grove of trees with leaves like tassels.

"We're here."

Kai thanked his aunt.

It was time to meet his grandma.

Kai knocked on the front door, rubbing off flakes of white paint. He heard his Aunt's car backing out of the driveway behind him, receding into the distance. He heard a squish and a rustle from inside the house, someone standing up from a couch. Slow footsteps walked to the door. Kai waited, wondering who Grandma would be. The door creaked open.

There was an awkward pause. Kai's first thought was that his grandma looked a lot like his dad, but old. She had dark brown eyes and wrinkly skin, a small worn face, and coarse gray hair tied back in a bun. She was overweight, and she was wearing a floppy dress, red with white flowers.

"Kai! You come see your grandma!" She gave him a loose, gentle hug. "I thought you'd be a boy, but you're a man. Uh!"

"Can I call you Grandma?"

"Yes. I am Grandma. Grandma Lokelani. Oh, I'm so happy you came. Lonely today. You make me happy." Grandma's voice was soothing and steady. Her accent was musical and stronger than Aunt H's.

"I'm glad that I could come see you. I...I've been sad ever since my dad died. I miss him all the time," Kai said.

"Don't make me sad. Not sad. Happy to see Kai. How is California?"

"California is good, but I like Maui better. It's so beautiful, and the people I've met...It even smells nice," he said, breathing deeply of the scent of flowers.

"You like plants?" Grandma Lokelani asked.

Kai smiled. "I like plants," he said.

Grandma smiled back. It seemed to be the answer she wanted.

She led him through the house and out the back door. Her backyard was a small nursery, several acres overflowing with flowers and trees. Potted plants were lined up along a shed, ready for sale, near a pile of rich dirt and a collection of shovels, spades, and pruning tools. Watering hoses ran from the shed to the rows of plants. A handmade sign lay on its side against the wall, advertising "Lokelani's Garden Flowers and Plants." Inside the shed he glimpsed a table and packing materials.

"These are for tourists," said Lokelani. "Apple bananas, coffee, banana, ti. That's taro," she said, pointing to a special small bed filled with water inside a little wall. They walked down a little path between the plants. "You know these?" she said, pointing to a delicate white flower. "Orchids. Twenty thousand kinds of orchid in the world. All different. More orchids than any other kind of plant with flowers."

She lowered her voice. "This is where I make all my money. More money than Grandpa makes at his bakery in Wailuku. Yah, really! No other place like this for growing orchids. Orchids love Iao Valley. And tourists, they love orchids. No other orchids like mine. For getting married. For take home." She paused. She seemed to size up Kai. "But you know what?" She lowered her voice to a secretive whisper. "I don't like orchids!"

Kai laughed. "Why?" he asked. What could be so awful about a flower?

Grandma Lokelani shrugged. "So easy to break. So weak. " She smiled at Kai. "I never tell anyone that before. You don't tell, either."

She gestured for him to follow, and led him down a row of plants. Kai recognized some of them. They were big, gaudy flowers with bright tropical-looking blossoms. "Hibiscus, torch ginger, heliconia," Grandma murmured as they passed. She pointed at a beautiful red hibiscus. "That one always lived right here. Before Kamehameha."

"Kamehameha came here?" Kai said. What was the great ruler of the Hawaiian Islands doing in this lush valley of flowers that felt so quiet, so forgotten by time?

"Big battle here, in 1790. Kamehameha killed warriors from Maui. Plenty killed. So many people died, the bodies dam up the river and it run red with blood. You know this place was always used for burying kings? Sacred river. I show you the place soon. Your Aunty Hepaula'ole, she told me you like old things. You want to see the heiau?" She looked at him closely, and seemed to decide. "You want me to take you? We can say a blessing together. We'll put your dad there..."

Suddenly, watching Kai, her eyes filled with tears. She hugged him hard, patting his back with her strong hands. "I miss him too," she said. "You're not the only one. You're not alone."

Kai struggled. He was so far from home. Yet his dad was present here. Everyone knew him. It was as if Dad was here, following. But Kai would never see him again. Dad would never know how much work Kai had done to do this right. Dad would never know how much Kai loved him.

Grandma Lokelani held him another moment. The feelings passed as quickly as they had come.

"Look, best part of the garden now. See the trees? Guava, Kukui nut, WiliWili, Lychee, Sausage tree…Trees are my favorite." They had reached the orchard part of the garden. But the trees grew close together, not in the neatly spaced rows Kai expected. "Trees don't need work like orchids. Trees live long. That one is sandalwood. Not many of those in Maui. In old times, sandalwood all over Maui. No more. That tree is special. My mother planted some that kind tree with me." The way she said "that kind" it sounded like "da kine."

"Grandma," Kai said softly. "Last night, I saw an owl."

He felt his grandma stiffen. She turned to him.

"It was…made of light. I was awake. I wasn't dreaming."

Kai's heart pounded. He hadn't told Aunty H about the owl. Why did he tell Grandma now? He hadn't thought it through. But he had needed to tell someone.

Grandma Lokelani nodded. "You no lolo --- not crazy. Don't be worried." She looked calm, even proud. "Plenty in our family see like that. That's nothing! Owls take care of you. Dead ones that love you, they come, looking like owls. Come to help. You need help? They hear you. Maybe your dad sent it. To watch over you. Lead you where you need to go." She smiled. "Maybe the owl brought you to me."

"Maybe." Kai nodded. He felt relieved. It was good to have shared his bizarre experience and to have someone understand. Grandma didn't seem a bit shocked. Not even surprised. Maybe it was some weird thing that ran in his family. Relief flowed through him like a warm wind.

"Come. I'll take you to heiau. I got to tell you something, though. In old days, it wouldn't be called a heiau. The one I'm taking you to would have been called waihau."

"What's the difference?" Kai asked.

"Now days, there's no difference. Everybody has forgotten the difference and just calls it heiau. But in the old days, a heiau was just for the chiefs and the ali'i. The one I'm taking you to, it's just for prayer. A family site."

"So should I call it waihau instead of heiau?" Kai asked. Which one had his dad meant? Probably the family site, or waihau.

"Call it whatever you want," said Grandma Lokelani.

They walked around the house to where a 70's two-seater pickup sat rusting in a mud puddle. The truck looked better outside than inside. The seat covers had ripped long ago. Chunks of padding had fallen out of the seat back and mixed with the sand on the floor. Dead cockroaches lined the crack between the dashboard and the windshield. The windshield was grimy and mud encrusted the wipers. The steering wheel was in excellent condition.

Grandma Lokelani closed her eyes and mumbled something in Hawaiian. Then she put the key in the ignition and turned. The truck started, and they headed up the road along the river toward Iao Valley State Park.

Chapter 13
GOD OF SQUIDS

The parking lot was partly empty when they reached the State Park. Kai followed his grandma past a small restroom down a paved sidewalk to a pedestrian bridge. The Iao River rushed in white rapids below them. A garden of native plants brought to the Hawaiian Islands by the first Polynesian settlers, and also plants found here before white contact, covered the hillside. The paved sidewalk meandered along the sparkling river with its clear, inviting pools. The sound of water tumbling over rocks filled the park. The Iao needle, a green volcanic structure like a thousand foot thumb, stuck straight up from beside the river like a primitive sculpture representing fertility and power.

Grandma Lokelani walked well for someone her size. Kai was amazed. Maybe she wasn't as old as she looked, or maybe her work kept her in good shape. Still, when they got there, she didn't want to climb the 333 steps to the highest viewpoint in the park. She sat on a bench and waited while Kai took the steps two at a time. When he got back, breathless, she led him down to the river. The paved sidewalk led to a dirt path. Ignoring the "No Trespassing" sign, Grandma Lokelani led Kai into the forest.

It was pleasant in the forest. Kai didn't like spiders, and there were many here, but Grandma Lokelani didn't seem afraid. "Nothing poisonous but one thing on land. Centipedes. They bite, and that hurts, but you won't die. Scorpions not good, either. But no bad snakes here. No bad spiders." She led the way, covering the uneven ground with sure footsteps. The trees were a tall green canopy shading them. The river murmured and rushed between deep dark swimming holes of polished rock.

The trail was overgrown but easy to follow. He felt his excitement growing. In his backpack, his dad's ashes waited. Soon, very soon, he would fulfill the promise.

They walked and rested, and walked and rested, sitting on rocks near the river to talk while Grandma Lokelani gathered her strength.

"What do you know about Hawaiian religion?" she asked.

"Nothing," Kai admitted.

"I got to teach you something, for the blessing." She paused, trying to decide where to start. "First, there were the old ways. You know in the old days, old Hawaii, the god Maui he pulled the island up out of the sea. He tricked the sun, too, so it would stay longer in the sky sometimes in the year. There were all kinds of gods in old Hawaii. Kane, Lono, Wakea, Ku, Hina, Pap, Pele…Many gods. Gods for all kine things. Got to respect all. Kanaloa, he was the god of squids."

"God of squids?" said Kai.

"Yah, squids. But that meant healing, too, and magic. Not just squids like you think…There were gods for sea. More kinds for sky. For earth. Thunder, rain, for having babies. For mana, and power, everybody got their own spirit. From their family. Spirit of ancestors. Aumakua. Some places had a spirit, too. Old Hawaiians, they pray to all kine. This was how they prayed. For Kane, they went to big rocks that stuck up like part of a man. Got to be near a river."

"You mean, like the Iao needle?" asked Kai.

She nodded.

"They ate special. Pork, kava. Prayed for forgiveness."

Grandma Lokelani stopped talking and studied Kai.

"Every family got aumakua. Sometimes from dreams. Or animals. Different way.   Our family has shark, and owl."

Kai met her eyes.

"When you told me about your owl, I knew you been chosen," she said.

They sat silent for a little, listening to the powerful rush of water. Kai felt easy, and glad. He was no longer worried. It was right to be here now, with this Grandma who loved him at first sight and understood.

Dad, I'm glad you asked me to come.

Grandma met his eyes with her own smiling ones. "But all that was old days. Nobody believes in those old gods in the same way anymore," she said. "Everybody believes some, forgets some. Now we're Christian. Your dad, he was Catholic. He believed like me."

"You don't believe in the old gods?" asked Kai.

Grandma plucked a leaf from a bush beside. On the forest floor, something quick and orange crawled out of sight. Grandma didn't seem to have seen it.

She balanced the leaf on the tips of her fingers. It moved slightly but she adjusted so it didn't fall. "We're Christian. But we're Hawaiian, too. Christian-Hawaiian." The balanced leaf fluttered to the ground. This time, Grandma let it fall.

"If you're Hawaiian, you know your ancestors, their mana. Your dad knew the ancestors. He loved Maui. That why he ask you to bring him home."

"This place was sacred to which god?" Kai asked. Somehow, it seemed wrong that an old sacred altar was now swarming with tourists who came to take photos but not for anything spiritual. Shouldn't there be a sign that asked visitors for a moment of silence, at least?

"Kane. The needle is sacred. Whole place here sacred. Plenty bones here. Plenty heiau."

Even before they reached the family heiau, Kai felt they were near. He could sense his Grandma's pace slowing, and her own anticipation. The heiau was a pile of dark rocks, like a raised rectangular platform, just to the side of the path in a level clearing. It was small, only the size of a long table, and stood about three feet tall. Kai wondered if any hikers had ever sat on it to rest. But there was something purposeful about the rock pile that commanded respect. No one would hurt it.

Grandma Lokelani raised her hands and began to chant. Kai stood beside her, letting the melodious sounds of the Hawaiian blessing wash over him. He could feel how hard she was praying. He could feel how much she loved him and his dad...

Was this the place Dad wanted? *Dad, am I here?*

Grandma turned to him. "I pray to God. I did old chant for healing, for forgiveness. I prayed that your dad be in peace, and know we love him. I did an old Hawaiian chant too, in the old way, calling the mana of our ancestors. Now it's your turn."

She waited.

Kai cleared his throat. He took out the box of ashes. He remembered his dad's face, the love in his eyes before he died.

"God, if it is possible, please let my dad know that I love him... Dad, I brought you here where you asked. I'm glad you asked me to come. I won't forget you."

Was this the right heiau? What had dad said? He had asked Kai to find the old one. Was this the old one?

"Grandma, is this old?" he asked. "Dad told me to find the old one. Just before he died."

"I built this one myself," Grandma Lokelani said.

Suddenly, a shape swept across the clearing above them. The bird seemed huge. Its wings were floppy and totally silent, the color of shadow.

Grandma gasped. "Pueo!" she breathed. Owl!

Like the owl of light I saw at night. But this is a real owl. Kai felt a chill pass through him.

"Don't be afraid," Grandma said, putting her hand on him. "It's good. Very good! You are watched over. Loved. By those from the past."

"In the owl?" Kai tried to get his mind around Grandma's belief. *Did she really believe a bird held their ancestors?*

"Do you believe God is in everything?" Grandma asked, sensing his bewilderment.

"Yes," Kai said.

"People we miss when they die, people from long time ago, old gods, old places ---- they don't go away. They stay. Keep us company. "

"So why did the owl come now?" Kai asked, trying to understand her.

"What do you think?" Grandma asked.

"So we'd remember the past?" Kai said slowly. "So you would teach me things? But what does it mean?" He still held the box of ashes.

"What do you feel?" Grandma asked.

Kai searched his heart for his most honest answer.

"I feel grateful to be with you," he said, "and that Dad is near, somewhere. This place is special, but I don't think it's where he meant."

Grandma nodded. "That's why the owl came," she said.

Kai nodded. Although his rational mind couldn't accept the sign as Grandma did, he felt he could imagine how she experienced it. A part of him resisted, and a part of him wanted to believe. *I'd like you to be here, Dad. I'd like to continue to get to know you and I'd like it if you could spend more time getting to know me.*

"So what do we do?" Kai asked.

"All of life is a prayer," Grandma said simply, offering Kai her hand. He took it. Grandma's hand was calloused and warm. Her nails were short, clipped for her work with plants and soil. They bowed their heads. "God, lead Kai where he is meant to go."

They left the heiau and hiked back down to the river. "How did you build it?" Kai asked. He was still mulling things over, trying to figure it out.

"We had another one, an older one in Wailuku town," Grandma explained. "Then they were going to build there. Big warehouse right on top! We had to do it fast. We got the rocks, brought them up here, found the place. We did all that. My mom, Meli, she was with us then. Nahoa, he was just a little boy."

"What do you think Dad meant about the old heiau?" Kai asked. "Do you think he meant the one in Wailuku?"

"No," Grandma said. "Wailuku was new, too. There are many, many older ones. You got to go where the family lived a long time ago," she said. She seemed more tired now, and Kai slowed his steps for her. "Go see Great-grandpa in Hana. He knows where family lived. He knows the heiaus, he'll help."

"I don't know why finding the old one mattered to Dad, but it did. He said to follow the chant..." Kai stopped.

"The chant?" Grandma looked blank.

Kai realized he hadn't shown it to Grandma. *How could I forget?* They had so much to talk about, it had slipped his mind. He took the paper out of his backpack and handed it to Grandma. "I forgot to show you! Dad gave me this. He said it would lead me to the right heiau. Do you know it?"

Grandma sat on a boulder beside the river and took her reading glasses out of her pocket. She squinted at the paper. "Oh, yes! This one, my mom Meli showed me. Long time ago. Special to our family.   It tells sacred places. Sacred to us. But I don't know how to read it. Just some. Here's Lono, see? Maybe a place for Lono?   I think different people added different places. You know most chants made not by one person? Many people. People keep on adding. But I don't know. Most chants, I just learn to remember, like a song. I don't read each word on paper. Take this to Great-grandpa. Maybe he will know."

Kai took the chant and put it carefully back in his backpack. He sat beside Grandma on the boulder. They listened to the fast moving water of the river beside them. It was pleasantly cool and peaceful in the green shadows beside the rushing current.

"If you go see him, bring Great-grandpa some candies. He loves candies. Spicy ginger. That's his favorite. And fresh chicken feet. He goes crazy for chicken feet!"

"Feet?" Kai said.

"Oh, yes. From Ah Fook's Market. Great-grandpa knows how to make them the best spicy feet," she said. "Just like my mom. Good cook!"

"Okay," he said. "But will I have to eat them?

Grandma laughed. "You never had chicken feet? They're good! Yes. Really!"

Kai smiled, unconvinced. Grandma's laugh --- an easy, relaxed sound --- reminded him suddenly of Mom in California.

"I should have brought you something," Kai realized.

"No, no! You brought me you," said Grandma contentedly.

Strangely, Kai did not feel disappointed that this was the wrong heiau. He liked Grandma Lokelani, very much. It had been a worthwhile day, and although he hadn't found the right heiau, he was on the right track. It wouldn't be long.

"I'm glad I got to come here with you," said Kai.

"Kai, you gave me a happy day," said Grandma Lokelani. "God blessed me, by bringing you today."

They stood. Kai followed his grandma back along the river.

Now he knew what a heiau was, and understood what it meant. Now he knew Dad's mom and sister. He was beginning to understand how his family could walk between old ways and new. It was strange that even Grandma, Dad's mom, didn't really know what the chant meant, but soon, Kai would find Great-grandpa. Having come this far, he would follow Dad's wish, and go to Hana.

Chapter 14
OLD WAYS AND NEW

Year 1790
Iao Valley, Maui

Today Kamehameha had realized a dream. The foreigners' weapons had given him a terrible power over his rivals. With the help of two strangers who had become his consultants, muskets, and their canons, Kamehameha and his warriors had killed thousands. The bodies of the dead lay piled in the river.

Thousands warriors had arrived with Kamehameha in hundreds of canoes from the island of Hawai'i. The invaders forced the locals into the blind canyon of Iao Valley. The local Maui forces had been confident that they would be safe in Ioa Valley, so much so that they had invited their women and children to watch the battle from the mountainside. No battle had ever been lost in the stronghold of Iao. What the Maui forces did not anticipate was the power of Kamehameha's weapons and strategy.   Now, the river was dammed with the bodies of Maui warriors.

Kamehameha the invader cried out in triumph.

His warriors answered. They marched out of the valley of death. In front of them, they pushed the lone survivor from among their opponents. They had kept this man for a special purpose which all understood. Now it was time.

The march was long. Kamehameha insisted they reach the sacred heiau. The men were spent. After hours of fighting, they struggled to march. Yet their leader was adamant. They must do this properly.

Kamehameha understood the importance of tradition and ritual. His bloodlines tied him to the highest chiefs. His mother had altered her entire life to follow traditional rules: she was so kapu divine that she could not live near other people, and

61

had to spend her life alone in a remote cave. He attributed his own power and success partly to her sacrifice. Kamehameha knew that he won battles not only through his own skills as a warrior, but because the gods favored him. In return, he carefully honored the gods.

At the end of the line of warriors, the chief's religious advisors and head priest followed. The kapuna was pleased. He had read the signs correctly, and advised his chief well on strategy.

Now the kapuna would perform the sacred ritual. In his hands he carried a red cloth bundle. Today would be a fitting time to unveil the object in ceremony. Like this battle, use of the object was not something that had ever been done before, or would ever be repeated.

Finally, the tired warriors and their captive reached the heiau. All sat around the platform and looked up at it. Many were bloodied. The kapuna began to chant.

The prisoner was brought forward. He knew what was coming. His eyes were wide. Several men held him down.

With a swift, practiced motion, the kapuna slit the man's neck. The man squealed like a butchered dog. The warriors held firm. The sacrifice's fresh blood flowed into the heiau rocks. The offering gushed and finally slowed to a drip. The man lay still.

The kapuna waved a prayer stick and lifted a gourd cup. The Awa had been prepared by chewing and spitting and was ready to drink. He passed the cup.

The kapuna took the red cloth object. He held it high above the sacrifice. In a quick gesture, he pulled off the cloth.

The warriors gasped.

"We take the power like the power of the waves, like the power that darkens the sun in mid-day, and use it to crush our enemies," the kapuna began. All the while, he held the object out for all to see.

Everyone stared. No one had ever seen anything like it. Some warriors averted their gaze. What was it? Clearly, it came from the strangers. Was it a weapon? More dangerous, perhaps, and therefore kept by the kapuna?

The kapuna waved the object. His meaning was clear. The strangers' power was now their own power, harnessed to crush their enemies. The power came through the mysterious object. Like the strangers' weapons that had become their own weapons, this thing had once given power to others. Now, the power was theirs. The object, their use of the strangers' weapons, and the war god's blessing had given a bounty of death.

Beginning to feel the first effects of the narcotic drink, the warriors watched the kapuna re-wrap the object in its blood-red cloth. They passed the Awa gourd. As they drank, each man contemplated what he had seen and its terrible promise, as they sank deeper and deeper into a shared dream.

Chapter 15
WHAT DAD'S PRIEST REMEMBERS

The present
Kihei

The next morning, Aunty H gave Kai directions to walk to Dad's Priest's home.

"You better talk to him," she said. "He might know something."

Father John was different than he'd imagined. He was retired, and lived near Aunty H.

"Hello! What brings you here today?" The man standing in the doorway before Kai had a soft, pudgy, wrinkled reddish face, medium-length graying black hair, and a stout build. He looked to be in his late sixties. He was wearing a brightly colored, loose T-shirt and long khaki cargo shorts.

Kai introduced himself.

"Father John. May peace be with you." The priest gently took Kai's hand in his large paw-like hand, sending love and comfort through his fingers. "Come in! Sit down! I can tell we have much to talk about!"

Kai walked through the white painted doorway and stepped into Father John's house. A fan was humming softly in a room somewhere in the house, and he could hear trees off in the distance rustling in a warm breeze. The house was shady, slightly stuffy and plain. Father John led Kai to a pair of wicker chairs beside a rectangular coffee table made of a dark hardwood.

"Do I know your father?" the priest said. "Are you Nahoa's son?"

"Yes." Kai paused.

"You look just like him."

"I wish I'd known him better," Kai admitted.

"Oh, I'm sorry. Is he deceased?"

64

"Yes, he passed away a few days ago. I was there."

"I feel your pain. That which is pure, clean, and holy will enter heaven, and God is merciful…Is his death what brings you to Maui?"

Kai thought back to the moment of his father's death, the slow breathing, life slipping away. *Promise, promise, promise…*He looked into the eyes of the priest. "Yes. Yes, I came because my father directed me here."

Father John gazed back comfortingly. Suddenly, a funny look. "Did you know that I knew your father when he was a child?" He did not wait for a response. "Ugh, he was such a screw-off. I was his teacher at the church school. He sat in the back corner of the room--" he made a loose gesture with his fingers, pointing to somewhere in an imaginary classroom, "and all day in school, he would jabber with his group of buddies. He had this loud, obnoxious deep voice…and he always had this smirk on his face, and I could tell he was thinking of something to tell his friends once they got out of school. He never paid attention in class for a single instant. Or so it seemed. But he must have been listening, because he grew…"

"I guess I never really knew my dad."

The priest laughed. "I guess so. So why did you come visit me today? Did you come all the way to Maui just to see me?"

Kai shrugged and slouched back in his chair. "I'm not sure. My father, when he was dying, told me to come here. He gave me this ancient Hawaiian chant, some kind of message. He told me to follow the chant and spread his ashes wherever the chant leads. The only problem is that the whole thing is written in Hawaiian. So I was wondering if you could help me figure out what it means."

Father John looked concerned. He bit his lower lip. "Yeah, that makes sense. Your dad and ancient Hawaiian religion. You don't get messed up in that ancient Hawaiian stuff, alright?"

Kai felt a sharp bristle in the back of the wicker chair. He scratched his back. "Why?" he asked cautiously.

"Oh, Hawaiian religion was evil, evil. People should never try to go back to the old ways. Hawaiians used to have huge ceremonies for human sacrifice. Part of the religion. They sacrificed at special heiaus, where the rulers slaughtered war captives and slaves. The sacrifices went on for a while even after Christian missionaries came to Maui, until finally the Christians were able to squelch out the religion.

"Hawaiian religion was the work of the devil. The chief of Maui at the time of Cook's arrival built a house out of the bones of his enemies. The ones he killed! He was awful, the whole religion was awful. If you lived in ancient Hawaii, either you belonged to the lower class, or you were one of the Ali'i, the rulers, the religious leaders, the privileged. If you were from the lower class, you couldn't even get near one of the rulers.

"Don't try to revive the old Hawaiian religion. It is all bad. Some people still secretly are superstitious. Some people still believe the signs. Some people are also ignorant of the bloody history of the islands. You shouldn't mess with the religion. Worship the God who is good, and only worship Him. Do not believe in false signs. Okay?"

Kai thought of standing outside Aunty H's house in the dark. He remembered the geckoes and toads, calling him, beckoning him outside. The moon, the stars, and the black silhouettes of the trees. And the owl. *Promise, promise*. His dad trusted Kai to make the right decision.

"Can I still show you the chant? Do you think you could help me translate it?"

The wrinkles on Father John's forehead became more prominent. Then he chuckled. "No, I don't know Hawaiian. No one knows Hawaiian anymore, it is a lost language. It is so much like your father, making it hard on you. He made everyone's life difficult, that's just how he was. Anyway, I can look at your chant. I knew your father pretty well, so I might be able to help you."

Kai pulled the chant out of his pocket and unfolded the paper. He placed it on the desk in front of Father John. The priest quickly scanned the page with a solemn expression.

"No, I'm sorry. This doesn't look familiar. Maybe a family chant, passed down through the generations. I'm guessing your dad never found its translation, he just kept it as a family treasure and passed it down to you. This won't lead you to a certain place where you can bury your father's ashes. Most chants are vague and repetitive. You are on the wrong path."

"I promised Dad," Kai said quietly.

Father John was silent for a moment. Then he sighed. "A promise to the dead should be honored. Let me make a call. I know a man who may be able to help you."

Chapter 16
TRANSLATING THE SECRET CHANT

T he next morning, Father John escorted Kai to David Hudson's office. It was near the priest's home, and Father John wanted to make the introduction.

David Hudson's office was neat and orderly. A row of organized filing cabinets lined the back wall, while Hudson sat at a large desk, reclining in a leather chair and facing a computer. "Hey, come in," he said, glancing up.

Hudson had short gray hair. He was about six foot two and looked to be in great shape. He wore loose-fitting jeans and a relaxed grin. "So I hear you need some help," he said in a deep, soothing voice, glancing up at Kai and the priest.

Father John spoke first. "David, this is Kai. As I mentioned, he's on a spiritual journey. He's visiting from California, but his dad grew up here. I knew his father Nahoa well. Now Kai needs an expert in the Hawaiian language to figure out something his dad left him."

"No problem," said Hudson, waving his hand. "It's the least I can do for you, Father." He had bright blue eyes, gentle, the color of clear ocean.

They shook hands. "David Hudson. Welcome." Hudson's grip was firm. Hudson saw Kai eying the blue logo above the desk. "I guess I should introduce myself a little bit," Hudson said. "I've been working with the organization since my family started it up in the mid-80s. We look at archeological sites. On Maui there are a lot of strict zoning rules, so we pass a permit if it's OK to build on a site."

"What do you find?" Kai asked. What artifacts could possibly be around in modern Maui?

"Oh, there are heiaus—Hawaiian temples—*all over* the island. You'd be surprised, we almost always find *some* kind of relic when we study a site. Famously, a team began construction on the Ritz Carlton down by Makena and ran into an ancient burial ground. Today, most of Makena is built on top of historical sites. Local Hawaiians have a lot of respect for their past, and there's been some powerful legislation. We do our best to make sure things are protected even as the island is more and more developed. Are you part Hawaiian?"

"Yes... Well, um...my dad was. But he passed away a few days ago."

"Oh I'm sorry," Hudson said. He swiveled around in his office chair. "Why don't you pull up a chair? Make yourself comfortable. Father, you're welcome to stay, too, if you want."

"I'll wait outside for you," the Priest said.

"I'll be fine," Kai said. "I can walk home. Thanks for everything, though."

"Oh, you're welcome. If you need anything else, you know where to find me. But I wouldn't recommend getting tangled in that Hawaiian religion. You should go on your own and find the right spot to spread your dad's ashes. Trust in God, and he will lead the way. Have a blessed day! Good luck on your journey!" he said as he left. "Good luck to you too," he said to Hudson.

"Great man," Hudson said quietly after the man had left. "Probably saved my life five years ago." *What kind of problems could* this *man have?* Kai looked at him inquisitively, but Hudson didn't explain. What could a priest help with? Alcohol addiction, maybe? "Anyway," Hudson was saying, "tell me a little about this chant."

Kai told David about his father and his dying wishes. As Kai spoke, David fiddled with his reading glasses, twirling them around in circles. "My dad asked me to go to the family heiau. He said the chant would lead me to the right place." Kai got the chant out of his backpack and handed it to the man. Hudson set his glasses on his nose and peered down at the sheet, deep in concentration. Then suddenly, he stiffened.

"Wow!" he breathed.

"What?" Kai asked.

David looked up. He seemed surprised he'd spoken aloud. "We've got to check this," he said hurriedly. "I'm not actually an expert in Hawaiian language, just in Hawaiian archeology. So I might be wrong. Just a second, I'll send it to one of my friends in Honolulu. She's a professor, and she's great at this stuff." He quickly scanned the chant and sent an email. Then he called his friend and chatted for a bit, explaining the situation in a flood of hurried words. Kai could tell from David's voice how excited he was. Perhaps the chant was more special than Kai had imagined. "Good," David said after a few minutes on the phone, "thanks again for taking time to do it now. I think this might be the most interesting thing to walk into my office in a long while." He laughed. "Of course. We'll wait on the edge of our seats. And honey, I owe you one…Okay, it's a deal." David put his phone down and turned to Kai. There was anticipation in David's face. A rush of excitement swept through Kai. Now he would finally learn the chant's message! But what was David excited about? "Can you understand any of it?" Kai asked.

"A little," Hudson said carefully. "Bits and pieces. There are only really two kinds of Hawaiian chants." He was holding back, waiting for the translation. He wasn't going to say too much until he was sure, but he looked like a kid before Christmas.

"So, what are you thinking?" Kai pressed.

"Well," David began, "there are chants that tell stories, like about sharks and the mythical birth of the islands and things. Lots of metaphors, if you know what I mean. But yours seems different. Unlike anything I've ever seen." He paused, and grinned at Kai. Clearly, David loved figuring things out.

"Different how?" Kai asked. Kai thought of what his grandma had told him about the chant identifying places sacred to his family. Why would that be of interest to David? Kai decided there was no reason to mention what Grandma had said.

David's eyebrows furrowed. "For one thing, the form," he said. "I've never run across one quite like it…" he seemed to want to say more, but to decide against it. He glanced at his computer screen. No answer yet. "Of course, it might be a genealogy chant. It's pretty short, but maybe. Ali'i used to make long lists of their ancestors."

"Father John was telling me about ali'i." *What would that mean?*

"Yes, the leaders. Ancient Maui was divided into two social groups, ali'i and commoners. Ali'i had sacred blood lines. They could be so pure they were untouchable, divine. The ali'i created long genealogical chants, whereas the commoners were only allowed to trace their ancestors back three generations. A way to control them, I guess." He paused. He was talking quickly, but his eyes kept going back to the computer. He could hardly wait. "If you were a commoner, you could be killed for stepping into even the shadow of an ali'i."

"Father John told me some history. About wars."

"Yep. Maui has had a long history of conflict. Some members of the ali'i, actually, were forced to go live in isolation to avoid being murdered." David tapped his fingers nervously on his desk top with nervous energy.

"But what you're saying is…if this is a genealogical chant, then I'm probably related to ali'i?" Kai sat up a little straighter. He felt a surge of energy pass through him. *I am about to figure out what Dad left me. Is it something to do with who I am?*

"That's what I'm thinking." Hudson grinned. "I don't know for sure yet, but that's what I'm thinking." David's tone indicated that he still hadn't told Kai everything.

"So if I learn I'm related to ali'i, what can I *do* with that?"

"You might get some land here on the island if you could prove it. What probably happened, though, is your great-grandparents had land and then sold it away for too cheap, before they understood its value. That's what happened to most descendents. You might learn that you're related to King Kamehameha, and that would be pretty cool."

"King Kamehameha?"

"The king who united the islands. I'll tell you more once we get the translation back. Why don't you come back at the end of the day, and see if I have it by then."

Kai said goodbye. He had some things to buy for Great-grandpa before he went to Hana tomorrow. He still had to figure out how to get to Ah Fook's grocery to buy the candies and chicken feet. Maybe Aunty H would help him.

When Kai returned three hours later, David was finishing a phone call.

"Oh, hi!" he said. "I've been too busy to check, but let's see if we got anything." David opened his email. His face broke into an electrified smile.

"Bingo!" he said.

He clicked a button and the printer came to life. "Got it!" he said. Kai felt excitement swell inside him. Finally, he could see what it meant!

Kai stared at the translation. Even in English, it made no sense.

The sand of fire leads to sand of night
Kihapi'ilani's road leads behind the father's house
Hear the echoes of our song

Above the land of the pineapple and the paniolo
Above the springs in the forest of ash
Hear the echoes of our song

Beyond the cruel sun to the land of the taro
The stream in the northernmost point beyond the mother's auwai
Hear the echoes of our song

Lono's treasure in the small shrine
Near the great shrine
Hear the echoes of our song

He who sees the owl possesses the power
Lono's treasure, power of the ancestors, power to find, power to protect
Hear the echoes of our song

Kai's heart sank. The chant was supposed to be a
message from his dad. It was supposed to tell him how to find
the right heiau. This was meaningless gibberish. Indecipherable.
He wondered if it were possible that the lady had translated it
wrong.

"What's it mean?" Kai asked.

Hudson didn't answer immediately, but he seemed so
excited he might burst. When he did finally speak, his eyes were
bright. He met Kai's gaze directly. "I was right," he said. "Your
chant is very, very unusual…It seems to be some kind of
directions," he said. "The bit about Lono, that's what intrigues
me. You know, when Captain Cook arrived on Kauai in 1778,
the Hawaiians welcomed him as their god Lono." He paused.
"Soon enough, they found he was just a regular mortal bringing
gifts of cholera, measles and gonorrhea that would decimate the
population." Hudson ran his hand through his hair. "I'm not
sure if this is right, but…"

"What?" Kai asked. Grandma had mentioned Lono, too.
But what did it mean? He was dying to know. What about the
chant was making this archeologist so excited?

"Cook had some things the Hawaiians had never seen
before. Iron. The Hawaiians were anxious to trade. There's
been speculation among historians about first-contact artifacts."

"What do you mean, first contact?" Kai asked. He hated
to sound dumb, but he still didn't get it. Why was Hudson so
excited about old Hawaiian history? What did it have to do with
his chant?

"First contact between the Polynesians of old Hawaii and
a modern European. Look, here's what I'm getting at. Some
people think there was an artifact. See, when Cook landed there
was a war going on here on Maui. Kamehameha, the guy who
united all the Hawaiian islands into one kingdom, hadn't united
them quite yet. He was here near Hana, fighting Kahekili for
control of Maui." Hudson pointed to a paper on his desk. "We
know quite a bit from Cook's journals…Here's the island of
Kauai," he said. He drew a stick figure man on the paper.

"Here's Cook, doing his thing." Hudson moved his pen slowly across his desk toward another paper, like a ship crossing between islands. "News traveled fast, even back then. People were probably canoeing between the islands as fast as they could, to let everybody know Lono had arrived. Then swarms of locals met the ships. Most of the welcoming committee merely looked. But what if someone secretly collected something? When Cook's men weren't looking. An object from Lono would have a lot of power." Hudson set the pen down.

"Like what?" Kai asked, breathlessly. Was there some kind of treasure?

Hudson nodded vigorously. He was so excited that his eyes shone. "Exactly. Like what? That's what all the historians would like to know. It would have to be something small, easy to transport. Easy to steal. Not missed enough that Cook would notice immediately. Interesting to the Hawaiians...But it doesn't really matter what the thing was, see. It would have significance because of its history. Say it was the first thing passed between the chiefs here and the Western world. An object passed between the new era and the old. A cultural bridge. A catalyst. Proof positive of the magical power that would soon destroy the entire culture of old Hawaii. A little piece of history." Hudson studied Kai. His voice dropped. "Some say the Hawaiians hid an object, and kept Lono's treasure for themselves," he said.

Kai tried to process it all. "You're saying the chant might be like a map to an artifact?" he finally managed. "To something valuable from Captain Cook's first contact with the Hawaiians? But I thought it led to my family's heiau."

"Maybe," David said slowly, "your family hid their most valuable possession in their most sacred place."

Suddenly, it all made sense. Kai bristled with Hudson's contagious excitement. Maybe his father had left him a valuable inheritance after all! All he had to do was find it. "Could you sometime...maybe help me interpret the chant?" he asked. "Where do you think I should start?"

David leaned closer, his blue eyes excited. "Do you think maybe...we could team up on this? I mean, I know a lot about the history of Maui. And I have a new employee who specializes in historical sites like heiaus. Maybe the three of us could work together."

Kai thought it over. Hudson obviously wanted a share in the profit of Cook's artifact. Kai kind of wanted to find it himself. However, he also realized that he'd have much more success if he had the help of an expert. Great-grandpa might know where to go, or he might not. It would be smart for Kai to take all the help he could get.

"I'd like to help you," David went on. "I love discoveries, and the chant might lead to something very interesting. Of course, if we find anything, you'll have to decide what you want to do with it," David paused. "You have a few choices. You can keep it, or loan it to museums. Depending upon what it is, you could auction it. I could represent you, if you want. My typical commission is 20 percent which is paid by the buyer. That's industry standard, but depending on the value, we could negotiate. When we know what we're dealing with, we can discuss the details --- there might be extra fees for marketing, restoration, shipping --- but let's leave it like this for now. I'll help you find it, if you'd like, and after we know what you have, you can decide if you'd like me to represent you."

Kai thought about it. It would be amazing if there were really something valuable. But what if it turned out to be something that had value only to Kai? Or if he found he didn't want to sell whatever it was? "Mr. Hudson, what if you help me and it's something that only matters to me? Like...an old skull? Or a book? Something sentimental that belonged to my family?" Kai said. "If it's something like that, I'll probably just keep it."

"Of course. You will decide when you find it," said David. "When we know what it is, I'll give you an estimate of what I think it might bring at auction. Then you can decide."

If Dad's chant really directs me to a valuable object, I could use the money for college! "Mr. Hudson, it's a deal. If you help me, and we find anything I'd like to sell, you can represent me at auction."

"Sounds good. And call me David." They shook hands again. Kai wondered if he would need to sign anything, but David seemed content with merely a handshake.

David scribbled something on a business card and handed it to Kai. "That's my cell. You should be able to reach me most of the time." Kai wrote his on another card and handed it to David. "I'll call you later today once I think through how we're going to tackle this thing."

"Thanks," Kai said. As he left the office with the chant and its translation in his backpack, he felt dazed. An artifact? Ali'i, noble relatives? A valuable object hidden and protected by his family from the time of Captain Cook?

The chant's final words were about an owl. *He who sees the owl possesses the power…*

Kai had seen the owl. The chant was for him, and so was whatever waited in the right heiau at the end. Kai could hardly wait to begin looking.

Chapter 17
SUE GETS HER SECOND ASSIGNMENT

David Hudson pulled off the dusty gravel road, parking his BMW next to two other cars. This stop off the road served as a temporary parking lot for Lot 11.

He found the project manager, close by. The manager had parked his pickup truck near the center of Lot 11, about a hundred yards off the road. Now he was sitting on the back of the trunk, feet dangling in the air, eyes glued on a thick stack of papers he was reading. The manager had loose grey hair, a bald spot, and thick-rimmed glasses.

Lot 11 was dusty and unremarkable, much like the road. Situated on the east side of the West Maui Mountains, near the town of Waikapu, south of Iao Needle and Wailuku, the lot had a good view down the rolling green hillside to the ocean at Kihei. The other direction, Hudson could see the intricate ridges and valleys in the West Maui Mountains. However, the lot itself was dusty and seemingly forgotten. It had been cleared for agriculture numerous times. Small warehouses faced both the western and eastern side.

"Oh, hey boss," the manager said, glancing up from his reading, startled. He had a slight southern accent. He jumped off the truck and they shook hands. "What brings you up here today?"

"I'm looking for Sue. How's the project coming along?"

"Oh, all right. Background and stuff, you know. We just GPSed it and made a quadrant map today. Tomorrow I think we'll start the GPR scan." Ground Penetrating Radiation was a

tool for creating underground maps of sites. "Hey, if you're
looking for Sue," the manager
continued, "She's down there, mapping the site." He
pointed and David started over to where Sue was working.

Although not aesthetically beautiful, Lot 11 was an
intriguing archeological site. A wireless service was planning to
build a 48-foot antenna pole and an equipment shelter on top of
the lot, but first the land needed to be checked for possible
artifacts, ruins, or even grave sites. It was his firm's job to
carefully map the region and label types of soil, animal and plant
life, and artifacts. David expected his team to find something
here. Local legends told of a conch shell used to call people
from miles around. Archeologists suspected that it was buried
somewhere around here. While many had tried to find it, no one
had succeeded. David wouldn't mind finding something flashy
like the conch shell. He was always on the lookout for items that
might interest museums and collectors. He loved the excitement
of his work. There was always the chance he'd discover a
significant historical find. That's why he was so intrigued by
Kai's chant.

Sue was kneeling and pounding stakes into the ground.

"Sue, I just found a great new lead for another project. It
was actually a walk-in --- a kid came in today with an amazing
request. I know you're busy, but with your expertise I thought
you might be able to help."

"Why, of course," she said right away. "How can I help?"

David explained about Kai's visit to his office and the
reference to Lono in the chant. "If we could find an artifact from
Cook, it would be *huge*. It would gain us so much respect. Plus,
it's probably worth big money. I'm willing to give you a share of
the buyer's premium."

Sue wrinkled her eyebrows and gave him a weird look.
"Are you sure about this? Maybe it's a scam."

That's what David liked about Sue. While most first-time
employees were wide-eyed and willing to please, Sue was
different. She was independent, critical. While she was just out
of college and in her late twenties, she hardly seemed new to the

job. "Yeah, I'm pretty sure. Actually, I was thinking the same thing when I first got the translation of the chant. But Kai seems genuine to me. You'll see what I mean when you meet him."

She remained critical. "And what if his dad just made up the chant?"

David sighed. "Kai was pretty sure that his dad didn't know anything about the chant. He merely passed it on, kind of as a father-son type thing. And anyway, Sue, I know this is a gamble. But that's the whole point. The reward would be so great if everything works out. We *have* to try. Here, I'll make you a deal. You work on this project for a few days. You help the boy figure out the chant and you find the heiau with him. I'll work with you guys too, off and on. If you find the artifact, we'll represent it and you get a piece of the commission. Let's say, five percent. If not, we pretend you were working here the whole time and I pay you accordingly. Sound good?"

Sue looked at him intently. "David, I don't understand. What are you going to get out of this project?"

"You don't get it, do you? Look, you know me. I could retire now if I wanted to. But I don't. Why? Because I'm trying to help *you guys* out. And I love this stuff. How can we possibly resist a historically significant find? If we find the artifact, you and I and the rest of our team will be famous. World-famous."

Sue nodded. "All right, then. When do I meet with Kai?"

"Good. Glad you're on board." David was obviously relieved. "I'll call you with Kai's number later today. Would you be up for starting later this afternoon?"

"I'd be happy to begin any time. I'll get in touch and start working."

"Sure thing. I'll see you later, Sue."

As David turned and left, Sue stared at his back, perplexed.

Chapter 18
KAI'S NEW PARTNER

Back at his aunt's house that evening, Kai felt his phone vibrate.

The woman on the other end spoke rapidly. "Hi, my name is Sue Olson. I believe David Hudson mentioned me?"

"You're the heiau expert, right? David called and told me about you."

"Well, actually, archeologist --- but I know a bit about heiaus. I help David evaluate the importance of sites, and protect artifacts. David told me about your visit to his office, as well. Are you busy? Would you like to meet tomorrow to talk about the chant?"

"Actually, I was going to go to Hana to talk to my grandfather tomorrow. About the chant."

She paused. "Would you like a ride? I can drive you to Hana. We can talk on the way. I have the day off from my regular work, and there's some great hiking. I can hike and then drive you home."

"I'm going to spend the night at my great-grandfather's house," Kai said, "but I'd love a ride there. Then my aunt doesn't have to drive."

The next morning, Kai stood near the speed bumps on the local road. An old Volvo station wagon pulled to the curb.

Immediately, he did a double take. Sue Olson was beautiful. She looked physically strong, like an athlete. Her thick, honey-brown hair glowed with gold in the sunlight. Her long, tanned legs looked like a dancer's. "Hello," she said through the open window.

"Hey...thank you," said Kai. "Thanks for the ride."

"No problem. I'm Sue," she held out her hand. "I should be thanking you. I don't normally do work this interesting."

She moved a book off the passenger seat. Kai glimpsed foreign writing on the cover. "Pleasure reading," Sue explained. "I'm Swedish."

Kai hopped in beside her, setting his backpack and the double-bagged iced chicken feet in the back.

"David told me about your chant and its connection to the god Lono," Sue said. "How exciting! You're very lucky your family kept your chant alive."

Sue pulled a tight turn and pressed on the gas, accelerating to fifty down the narrow street. "You think the chant's really about Captain Cook?" Kai asked.

"I'm not sure, although David has his heart set on Cook. There were so many explorers who actually set foot on Maui, like La Perouse, for example. So even if we don't find a Captain Cook artifact, there's a good chance we will find something from another explorer. Or maybe Lono is just a religious word, and we won't find anything at all." Kai was about to ask a question, but she jumped back in. "So are you really Hawaiian?"

The question caught Kai off guard. *I'm not used to thinking of myself as Hawaiian. Is that what I am?* "My dad was part Hawaiian. I'm still pretty new around here, though."

"You're lucky," Sue said. "You're probably already accepted by locals. Me, sometimes I don't get what I want just because I look like a tourist. Plus, if you decide to stay here, you'll get all those benefits."

"Benefits?"

"Yes, you haven't heard? Just as an example, your kids would get free education, just for being part Hawaiian. Didn't you know? People of Native Hawaiian ancestry get to go to elite schools on Oahu for free. Under the Kamehameha system. Then there's the Bishop Trust. Huge."

Kai noticed how she enjoyed talking, leading the conversation. She was sure of herself. "There was a scandal recently. It's rumored that the members of the board of trustees got paid more than the President of the United States. Incredible amounts of money. The money is supposed to ensure that Native Hawaiians get accepted into colleges first. Of course, it's rumored that the members of the board didn't use the money for students at all."

Kai realized his dad must have turned down Hawaiian scholarships for school and maybe even to go to college on the mainland. "Not very fair, but that's how things work around here." She lowered her voice. "And it's possible you might be very rich from this chant."

They had reached the central basin of Maui. Sugar cane fields stretched in either direction. The West Maui Mountains and white windmills stood on the left, while Haleakala, topped by its crater, towered to the right. Sue drove as fast as she could, tailgating the cars in front of her and passing cars as they moved at forty miles per hour down the congested four-lane highway. Kai unrolled his window a crack and a gust of warm air entered the car, carrying with it the earthy smells of fertilizer and sugarcane.

Sue told him to read the chant twice for her, then to repeat just the first few lines. A look of concentration crept across her face as he read.

The sand of fire leads to sand of night
Kihapi'ilani's road leads behind the father's house
Hear the echoes of our song

Above the land of the pineapple and the paniolo
Above the springs in the forest of ash
Hear the echoes of our song

Beyond the cruel sun to the land of the taro
The stream in the northernmost point beyond the mother's auwai
Hear the echoes of our song

Lono's treasure in the small shrine
Near the great shrine
Hear the echoes of our song

He who sees the owl possesses the power

Lono's treasure, power of the ancestors, power to find, power to protect
Hear the echoes of our song

Finally, she said, "Well, that's tough."

"I know. I've been kind of confused ever since David showed me the translation."

Sue laughed. "I feel your pain. I really can't help you with most of that yet. I need to do some research. It looks like there's a lot of references to Hawaiian history."

"So no ideas?"

"Well, just one, about the first line," she said. "It could be wrong, though."

"About the fire sand?"

"Yes. Hana is famous for Kaihalulu beach and Honokalani beach, beaches of red and black sand. The colors are very rare. Maybe that's what that line refers to?"

"Yeah, that makes sense. Maybe the heiau is on one of the beaches."

"Or nearby."

"So it's looking like we're going to have to rely on my relatives mostly," Kai said. "The chant might provide us kind of a general picture, but to find the exact location we're going to have to talk to my great-grandpa."

"Exactly," said Sue. "Except you misspoke. Your great-grandpa will help you, not us. There's no way he's going to help if I'm with you. Remember, I'm not Hawaiian. I look like the enemy. Don't let your family know that you're working with me and David. Remember, your family wants to protect your family sites, not excavate and research them." For a second, her words sparked a feeling of guilt. Would Great-grandpa be disappointed if he knew Kai was seeking a possible artifact as well as a place for Dad's ashes?

But I'm doing all this for Dad, just the way Dad wanted. Kai would figure everything out when he met Great-grandpa.

Sue was right. Great-grandpa would be willing to help Kai alone.

Chapter 19
THE MAGICAL FRUIT STAND ON THE HIGHWAY TO HANA

"There's a famous restaurant," Sue said, pointing out Mama's Fish House near the beach at Ho'okipa. "Celebrities come here, when they want privacy. You eat near the beach, in kind of a garden, and watch the big waves. Some of the best windsurfers in the world come here to Ho'okipa."

Sue pressed on the gas and the car accelerated. Now the landscape changed and they drove over hills near the ocean. "That's Kite Beach," Sue said, pointing. "There's one area designated for kite sailing, and another for windsurfing. Right near shore there's a protected place for beginners." Ripples of whitecaps slowly approached shore on top of turquoise water. In the surf, wind filled colorful kites and sails. "It's one of the best kite surfing locations in Maui. It's always windy here."

Soon they passed through the small town of Paia on the highway leading to Hana. Shops crowded the main street. Expensive glass art and paintings filled in the windows of some shops, while cheap touristy gifts were showcased in others. Two middle-aged women with long gray hair and sandals, wearing matching peace-sign tie-dyed shirts, emerged from a health food store. A family with sunburned pink faces and bright t-shirts and shorts crossed the street carrying shopping bags. A deeply tanned blond-haired girl and her mother, both barefoot, stood under the entrance to a shop advertising yoga therapy and New Age healing crystals. Beside them, a surfer carried his board into a windsurfing shop.

"This used to be a plantation mill town," said Sue. "10,000 workers lived around Paia in camps."

Almost as soon as they entered the lively little town, it was behind them.

They passed a Buddhist cemetery near the sea. "Matokuji Mission," said Sue. "Built by Japanese-Hawaiians."

A steady stream of traffic was slowing them down.

The Hana Highway became a two-lane road next to a cliff that dropped to the beach, where windsurfers readied their boards on the edge of the surf and judged the developing breeze.

They passed pineapple fields, dark furrowed earth with rows of spiky leaves rolling into the distance. Kai saw banana trees and coconut palms. Maybe because of his visit to Grandma Lokelani, he found he was beginning to recognize some trees: mango, plumeria, and African tulip. They passed bamboo forests.

"I've heard there is a species of bamboo that can grow a foot in one day," she said. "You can almost see it growing."

Gradually, the landscape changed. Everything became damper and greener. They were no longer driving through open fields. They were in a rain forest. Dark green branches formed thick canopies. The treetops were studded with bright orange blossoms. A moist, earthy smell hung in the air.

They crossed a one-lane bridge near a waterfall. Kai heard the roar of water.

"Tell me what you know about heiaus," Kai said. "Aren't you a heiau expert?"

Sue laughed. "There's so much to tell you," she said as she navigated another turn. "Have you heard of Halekii-Pihana State Monument?" Sue asked.

Kai shook his head.

"Okay, let's start there. Halekii-Pihana is above Wailuku. It was overgrown until the 70s. Which means it's one of the best preserved sites. They were Maui's two most important temples at the time of white contact. Pihana is kind of like a pyramid, hidden under some bushes. Both Pihana and Halekii are above Iao stream, built from the stream's stones. Originally, they would have had the features of heiau used by royalty in the pre-contact era."

She paused.

"Of course, Halekii is most famous for being the site of the most recent recorded human sacrifice by Hawaiians, in 1790. You've heard of the battle that filled Iao river with blood? After Kamehameha won, he worshipped Ku, the war god, at Halekii heiau with human sacrifice."

Human sacrifice as recently 1790? "Wasn't that after Captain Cook came to the islands?" A little after the era of the Declaration of Independence, in the era of Mozart, Hawaiians still performed human sacrifice? That would be the same time his family was maybe hiding whatever it was --- the artifact --- and creating the chant.

"A prisoner of war was killed to appease the gods," Sue said, "in one of the last powerful actions by a Maui chief showing total disregard for the cultural norms and religious preferences of Europeans. After that, Maui's leaders became puppets to various European settlers. Missionaries were extremely powerful, exerting their influence over all aspects of life, setting the rules, breaking the old taboos...even controlling those leaders the Hawaiians considered divine."

Kai was speechless. He felt strangely culpable, as if he had something to do with all this. Any system that supported human sacrifice was barbaric and deserved to be overthrown. And yet, he wished his ancestors had not let themselves be taken over so completely. Maybe they themselves had been ready to give up the system involving sacrifice...But no, that wasn't it. How had Aunty H explained it? The Hawaiians had been wowed by the newcomers' guns. Then they had been wiped out by disease. The leaders who were left had been converted to Christianity, and then missionaries had taken control of everything.

The weapons the Europeans had must have been so tempting. The Europeans were like magicians with shiny toys. They had so many things the Hawaiians did not. Not just steel, but knowledge.

Yet although he could understand how such things had impressed his ancestors, it was still hard to fathom how quickly they had shed their whole culture. Why hadn't they fought harder to keep some of the old ways?

Had they felt…ashamed?

"Look in the backseat," Sue said. "I think I have something back there for you…" she glanced over her shoulder. "That blue folder," she said.

Kai found it. He read aloud, feeling a bit sick from the turns the car was making.

The heiau complex near Wailuku is quite large, and relatively intact…The largest heiau in Hawaii is Pi'ilanihale Heiau near Hana. As is common, the monument includes a large stone platform where there were once structures where the kahuna, or priests, stored drums and other sacred objects. When the heiau was in use, religious figures composed of tall carved wooden statues stood upright around the platform. A special part of the heiau was used for the sacrifice of plants and animals. The one in Hana was started in the 13th century. Of course, smaller family heiaus deviate more from the strict traditional patterns of structure and use one finds in those heiaus used by royalty.

"Oh, yeah, that's the important part," Sue said. "Family heiaus. They were casual. And quirky. When I'm on site trying to hypothesize the age of a particular heiau, I always keep in mind that all heiaus were works in progress. I mean, each generation added what it needed on top of the site. So each heiau changed over time from when it was built until its last use as a religious site. It was the site itself, not the structure, which was sacred."

They talked about the Hana heiau. Like the ones in Wailuku, it was forgotten until about thirty years ago, when it was rediscovered after becoming totally overgrown.

"Only the heiaus that were forgotten survived," Sue explained. "The rest were destroyed. People took them apart when they knew about them, or built on top of them."

"So my heiau might be overgrown," said Kai. *If it's still there.*

"Tell me about your grandma's heiau," Sue said. "Was it the typical rectangular raised platform altar composed of volcanic basalt? Aligned parallel or perpendicular to the makai-mauka axis?"

"It was a rectangular pile," said Kai. "What's makai-mauka?"

"Oh, sorry! You look so much like a local, I forgot. Have you noticed that people on Maui give directions in terms of the sea -- makai-- and mountain – mauka?"

She explained that traditional land divisions for agriculture were based on each family owning a strip running from the mountainside to the sea. Families owned long, thin parcels and rotated the parts they used for growing taro. Heiaus were usually by the sea, or at the top edge of the parcel on the border between cultivated and untouched land. Most heiaus were built either parallel or perpendicular to the imaginary makai-mauka line running from the summit of Haleakala or the nearest mountain peak to the sea.

"My grandma's heiau is way back in the forest," said Kai.

"Hmm," said Sue. "Well, they're all over the place. But it was a family site?"

"My grandma built it."

"Well, the location might be a clue to your chant. Maybe other family members in the past chose sites back in the forest, too."

"I don't know," said Kai. "I don't think my grandma's heiau has anything to do with the chant. She built it herself, and when I showed her the chant, she didn't really know what it meant, just that it had to do with places sacred to our family in the past. But she thought Great-grandpa in Hana might know."

They drove in silence. Kai tried to imagine his family heiau, an intricate assembly of rocks deep in the rainforest, shaded by trees. He wondered what Sue liked to do in her time off. Maybe hike or rock climb? Something adventurous and challenging. Maybe deep-sea diving?

The rainforest grew thicker and darker. Kai felt he was entering a different Maui. Secretive. This was the windward side, the side his grandma said belonged to Lono, god of fertility and rain, and to the pig-god, Kamapua'a. What was out there?

Rivers? Animals? Kai opened the chant and tried to focus his thoughts around the next line of the chant: *Kihapi'ilani's road leads behind the father's house.* What could that mean?

Up ahead, Kai glimpsed a small farm stand in a wide place beside the road. The stand sold pineapple, fresh coconut milk, and raw sugar cane to tourists. A few locals wielding machetes stood near a cutting board, ready to prepare the fruit for customers. Kai felt drawn to them. There was something about this place.

Had he been here before? That was impossible. But it looked vaguely familiar. The feeling was ridiculous, irrational. Still, he couldn't shake the feeling. He felt as if he were falling. His link to this place was irresistible. A force was pulling him closer, wrapping him in...

A man stepped from behind the stand. He was a big man, with broad shoulders and big hands even for the rest of his body. He moved easily, comfortable with himself and the people he was near. Kai gasped.

Dad?

"Stop!" he said.

Sue slammed on the brakes.

Without waiting, Kai jumped out of the car, and ran to the fruit stand.

A family of tourists got out of his way. The group selling sugar cane included two teenage boys with tattoos and an older woman. But there was no man.

Suddenly, it seemed so silly. What was wrong with him? It was crazy. His dad was dead! He had seen some guy that looked like Dad. Maybe a relative?

But where'd the man go?

Behind the stand, a path led across a little grassy clearing into the rainforest. A few tourists were walking down the easy slope back to their cars. The hiking trail was so mild it was almost like an access road.

Kai glimpsed a figure. He stood at the edge of the forest where the path disappeared.

Kai's heart pounded.

The shadowy figure stood very still, staring intently at Kai, watching him. Kai saw him lift his hand and set it over his heart, as if he were reciting the pledge of allegiance, just the way his dad always said goodbye in sign language when they were too far apart for words.

A memory came flooding back.

Kai was six years old. His dad was teaching him to ride his bike.

"You got to feel the ground," Dad said.

"I can't!" Kai said.

"Like surfing. Feel the grass up through the bike. Don't fight the ground. Go with it. The ground is bigger than you. You ride the ground. If you try to fight the ground, you're not going to win."

His father grabbed the bike. "You ready to fly on your own?"

Kai was afraid to move a muscle. Afraid to speak.

"Okay. I count to three. One, two, three…"

Kai was flying over the grass, actually soaring it seemed, with the wind in his face. Dad was cheering. Kai bumped along, holding on tightly. After a long time his bike slowed of its own accord and he put his feet down and looked back. Dad was far away on a little hill.

Kai held his hands up in victory.

His dad smiled back and put his right hand over his heart.

The figure near the forest's edge disappeared.

Sue. She would be waiting. Kai looked back. She was watching him. She looked perplexed. He waved, held his finger up for her to wait a minute, and pointed to the forest. That was all he could give her. At least she would know where he'd gone.

He started up the hill.

He rounded the corner. Banana trees with big gaudy blossoms and guava trees lined the road. Rotten guavas had fallen to the ground and lay smashed, stinking sweet. Tourists strolled.

He hurried. It made no sense. He knew that.

He heard a noise beside the trail. It was someone yelling, whooping. A man's voice in the woods.

Dad!

Kai was nine. He'd finally made a shot in basketball. After all those tries, those wishes that it would go in, those calculations about the angle the ball should follow, the secret tense prayers… After all that, it

90

had actually gone in, right when it mattered most in the game, and like a miracle, Dad was there to see it and he was watching as it arced up, up, and in! Three-pointer swish shot!

Woo-hooo-yeah!

Dad's voice rose above everyone else's. His powerful pride filled the whole gym. He wouldn't stop. Even when the rest of the crowd quieted, Dad was still cheering.

Woo-hooo! Way to go, Kai!

Dad, I wish you were still watching.

Yet dad had missed so much of Kai's life, even when he could have been there.

Woo-hooo! It was coming from the woods. He followed the sound. A smaller path branched into the darkness under thick trees. He reached a precipice. The cliff dropped to a black pool below. Across the pond, a group of local boys clung to some roots at the edge of the cliff.

Suddenly, a boy broke loose and threw himself far forward away from the mud cliff.

Wooooo! He yelled as he dropped. The drop was spectacular, at least twenty-five feet. There was a huge splash. The jumper disappeared and then popped back up and wiped his face and laughed. He gave his friends the hang-loose sign. As he swam across the pool and climbed out onto a bundle of roots, his friends cheered.

There was no man.

Kai felt warmth from behind him. He whirled around.

 "Kai?"

Kai was startled. It was Sue.

Kai nodded. His heart was still beating fast.

"What's wrong?" she demanded.

Kai struggled to answer. "I think I've been here before," he said. "I thought I saw someone."

"Really? From when you were small?" Sue raised an eyebrow. "I didn't know you'd ever been to Maui. But I don't think this place has anything to do with the chant, do you? You alright? You ready to go now? Next time, let me know what you're doing."

They hiked together back to the car, and climbed in. Sue turned the key in the ignition.

Nothing happened.

"That's strange," she said. She tried again. Still, nothing happened. The ignition wouldn't even turn over. Her brow furrowed. "I don't understand," she said. She tried again. "I wonder if I've flooded it or something," she said. "Okay. Let's get something to eat. Then I'll try again."

The raw sugar cane from the fruit stand was tough and tasteless, like strips of fiber in Kai's mouth. He tried to suck on it but found he didn't have the patience. He bought a coconut, which the local boy split so he could sip the thick, greasy cream-colored milk inside.

Sue tried the key again. She couldn't move it in the ignition. "Maybe I locked the steering wheel?" she said.

Kai couldn't help her. He rarely drove at home. Plus, he didn't think Sue actually wanted any help. She was too frustrated. He sat quietly.

"This is making me crazy!" Sue yelled suddenly. She got out of the car and walked away. They were already quite a drive from Kihei. If they needed to call for help, it would inconvenience whoever came.

Kai felt strange. Why were they still here? Was he supposed to find something before they left?

"Could it be out of gas?" he asked, when Sue returned.

"No!" Sue muttered. She closed her eyes and concentrated.

It's like we got sucked in to this place by something strong and now we can't leave. It's holding us. But what?

A man stepped out from behind the fruit stand. It was him, but he wasn't much like Kai's dad after all. He had the same build, but a different face. Kai watched him laughing with the local boys.

How had he been so mistaken? Kai felt shaky. Everything was so different here. Almost like he had entered a different reality. Now that he saw how little the man resembled dad, he felt embarrassed. He was glad he hadn't told Sue.

Suddenly, Sue opened her eyes and smiled.

"It's the key!" she said. "I'm using an old key ring." She held it up. There were six keys on it. "I'm using the wrong key!" She put the right key in and the car started. "I don't know what came over me," she said, as if to herself.

"Strange things happen sometimes," said Kai.

Chapter 20
MENEHUNE'S GARDEN

The road was all hairpin turns. There were so many that Kai couldn't believe it. The first few were fun. He enjoyed the carnival-ride sensation of being pushed against the side of the car. Sue had to slow down to take the one hundred eighty degree turns, just as all the cars ahead and behind did. But soon enough, even with Sue driving slowly, he was tired of them. In fact, he felt sick. The air was sticky, and heavy, and the smells of rotting fruit and wet soil was strong.

Rain hit suddenly, with force. It fell so hard it was impossible to drive. All the cars in the long line of traffic pulled to the side or waited out the storm in the middle of the narrow road. The sound of rain smacking the car's roof was deafening.

"There'll be some flash flooding," Sue said. "It can be dangerous in the lowlands if it's raining like this on the hillsides above us." She gestured toward the dark, impenetrable hillsides rising steeply around them, now hidden by sheets of falling water. "Hikers can get caught if they're not careful. You don't want to be near a river, or in a gulch." Some hikers had died here, unaware of the rainstorms raging higher up the mountain.

"So we'd better not stop to hike right now?" Kai said. The tropical downpour continued to rage.

Sue laughed. "It'll pass soon," she said. While they waited for the rain to subside, she explained the rain patterns on the island. "In Kihei, less than 15 inches of rain falls a year. But the West Maui Mountains get more than 400. So there are all these interesting mini-climates," she said. "Sub-alpine zones and subtropical zones, just a short drive from each other. And there are so many species of flora and fauna that no one has identified them all. Some of the plants, like silversword, grow only in a tiny climate zone --- only in Haleakala's crater, nowhere else in the world. And there are surprises. Did you know there's a redwood forest on Maui?" Kai hoped he would get to explore them all.

As suddenly as it had come, the rain slowed to drizzle. They started to drive again, but a bit more cautiously on the soaked roads. Kai braced himself for more of the annoying hairpin turns. Soon, the scenery became monotonous. Of course the rainforest was beautiful, and the steep black and green cliffs that occasionally dropped below them to the ocean were spectacular. But it seemed like they had been in the car for hours.

"We're about half-way," Sue said, reading his mind.

Finally, it stopped raining. Kai opened his window and gulped in the fresh, fertile smells of the washed rainforest.

"Look," Sue said.

The view was picturesque. A steep green hill dropped away from the road down to a dark, choppy sea. Splashed by waves, a point of black rock and coconut palms protruded into the sea. A small church and a cluster of homes clung to the point of land like a miniature village from a distant, isolated time in the past.

"Keanae Peninsula," she said. "I'll bet it's looked just like that for a hundred years."

"What was Hana like, one hundred years ago?" Kai asked. His great-grandpa's parents would have been living there then.

"It was a boom town!" said Sue. "Maybe thirty-thousand people lived in Hana then. Now it's more like a few hundred."

Hana's a ghost town.

Sue told him what she knew about Hana's history. Before Captain Cook, Hana had been one of the largest and most important cities on the island. It alternated between alliance with other cities on Maui and cities of the Big Island of Hawaii. It continued to be an important city until around 1940. From around 1880 to 1940, it was a bustling modern city with two movie theatres and many stores. Then the sugar cane industry closed. In 1946, a tidal wave hit Hana and killed eight people. Without the sugar cane and after the devastation from the tidal wave, Hana was reduced to a small tourist town. Many families left to find work on plantations in other parts of Maui.

"Hana is special," said Sue. "It's so different than the rest of the island. Quiet. Like going into the past. The beaches are gorgeous. Dark blue water, and red or black sand. The red beach is by Hana Harbor, but really secluded because of the trail. It's in a volcanic cinder cone and the sand is really rough, just pieces of cinder. But it's so calm that people like to snorkel there. Nude," she added.

"Have you tried?" Kai asked.

"Not yet," said Sue. "Then there's the Seven Sacred Pools, these deep pools connected by waterfalls where you can jump and swim. There's a place I've hiked by the pools where you go through a bamboo forest, on a wooden boardwalk. When the wind passes through it, the bamboo sings, like chimes."

The way Sue described Hana, it sounded delicious and secret.

"I'd try snorkeling with you," Kai said.

"Let's stop here," Sue said, ignoring his offer. She pulled off at the Keanae Botanical Gardens. "Stretch our legs, okay?"

Kai was grateful. They parked under giant monkeypod trees.

The garden was lovely, and strange. Impatiens bloomed on the forest floor. Other plants had leaves the size of shields. There was taro. Papaya fruit bulged like warts on the trunks of trees. Mosquitoes swarmed.

Water dripped. Although it was still early in the day, it was strangely dim here, like dusk under the canopy of branches and rising mist. They were the only ones in the rain-washed garden.

"It's beautiful," Sue said softly. "I've been to Hana a few times, but I've never been here before. I didn't know this even existed. Maui is like that…You're just going along, and you think you know where you're going. Then, boom! You're somewhere completely different from where you just were, doing something you never expected. As if the island had its own plan for you. Like time travel. Like a children's story, where you pass through a door. Only the people who go know about it." She smiled at Kai. "To everyone else," she said softly, "what happens remains a secret."

Sue sounded strangely spiritual. Like the power of this place was getting to her. He felt it, too. The heavy stillness pressed against him.

"We're the only ones here," Sue murmured. Her words hung in the muggy silence. "Except the menehune," she added. "You know, the little magical people."

Kai was surprised. Sue, who had been so professional all morning, sounded kind of dreamy.

"What do you think? What do you feel? Be honest." She asked, studying him. She dropped her voice. "It's a menehune place, isn't it?"

"Are menehune good or bad?" Kai asked.

Sue considered, and looked playful. "Both," she said. "They can do good things or bad things. They're powerful."

Kai felt uneasy. There was really something weird about this place. There was something lurking here. Hidden in the brush at the edge of the beauty of the garden, where the garden stopped being a park full of flowers and became the forest. Was something watching them?

Just then a family of tourists came down the path.

The spell was broken.

"You ready to go?" said Sue. "I'm excited about the chant. I think together we can figure it out. And I can't wait to hear what your great-grandfather suggests."

As they started back to the car, mosquitoes descended with a vengeance. They came like a shadow. High-pitched whining filled Kai's ears. As one, they ran back to the car and slammed the doors shut.

They got back on the road to Hana.

The same scenery they had been watching for hours closed around them again.

Chapter 21
THE TEAM

The investor called the developer before lunch. "How is everything? No delays?"

The developer made a face. Why did this investor think he would hurry more if prodded? Hadn't he already guaranteed that he would hurry? "Everything is going well," he said calmly.

"On track? I learned today, zoning decision very soon. Our requirements may change. We need everything permitted. As soon...as...possible." The investor spoke the last three words very slowly and clearly.

"I know. I heard the same," the developer reassured him.

"Good," said the investor. "I'll check with you tomorrow."

You do that, the developer thought. He hung up the phone and wiped the sweat from his brow. How was he going to make the process faster? The archeological inspection was sure to slow things down. All the sites in that part of the island were loaded with archeological obstacles that forced developers to redesign and receive special permits with conditions set by the Corporation Counsel and the Planning Department.

If he could get a certain inspector he knew, everything would move as smoothly as possible. He had worked with David Hudson before. David was great. David understood how things really worked around here, and how to get permits quickly for whatever you wanted. David knew all the important people. If he explained his constraints, David would understand. And David would do everything necessary. To make sure this would happen, the developer needed David on his team. He picked up his phone.

Chapter 22
WHAT TREASURE CAN BUY

During Kai and Sue's brief stop at the garden, traffic had worsened. Now there was a slow line, like a parade procession, of road-weary tourists navigating turn after sharp turn. Often, Sue was touching her brakes.

"How many more hairpin turns?" Kai asked.

Sue laughed. "Hundreds. We've probably done half. And then we'll do them all again on the way home." They slowed for another one-lane bridge, and waited for the oncoming car to cross before they could go.

Sue pointed out the date engraved on the bridge as they crossed. The bridges had been built mostly in the early 1900s, in the days when the road was a horse and wagon trail.

Sue kept talking. She seemed to want to keep a conversation going. "I know an old man who worked in construction at the time. Must have been in the '30s. He told me this funny story. There were a number of construction companies competing at the time. They all wanted the job of building the highway. So the government came up with a plan to divide the work up. Each company could bid their price to construct a section of the highway. But they wouldn't find out until after they were awarded the work and accepted it which section they were going to do. So some companies got the easy part, near Paia. Others got the hard part, near here, where they needed lots of dynamite. The extra costs above what he bid drove the man I know out of business."

Sue glanced at Kai.

"So," she said, changing the topic of conversation, "Tell me what you'll do with the money."

Kai smiled. "You think we'll find something?"

"I wouldn't drive all this way if I didn't," said Sue.

"How much do you think it will be worth?"

Sue considered. "Depends what you uncover, of course. A Civil War flag sold for almost one hundred thousand dollars recently. Even the spades used by John Brown's violent abolitionists sell for thirty thousand. But each artifact is different. Collectors tend to have highly personal interests. Even something which seems valueless can sometimes command a good price in a private sale to the right collector."

"Thousands?" asked Kai.

"That's a given," said Sue. "The artifact you find, if you find it, will be one of a kind because of its historical significance. If it belonged to Cook and was one of the first items from the outside world that old Hawaiians saw, it will fetch a high price at auction."

"What do you think it could be?" asked Kai.

"A plate. A sword…I don't know. He had a few items of great value on the ship. One was his ship's log. Another was his chronometer."

"What's a chronometer?" asked Kai.

Sue explained that the chronometer was a special timepiece. Cook's was designed by John Harrison to withstand sea voyages. Just before Cook's second voyage. Harrison, a clockmaker, won a prize from British Parliament comparable to several million dollars in today's money for designing the best sturdy, accurate seagoing watch. Harrison's chronometer ended up revolutionizing sea travel, allowing explorers to accurately calculate their longitude and, as a result, go much farther in their exploratory voyages without getting lost.

Cook was the first to test out the prize winning chronometer, and prove it worked. He traveled with a copy of Harrison's, the Kendall K1 chronometer, and it worked perfectly.

"So the chronometer was an experiment?" Kai said.

"It needed to be demonstrated. Cook used the chronometer to determine his longitude and it proved extremely reliable and exact. It worked."

"What did explorers do before chronometers?" Kai asked. He imagined setting out across the wide ocean without tools or modern navigational equipment. It must have been terrifying.

"I studied that, too," she said. "Before chronometers, people had come up with different ideas about how to determine longitude at sea, none of them very accurate. Obviously, they needed to keep track of longitude so they could return to places, and make an accurate map. Chronometers were a huge improvement. They allowed Cook to make fabulous, accurate maps of the places he visited --- so accurate they were not replaced until the twentieth century.

"The chronometer kept perfect time. It was built and set to London time. Cook could travel anywhere in the world and compare noon, when the sun was high in the sky wherever he was, with what the clock said. If the London clock said midnight when it was noon where Cook was, he knew he was half-way around the world.

"Once Captain Cook had returned to London, he published his ship's log, and celebrated the chronometer to great acclaim. He called it 'my trusty little timepiece.' It wasn't until later, on his third and final voyage that he discovered Hawaii. But you can bet that he brought his trusty little timepiece on that voyage, too," Sue said.

Sue's eyes were bright.

"As I was thinking about your heiau, I started wondering...What if he had a back-up? An extra chronometer provided by the watchmaker in case something happened to the first one. After all, the watchmaker was getting tremendous free advertising from every early voyage. After Cook demonstrated the chronometer's success in his voyages, every single long-distance voyage that could afford it took a chronometer. Every single voyage until the twentieth century!

"The producer of Cook's chronometer was named Kendall. If I were Kendall, I would have sent two chronometers with Cook every time, just in case. The chronometers Cook had were copies of the prototype prize-winning one, anyway. Why not produce two copies and give them both to Cook?

"No one says anything about a second chronometer in the records. But why would anyone mention that? The voyages were meant to prove that explorers could trust their lives on the reliability of the product. If I'm right that there were two chronometers on his voyages, one might be here, in your heiau, a place no one would look, neither Cook nor his crew nor the Hawaiians themselves, an untouchable place of sacred safety."

"How would my family have ended up with it?" Kai asked.

"That's easy. Maybe Cook and his crew were distracted. You know, many Hawaiians actually visited the ship at the beginning, before things got out of control. The chronometer wasn't large, and it was shiny, eye-catching. I saw one online. It was recently up for auction. It wasn't on any particularly famous voyage, and it was from several decades after Cook's revolutionary, experimental model. Yet it commanded over one hundred thousand dollars among clock collectors. Another famous watch from 1779 – Captain Cook's era – sold recently in Paris for well over a million dollars."

"What if the artifact at my family heiau isn't the chronometer?" Kai asked.

Sue shrugged. "There's a good chance it's not. But I think it is something important like the chronometer. You said your grandma thought the chant was about places sacred to the family? So it's probably been in your family for a long time. One of your relatives, or maybe successive generations of them, went to a lot of work to create the chant to keep track of the places. My guess is that it developed and grew over time, like a story told by successive storytellers, each one adding embellishments --- if it's as old as it seems, and started as an oral tradition. Once it was written, of course --- or if it was always written --- it wouldn't change as readily. People would just pass on copies to other family members. But your relatives still had to work to keep it safe in the family. At least a few people were involved over the years. Why would they go to so much work if they didn't have a valuable treasure?"

"What did you say the chronometer in Paris sold for again?"

"More than a million dollars," said Sue. "Your chronometer would be worth many times more."

Kai whistled.

"So," Sue continued. "How are you going to spend it?"

Kai hadn't thought much about it. There were so many things he needed. A college education. A motor-cross bike. Surfing lessons. A new ipod. His inheritance would buy them all.

"I'd like a car," Kai said suddenly. "A Porsche 911." He imagined the svelte lines of the car's polished body. "Blue," he went on, warming to the idea. "They handle really well."

Sue laughed. "I don't know," she said. "You don't strike me as a race car driver. I actually thought you've been looking a little green on some of these hairpin turns."

Kai felt embarrassed.

"A car might be fun," Sue conceded. "But what about travel? Don't you want to see the world? Wander through India, camp in Croatia? Maybe Thailand?"

Kai wasn't sure. He'd never been anywhere outside California, except here. His mom was always busy with work, and there hadn't been much money. It would be fun to see New York City, he thought.

Sue nudged him. "Just messing with you. But seriously, if you get a chance to travel, you should take it. After I finished studying Art History at university in Stockholm," Sue said, "I spent a year going around the world. Just to see everything. To meet people who couldn't speak my languages, who had different approaches to life. It was such an adventure. I never knew who I would meet next, or where I would sleep. I had a backpack, and all my things fit in it. It was incredible. Hiking the Himalayas. The Vatican museum. The hill towns of Spain. The Great Wall of China. Whenever I got to a place I loved, I found a job and stayed a while, to get to know it better. Kai, you should do it," she finished.

Kai was speechless. Had she really been to all of those places?

"After a while," Sue said, "I got tired of traveling. I longed to unpack, and have a hot bath. I wanted to cook in my own kitchen. I was lonely. I wanted to make friends I could keep and continue to see instead of always moving on, going our separate ways. I came to the islands, on my way back to Europe. And I never left."

"How long have you been here?" Kai asked.

"Maui, only a year. But I was in Oahu, working for the Bishop Museum before that, mostly with documents from the early period of European contact. Artifacts from Hawaiian prehistory. That job led naturally to this one, where I get paid to help identify and preserve previously undocumented archeological sites. I like the mix of being out in the field and in the office writing reports. I feel like my own boss. And I like the feeling that I'm contributing, preserving a lost culture for the future."

Kai wondered briefly if there was any conflict for Sue between preserving ancient Hawaiian culture and selling the artifact his family had taken from Cook. Apparently it wouldn't bother her if he dug up a heiau, as long as it was his family's property and she got to help.

For the rest of the drive to Hana, Kai imagined driving a Porsche.

Chapter 23
NO TRACE

D avid felt an annoying vibration in his thigh. He sat up in the comfortable office swivel chair. Then he reached down into his pocket and flipped open his phone.

"David, bad news. There are complications at the site. We need the survey done faster. Is that possible?"

"I'm not sure. Right now, we're working as fast as we can," said David.

"David! Listen to me! I need the survey completed as soon as possible. It's a zoning issue. We don't have much time," the developer demanded.

"Yes… yes. I will form a committee immediately. We will have the survey finished in a few days," David reassured him.

"Great. Remember, this absolutely has to get done. And there must be no trace of our work."

Chapter 24
GREAT-GRANDPA'S GIANT SECRET

Sue dropped Kai off at his great-grandfather's house. "Give me a call later," she said. Kai would spend the night with Great-grandpa, and then ride home with a friend of his who was headed toward central Maui.

Great-grandpa Ku'ukia lived off a quiet street in a narrow one-story white house. A row of palm fronds stood before a small porch. Peeling green paint covered the short stairway and outlined the front door. Cautiously, Kai mounted the steps and tapped twice on the front door. Kai wondered what Great-grandpa would be like. Would he know about the heiau?

An old man opened the door, bringing light into the dark house. He had wrinkled brown skin and strands of gray hair on his head. In his hand was a battered ukulele. He walked with a hunch but was surprisingly nimble for a man of his age.

Kai introduced himself and gave Great-grandpa the bag of food. Great-grandpa set the ukulele down and looked in the bag. His wrinkled lips parted into a smile, revealing uneven teeth that were separated like fingers. He let out a throaty chuckle. Then he spoke, slowly, methodically, with an accent. "Did Lokelani tell you to bring these? Thank you! Thank you. Welcome Kai. I've heard about you. Come in. Call me Poppy."

"Nice to meet you," Kai said, following Poppy inside. "Do you play ukulele?" It was dimly lit inside and musty. Daylight seeped through the few windows to the outside. The house was in a state of disarray. A white cat lay curled on one end of a sofa. Sheets and blankets were scattered throughout the room.

"Oh, yes! I love ukulele. All my life. Here, you sit down." Kai found a chair at the kitchen table. "We talk. You

106

had chicken feet before? Hawaiian delicacy." Poppy began to wash the chicken feet. Kai watched the old man pour two cans of Coke into a sauce pan, followed by sugar, soy sauce, and something else from a can. Then he set put the feet into the mixture and turned the heat low.

"Cook a long time," he said, joining Kai at the table. As Poppy lowered his body into the chair by leaning on the table, Kai noticed a slow carefulness due to his age. Poppy must be in his eighties. Yet he seemed young for his age. "Tough!" Poppy elaborated on the chicken feet. "I let them get soft."

"Poppy, how old are you?" Kai asked.

Poppy stared at him with dark brown eyes. "Older than you'd think, Kai. Oldest in family now. But not as old as you'd imagine."

Kai laughed. "And how old is that?"

Silence filled the room momentarily, and then Poppy chuckled. "If I told you a number, Kai, I would be lying. World is full of numbers, every number a lie. People aren't numbers. I'm not a number. Me, work the fields kept me young. You either got tough, or fell down dead. I was tough. Like chicken feet. Tough people are younger than their numbers."

"What did you do in the fields?"

Poppy chuckled again. "Kai, so many questions! Are you thirsty?" Poppy got them each cold cans of soda. "First, you tell me about yourself."

Kai told about himself and his life in California. Poppy listened closely, nodding.

"When I was young, it was all work," Poppy said. "Nothing but work. Hot!" Poppy explained how plantation managers didn't want too many of any one kind of people. "They didn't want us to ask for more pay. All from different places, we couldn't even talk. Had to invent pidgin language. Such bad work. Sharp stuff. Hard on the hands. Hard on your Grandma. But life has also been very good."

"What do you mean?"

"Good family. Nahoa, your father, he was a great boy," Poppy said. He revealed his ancient teeth in a half-smile. "He never complained. Never. Just took what he was given."

"You mean he was talented?"

"Very. Hula, surf, ukulele. Everything he did, he was good. Kai, let me show you something." They left the chicken feet boiling in the kitchen, and Kai followed Poppy through the dark room and out the screen door on the back side of the house. In the small backyard tall grass grew alongside small colorful flowers. A morning dove cooed.

"Kai, whenever someone visits, I show this to them. I remember showing this to your father, years ago." Kai looked around, wondering what his great-grandpa was talking about. Nothing stood out in the small backyard. "Kai, you see that tree up there?" He pointed. A tall, leafy tree swayed in the light breeze. "Look at it for a while. Don't look at anything else. Give the tree your full attention." Kai looked at Poppy, expecting something more. Poppy stood still, his gaze transfixed on the tree.

What was this all about? What was Poppy showing him?

Kai tried looking harder. There was nothing up there, was there? The morning dove cooed again. A breeze rustled through the tree. He waited for Poppy to explain.

"Now close your eyes," Poppy said. "What do you see?"

"I see…" Kai searched for words. He noticed the outline of the tree on the inside of his eyelids, in purple. "I can still see the tree. It's…still there."

Poppy chuckled to himself. "Kai, you are just like your dad. Absolutely right!"

Apparently, Kai had passed the test.

"Come back inside."

Kai wondered if Poppy often gazed at trees, or only with visitors. *But I'm in a hurry to find the heiau!* Maybe Poppy could sense Kai's impatience. Was Poppy insisting that Kai slow down and take notice? Kai took a deep breath. *Why am I in such a hurry?* To hurry was mainland-style. To take time was island style. *To learn from Poppy, I need to do things his way and pay attention.*

They sat down again in the moist air by the boiling chicken feet. Kai's eyes rested on the ukulele.

"Can you play for me?" Kai asked.

Poppy grinned. He took his instrument and began to strum. The sound was soothing, and to Kai's ears, strangely like the sweet, tinkling melody of a far-off ice-cream truck --- the sound of childhood. Then Poppy changed chords and the ukulele became mournful. He began to sing, with perfect pitch but in a raspy voice weakened by age. The Hawaiian words tumbled over one another, mixing in a current of rounded vowels as his old fingers worked the strings. Poppy's wrinkled thumb strummed with gusto. Occasionally, he slapped the wooden box of the ukulele with his fingers, adding rhythm in the midst of the song. The strumming gained momentum. Poppy's voice rose and swelled, filling the kitchen. Then he stopped suddenly, and smiled.

"Long time since I sang that one. I almost forgot it! That song was Meli's favorite. Come, I can teach it to you."

Kai took the ukulele. It felt so small and light in his hands.

"It feels like a toy," Kai said.

Poppy shook his head with disapproval. "Ukulele is serious," he said. "Best musicians on the island play ukulele."

"I don't know if I can do it," Kai said.

"You can do it. Just like Nahoa. He won a competition once, at school. Did you know that?"

"No," Kai said.

"Here," said Poppy. "I will show you."

A half-hour later, Kai had mastered the chords of a simple song. Poppy set the ukulele away.

"Kai," Poppy said, "you've come for a reason besides ukulele. I can tell. I am so glad for that reason, whatever it is. Tell me what brought you here."

Kai gulped, searching for the best way to tell. "Before my dad died, he told me to leave his ashes in a special place. A place

109

special to the family. I was wondering if you could help me find it. It's a heiau," said Kai.

Poppy nodded. At first, it seemed like he was going to speak, but he said nothing.

"Where do you think my father would have wanted me to put his ashes?"

Poppy looked thoughtful. Then he shrugged. "Don't know. What did he tell you?"

"That's the problem. I hardly knew Dad...I never got to see him much." A knot of sadness was growing in Kai's chest. "You actually knew him a lot better than I did," he said softly. "He left Mom and me."

"No, no. Not *knew*," said Poppy. "*Know*." He put a fist on his chest. "You know him. Not something you can lose. Why else he ask you?"

That didn't help at all. Kai couldn't just feel his way to the family heiau. "Do you know of an old family site where I could put his ashes?"

Poppy paused. "Kai, you ask, find out. You look, you find it."

"I want to put my father's ashes in a family heiau, an old family heiau."

"Yes. Why? Many heiaus. Great heiaus. Many on the island. Why an old family heiau? Why not a heiau you make?" Poppy seemed to be sizing Kai up, deciding something about him.

Kai sighed. "My dad only left me two instructions when he died. He told me to deliver his ashes to the old family heiau. He made me promise. Then he gave me this, to keep." Kai slipped the chant out of his pocket and handed it to the man. "I promised."

Poppy got his reading glasses. He looked at the translated chant for a long time. Then he whistled. "Your Dad gave you this one?"

"Do you know it?" Kai asked.

"Yes." Poppy stood, and found his keys. "Come, I will take you to the great heiau. Come with me."

Kai was relieved to find that Poppy was a good driver. Kai felt at ease. As the old car picked up speed around a curve, Kai stared out the window. Vines hung from the branches. They passed eucalyptus and guava. He found himself thinking about his dad again.

"Nahoa is with us," Poppy said softly, startling Kai. "Don't worry. He tells you where to go."

"How did you know what I was thinking?"

"We are family."

Now they drove on the Hana Highway, back towards Paia. Hana was much smaller than Kai had expected. It felt more like a collection of houses and stores scattered across the exquisite landscape than a real town. "Poppy?" said Kai, remembering what Sue had told him about the chant. "Where are the red and black sand beaches?"

"Red sand, back there. Black sand, up there." Poppy gestured.

The sand of fire leads to sand of night. Maybe Sue had been right. But instead of the heiau being literally on the beach, maybe "leads" meant that you had to *pass* the red sand and black sand beaches to get to the heiau.

"Are those the sands in the chant?"

"Yes," said Poppy.

Looking at the chant again, Kai asked, "And who is Kihapi'ilani?"

"The son of Pi'ilani. Pi'ilani, the great father. Ruler of Maui. Brought everyone together."

"Are we related to him?" asked Kai.

"No. But everyone respects the great king," said Poppy.

"So his son built a road?" asked Kai.

"Yes. The Great King's son built the road to Hana," Poppy explained.

"The road to Hana. The one we're on right now," said Kai.

"No. We are very close to Kihapi'ilani's road. But this is the new road. That's the old road. They built them next to each other." The road to Hana must be ancient.

Kai imagined teams of Hawaiians with simple tools building a road that stretched around the entire island to fulfill Pi'ilani's vision. "And where is the father's house? Does that refer to Pi'ilani again?" asked Kai.

Poppy smiled and said, "You'll see."

They turned right at Mile Marker 31 and drove down a small paved road. Soon the pavement turned to gravel and then they crossed a small stream that covered the roadway. On the right, a sign read, "Kahanu Gardens."

They paid admission and entered the park.

"Where are we going?" asked Kai.

"We are there," said Poppy, parking the car.

They walked on a level trail through rows of hedges, under a green tunnel of plants, and past spiky green nuts hanging from breadfruit trees. They reached a vast open lawn partly covered by heart-shaped leaved taro plants. Behind the taro, coconut trees swayed in the wind. In the distance, Kai glimpsed foamy waves crashing into shore.

Kai glanced at Poppy, amazed at his strength. He was breathing heavily now, and had a bit of unsteadiness in his walk, but they had not stopped once to rest.

"Do you want to rest?" Kai asked.

The old man looked insulted. "Not far now," he said.

The dirt trail led through dense forest.

"Hala trees," said Poppy, pointing up at the canopy. The trees looked pre-historic, with thick round limbs and bunches of pointed leaves that hung loosely. The forest ended at a clearing.

"Here! The great place." Poppy gestured.

The heiau was massive. It threw off Kai's sense of scale. Tall steps made of porous lava rocks stretched fifty feet up into the sky. Its foundation was larger than the size of two football fields. Kai stared, breathless.

"Pi'ilanihale heiau," said Poppy. "I feel it, too. Every time." Kai basked in the beauty of the scene for a moment. Everything except the heiau was green: the lawn, the trees, the mountains in the background. Only the heiau was dark brown.

Four coconut trees, oddly placed, stood together on top of the vast and mysterious platform.

"All covered in forest, overgrown, for many years. Then a few years ago, it was found, turned into a park. The largest heiau of all the islands."

"Did you know about it before it was discovered?" asked Kai.

"Yes, many knew," he said softly, "since a long time ago. Never lost to us." Kai understood. Poppy and other locals must have known about it but kept the location a secret for years to protect the sacred site. Kai asked if they could move closer. "No," said Poppy. "This is good."

"So is this also our family heiau?"

His great-grandpa paused for a long time. He fixed his gaze on the heiau across the lawn. "No, not our family heiau."

Kai sighed. "Poppy, I want to find the family one."

Poppy remained rigid. "Kai, did you ever go on a journey?"

Kai grinned. What was that supposed to mean? "I'm on a journey right now."

"Good, good. A journey to me! On this journey, what happened?"

So much had happened. Should Kai tell Poppy about the stories he'd heard about Dad at Aunty H's house? Or about hiking to the heiau with Grandma? Should he tell Poppy about his vision of the owl? "A few nights ago, I went outside at night. I saw something -- an owl -- in the trees. And then I saw an owl with Grandma Lokelani." He wondered if he needed to explain more. No, Poppy would understand.

Poppy nodded. He seemed to decide. "I'm glad. You are meant to see. I will bring you to the family heiau. Follow me."

The family heiau was behind Pi'ilanihale heiau, in the thick forest away from the dirt trail, hidden between two trees with roots that stuck up out of the earth like brooms.

"Poppy, what does Pi'ilanihale mean?" Kai asked.

"It means the Pi'ilani's house," said Poppy.

Kai thought about the chant. An entire chunk suddenly made sense:

The sand of fire leads to sand of night
Kihapi'ilani's road leads behind father's house
Hear the echoes of our song

Of course! First Sue had guessed, and then Poppy had confirmed, that the sands were the red and black beaches they'd passed on the way here...The next part of the chant was: *Kihapi'ilani's road leads behind the father's house.* The great heiau, the largest heiau in the Hawaiian islands, was called "Pi'ilanihale." "Hale" at the end of the name meant "house." Pi'ilani was the king and symbolic father...the big heiau was the "father's house" that Poppy's heiau was behind! The chant was a poetic riddle that could not be solved without knowing both the history and the landscape.

Kai drew near the family heiau. The pile of pebbles and pieces of lava was stacked without mortar. The structure was rectangular, about four feet long, three feet wide, and two feet tall. Another mound stood on top of the center of the heiau. After examining it from above, Kai realized it was a symbol. A small indent in its top looked like an eye. On the left side was a beak, and on the right a small tail. *A symbol of a bird. The owl!*

Poppy spoke. "Special heiau. Special to us. See how they don't line up? Most heiaus mauka-makai, mountain-sea." He motioned with his hands, putting his arms in line. "But our heiaus are different, off a little." Now he angled one of his arms.

"Our *heiaus*? So there are more like this?" Kai asked.

"Yes. This is a new heiau," answered Poppy.

"And do the older ones look the same?" asked Kai.

"I know one," said Poppy.

"When was this one here built?" asked Kai.

"More than fifty years ago."

The place for Dad's ashes and the Cook artifact, if it existed, must be near a different, older heiau that looked like this one.

"Poppy, can you take me to the older heiau?" asked Kai.

"Yes, Kai. I will take you. " Poppy's eyes sparkled. "But first, we go home and eat chicken feet."

Chapter 25
THE END OF THE WORLD

Year 1819
At a Sacred Site on Maui

Today the familiar world would disappear forever.
The messenger arrived at the sacred altar out of breath.
"Hurry!" he told the priest. "A mob of people is coming.
They destroyed the other heiau. They burned the figures of
gods! Anything you want to save...Hurry!"

The kapuna-priest was dumbstruck. Burned the gods?
Since King Kamehameha I died, nothing had been the same.
The new ruler, Queen Ka'ahumanu, had no respect for the way
things had been done for centuries. She decreed drastic changes.
Her mind had been poisoned by the foreigners and their strange
ways. As a woman, she wanted men and women to eat together!

Not only were the sacred rules about eating to be broken,
but all rules. The Queen had decreed an end to kapu, the entire
system: no more Hawaiian religion and moral codes. No more
of the rules that had bound society since before memory!
Thinking she was being innovative, modern, and open-minded,
she had decreed the end to everything.

The kapuna-priest stood frozen, stunned. Of course he
had heard the Queen's decrees, but he had thought them
impossible to enact. The gods would surely rise up and take
vengeance on anyone foolish enough to try to eliminate their
ancient laws. The people would surely prevail on such a queen
to change her mind. The forces of nature would bring
unprecedented storms and tsunami waves. She would be struck
dead, or killed.

Everything was off balance, misaligned. The world had
gone wrong. Since the strangers had come, the Hawaiian rulers
had raped the land. The forests had become stumps. All the
beautiful sandalwood trees had been logged to trade with the

foreigners. The common people had become slaves to sandalwood, hungry because all had to log rather than farm. An evil, insatiable greed had infected the leaders.

We have forgotten everything we knew to be right, the kapuna thought sadly. We no longer remember what is important. We have even forgotten to tend the taro plant that sustains us.

The trees were gone, and the sacred o'o-i'i-a'a birds that lived in them were gone, too. The ruling class ali'i could not even make themselves power capes or feathered helmets, because the birds were gone! How would they do battle? Everything was ending. All was lost.

What lack of foresight the leaders had shown! Could they not see that the sandalwood would disappear? Then what? What part of Hawaii would they sell next to support their purchases of ships, iron, goods, and weapons?

"They're coming!" the messenger repeated.

He was right: the sound of the crowd was startlingly close.

The kapuna looked over his magical things. What a foolish thing his Queen was doing! Didn't she realize that it was the system itself that gave her rank and power? How could she eliminate her own importance, and his importance, merely to follow her love affair with the strangers' odd ways? If she destroyed the kapu system, she would destroy her role as ruler. Surely, something would happen right now to prevent the end of the world!

The mob was closer. He felt forsaken, and powerless.

As a priest, he should protect the heiau. But what could he possibly say to disperse the mob? He had to do something! Was this to be his job alone? Would no one else stand up for all that was important?

"They will harm you!" The messenger looked ready to flee. The kapuna realized he was waiting.

Would the mob really beat him? Would they really dare to touch him? They had already dared to burn the gods...

"You go. I will follow," said the kapuna.

The messenger disappeared.

The kapuna looked around desperately. The crowd climbing the hillside was large. There would be no stopping them. He must hurry. He grabbed wildly at prayer sticks, drums, rattles, and small gods. His arms were loaded. His eyes filled with tears. He must not delay.

How had it come to this? How had foreigners reduced his people to destroying themselves? Which stranger had planted the evil seed inside the Queen that had caused her to do such a thing? Where was his strength? Why weren't the gods helping him? To what purpose had he studied and trained if the world was to be without religion?

His eyes fell upon the sacred object, wrapped in red cloth. He hesitated. He had handled it many times, but now he suddenly saw it with new eyes: it was something of the foreigners that had been brought to the inner sanctum. It did not belong here. It was like an evil invading disease that had found its way to the heart of Hawaii. Maybe all the turmoil would end if he got rid of it. The whole society needed to be purged of strangers and their ideas.

In one swift angry movement, the kapuna set down his load, grabbed the object and hurled it as far away from the heiau as he could.

The sacred object flew like a stone. He did not care if it broke! He heard it hit the ground. He thought of all those who had used and protected the object. He thought of its history. Then he felt a moment of sharp regret, but it was too late.

The crowd was almost here. They carried sticks and clubs. The kapuna scooped up an armful of sacred things and ran.

As he ran, he breathed a secret prayer. He would come back later and save whatever was left. He would rebuild. He would practice the rituals and healing arts, secretly if necessary. He would teach others. He would restore the correct order of things, bring back morality, pride, and power to his people. He would search the hillside for the object he had too hastily discarded.   He would find it, protect it, and use it to save the world.

Chapter 26
KAI REPORTS

The present
Hana

Kai stood behind a tree and texted David. *Call me.* Kai glanced around the corner to make sure Poppy wouldn't hear. Kai thought Poppy would understand about searching for a possible artifact, but Kai hadn't explained anything about this to him yet and he wasn't sure how it would sound. Somehow, Kai wasn't ready to talk through everything. He felt he was just getting to know his great-grandpa. What if Poppy didn't understand? Poppy had taken such care to hide his heiau. It was a private, spiritual place. Poppy might not like Kai telling people outside the family about it. After all, Poppy hadn't met David and didn't know how David and Sue were helping. No, it would be better to come back and visit Poppy again later and explain about the artifact then, if Kai found anything, and thank Poppy for his help.

David called.

"I just figured out something about the chant," Kai said.

"What did you find?" asked David.

"I just talked to my great-grandpa. He took me to a family heiau built around 1945. And there's an older one, like Sue was thinking. He said it looks like this one. So maybe we can find the older one that looks like this one. The older heiau will be the one in the chant."

"Excellent. What did the heiau look like?" asked David.

"Rectangular," said Kai. "About four feet by three feet, and two feet tall. A small dome on the top that looks like a bird."

"Great, Kai, this'll help. I was just going to start helping out today, actually. Could you give me directions to one of your relative's houses? I thought I'd talk to someone in your family. I bet your relatives know something else that'll help us."

Kai hesitated. Would Aunty H and Uncle Mano want to talk to David? Of course they knew that Kai had visited David for help with the translation –- in fact, Aunty H had picked him up at David's office to get the presents for Poppy. Kai had mentioned to Uncle Mano that David and Sue were willing to help with their expertise, and of course Aunty H knew that Sue was giving him a ride to Hana, but his aunt and uncle had both been a bit preoccupied with work and he hadn't gone into it any more than that. He'd told them, briefly, that David thought Lono in the chant might mean something about Captain Cook. But while Kai had told them it was possible there might be some object the family had protected for generations, he hadn't yet talked to them yet specifically about how much the possible artifact might be worth.

"I don't know if that would be a good idea," Kai said. "We didn't have much time to talk the last two days. I haven't told them much, and Sue said---"

"Kai, I'm sure it will be fine," David said.

Kai wished he had found time to talk more to his aunt and uncle, but he'd needed to think things through by himself. To be honest, he'd also hesitated to emphasize the monetary value of the possible artifact because he was afraid they might have a lot of advice. They might want to handle things for him. Kai suspected they would take longer than he would to follow the chant. He liked being free to follow the chant however he wanted.

"I'm good at this, Kai," said David. "If we're going to find this thing, we need to follow every avenue."

"Okay," Kai said. He gave David directions to Auntie H and Mano's house. "They're really nice," Kai said. "But I don't think they know anything that will help."

"I have to admit that it's a long shot," said David. "You have to try everything, though, if you know what I mean. Maybe they'll repeat something to me that you've forgotten, or didn't understand. We have to try everything."

"I just remembered something else about the heiau," Kai said. "My great-grandpa said it's on a weird axis. Most are parallel to the ocean and the mountain. Not my family's. It's very rare," said Kai.

"Interesting. That should make our task a lot easier. I'll call you if I find anything," said David.

Kai called Sue, and explained what he'd found, and that he would not need her help getting home. "My great-grandpa has found a ride for me," Kai said. "He wants to show me another place before I go back to Kihei. I'll call you tomorrow morning and let you know. Thanks for the help."

"Be sure you call," said Sue in an excited voice. "I can hardly wait to hear."

Chapter 27
THE SECRET COLLECTION

T hat night, the collector and the wealthy client met in a quiet neighborhood. The collector was nervous. A whole life's work lay in a safe behind a framed Hawaiian print in the far corner of the office. The print was dusty, seemingly forgotten. Finally, the collector would share the safe's contents.

Walking cautiously over to the safe, while the client waited at a respectful distance, the collector glanced around and then blocked the client's view of the lock. There was a satisfying click. The collector turned. Now the safe would display its secrets. One person only would see the achievement. The world would remain oblivious.

The collector slowly opened the safe's door, as if the safe contained a wild animal, coiled and ready to pounce. The fluorescent light of the office streamed into the safe, glistening off recently polished artifacts. The client stared inside.

An ancient poi pounder from pre-contact Maui. Smooth black stone. A gourd-shaped tool with a rounded top and bottom. Hundreds of years ago, a man labored over a board, using this tool to press poi into a fine powder. This poi pounder had been a family heirloom, an object of religious importance…

Six fish hooks from c. 1600 A.D. Glossy white bone carved into j-shaped hooks. A small hole, a loophole for a cord, at the top, and a delicately carved spearhead at the other end.

A stone adze, 9 inches long. In ancient Kihei, a woodcarver smoothed the surface of his sculpture until it shone with the fire of the gods. The family treasured the artifact, and eventually the family placed the artifact in the family's most sacred location…

"What do you think?" the collector asked the client.

"Wow, I'm astounded. How much are you asking for it?"

"You have no idea of its value. You have seen nothing."

"Who did you purchase these from? How did you get it?"

"I think we both know."

A silence hung in the air. After a few moments, the collector pulled a suitcase out of the back of the safe, unzipped the top and pulled open the cover. Inside was a two-foot-long wooden statue. A scalp of spikes. A burnt and carved face with an elongated snout. A squat mid-section, large hips, large feet. Kamapua'a, the hog, ancient Hawaiian god of fertility. Counterpart of the great god Lono.

Here was the heart of the collection. It had been an amazing find, an experience of a lifetime. Museums would pay dearly for this artifact.

The collector gently stroked the grainy wood. Placing one hand under its neck and the other hand under its legs, the collector gently lifted the idol. Cradling it lovingly, as if it were a child, the collector admired it. *You are my passion. I would sacrifice my livelihood, my reputation, every other one of my possessions for you. You are mine.* The museums would pay big money for this type of artifact, but the collector would never sell. Unless the price was right. Big money, but wait until the collection was complete. If only the collector could find the missing piece...

"So when will you be ready to sell your collection?"

"Soon. I can feel that I am close. This may be the last site. I'm hoping." *Soon, I will realize my dream.*

Chapter 28
OWLS IN THE FAMILY

Around lunch time the next day, after another ukulele lesson, Poppy's friend arrived at the house. She was a neighbor of many years name Ruth. Ruth was plump, with brown freckled skin and dark hair with glints of gold and red.

"No problem!" Ruth reassured Poppy. "You do so many nice things for me! I'm happy to give you both a ride. You know I need to deliver the baby quilt to my daughter anyway. Sounds like this will be on the way. We'll take Kai where you want, and then you have dinner with me, Ku'ukia, at my daughter's place. After dinner, I'll bring you home."

"Are you sure you want to come?" Kai asked Poppy. The old man would have to sit in the car for many hours to deliver Kai and return home. They were going some distance, to Makawao. First, they would have to drive back through all the hairpin turns Kai had taken in the morning. Then, they would drive upcountry, up the foot of the volcano.

"It is the only way. You need me," Poppy said.

At the car, Ruth insisted that Poppy sit in the back beside Kai. "So you can talk," she said. "It's a long drive, and you two need to talk. I'll listen to music." She put her headphones on and fiddled with her iphone.

As they wound through the rainforest, Poppy told Kai about the past. "I was born in Hana. Sugar plantation. Before that, my family was in Makawao with the pineapple. Great-Grandma Meli's family, too. We go there now --- to Makawao. The family place. Both sides of the family. Back then, it was paniolo -- cattle ranchers. Horses."

That was part of the chant: *Above the land of the pineapple and the paniolo.* "So your parents built the heiau up in Makawao where you're taking me?"

"Not my parents. Your great-grandma, Meli's grandma. She saw the owl. She built the heiau."

She saw an owl, too? And it led her to build a heiau? Did family members who saw visions of owls build new heiaus? He thought back to the chant: *He who sees the owl possesses the power...* Was Kai supposed to construct the next heiau? So he would find the heiau where a family member who had seen the owl used to live...

"She took me. She kept the chant."

"But why did she take you to the heiau?" Kai asked. He was confused because Great-Grandma's Grandma wasn't a direct blood related to Poppy.

"I listened to old ways," said Poppy. "Meli chose me, and I saw the owl."

Something was nagging at Kai. He couldn't figure it out. If Meli's grandma had built the heiau they were going to see, who had built the one in Hana? "So the heiau in Hana?" asked Kai. "Who made that?"

Poppy grinned. "Me," he said.

Why didn't you tell me until now?

Poppy seemed to understand. "Kai, let me tell you a story. A long time ago, when I was about your age, a little younger maybe, in Hana, I went on a journey. Long journey. I was seventeen. I had a feeling to go. I went into mountains. Little food. Lost, many times. Seven days up there. And on the seventh night, I see something."

"Like I did?" asked Kai.

"Yes, an owl. Over water, far away. It showed me the way home," said Poppy.

"So you built the heiau?" asked Kai.

"Yes."

"And you wrote some of the chant?" asked Kai.

"About my heiau," said Poppy.

"In Hawaiian? You speak Hawaiian?" Kai asked. *Why hadn't anyone told him to have Great-Grandpa translate the chant?*

"No, no. I only sing a little Hawaiian. Meli's grandma, she spoke Hawaiian. She helped me."

"So Meli's grandma gave the chant to you, and you added to it in Hawaiian, and then gave the chant to my dad?" Kai asked.

"Meli gave it to your dad."

"How did Meli's grandma get it?"

"That I don't know."

"What did it look like, the copy you got?"

"I have it," Poppy said.

You have an older copy of the chant! Why didn't you show it to me?

"I will show you, when you visit again," said Poppy, reading Kai's mind.

"Who wrote it?" Kai asked. "I mean, it was an oral chant in our family at first, right?"

Poppy nodded. "Many people wrote it. Different handwriting."

"Is your chant the same as what Dad gave me?"

"The same."

"And you never tried to follow it?"

Didn't you want to find the oldest heiau? Didn't you think about the Lono clue?

"I have followed it," Poppy said.

He kept it safe, and built the heiau and added to the chant.

"I mean, do you think it leads to anything?" Kai asked carefully.

Does Great-grandpa know anything about the possible artifact?

"It helps us remember," said Poppy.

Kai let his questions rest. How would Poppy feel about Kai collecting the artifact? Kai was afraid to ask. Dad had something in mind, perhaps something that Great-grandpa didn't know.

"Poppy, why did you build your heiau in a park?"

Poppy laughed. "I didn't! Not a park. Big forest! Where no one would see."

"But why did you choose that place?"

"I felt it was right."

"So we're going somewhere in Makawao that's really hard to find...somewhere that Meli's grandma thought would be safe?" asked Kai.

"Yes."

"Thank you for taking me," said Kai.

Poppy reached out and squeezed Kai's hand with fingers as old and tough as a well-worn work glove. "I hope I don't forget now where to go. So many years now! We will see if I still know."

"You haven't forgotten anything else," Kai said.

"That is true. But places change."

"I think we'll find it," said Kai.

"Your name means seeker," said Poppy. "Do you know mine?"

Kai shook his head.

Poppy smiled. "My name, it means guide."

Chapter 29
TRUST YOUR INSTINCTS

T hey left the rainforest and crossed a small bridge. The road climbed through Haiku. Poppy explained that pineapple had started on Maui around 1890. As they gained elevation, the landscape transformed. Rolling hills covered with tall grass and bushy trees replaced the rainforest. Soon they entered a town. Although it was still warm, compared to Hana it seemed crisp and invigorating.

"Nice and cool here," observed Poppy. They opened their windows and Ruth turned off the air conditioner.

A gentle breeze rustled the tall grass, laced with the brisk scent of eucalyptus trees. Colors looked vibrant. Where Hana had seemed lush, lazy, wet, overgrown, and sometimes sweetly over-ripe and rotten, this place had a different feeling. It had the perfect temperature and Kai felt relaxed, but energized.

"Makawao town," said Poppy. "Still a little bit cowboy up here." Puffy clouds hung low above them. Off in the distance, the West Maui Mountains were shaded light blue and looked very far away. To the left, a steep incline led up to the sky. More than eight thousand feet of Haleakala rose above them.

As they drove through the central street, they passed parked cars, coffee shops, bakeries, funky clothing boutiques, and an organic grocery store. They passed the Aloha Cowboy, Rodeo General Store, and small shops. A local walked leisurely, wearing flip-flops, a loose flowered shirt, and a cowboy hat.

"Makawao is old," said Poppy. "King Kamehameha got cattle, horses. Then the vaqueros came. They turned Makawao into cowboy town. Now they have rodeo. Hawaiians called the vaqueros paniolo."

They turned onto another road.

"Your Chinese Great-Great-Grandma lived here," Poppy said. "Her whole family was butchers. Delivered meat on horses."

Suddenly a line of bicyclists in single file appeared from around the corner. They wore colorful clothes that looked like spacesuits. The man in the front wore red, followed by about ten riders in neon yellow and then twenty more in dark blue. Each rider wore heavy white helmets, thick black gloves, and white shoes. Kai laughed. They looked like they were on the moon.

Poppy shook his head and said, "Tourists. Big money. Ride all the way down the mountain."

"Oh, don't be so hard on them!" said Ruth, laughing. "At least they're not crowding the Hana highway. Hey, how're you guys doing back there? We're getting close, am I right?"

Kai pulled the chant out of his pocket. "Poppy, you said it's near a spring, right?"

"Yes. Waihou Springs."

Kai studied the chant. He read aloud to Poppy. "Above the springs in the forest of ash…"

"Will be hard if the forest is gone," Poppy observed.

Kai read onward. If he knew what he was looking for, it would be easier to recognize. Once Poppy and Ruth dropped him off, he would be on his own.

"Will this be the oldest of our family's heiaus?"

"No. Many older."

"Have you been to them?" asked Kai.

"No. Makawao is the oldest I have seen," said Poppy.

"How do you know there are others that are older?" asked Kai.

"I feel them."

"Do you know anyone I could talk to? Anyone who knows?" asked Kai.

Poppy grinned. "I am oldest. No one else left." He lowered his voice. "Listen. You must trust. Trust the chant. Go to the heiau. Take your time. Hear the heiau. The heiau will show you."

"So if there's an older heiau than this one, I'll know after visiting it?"

"Yes, the heiau will show you the way. You have to go to know. Each will tell you if you listen. Trust," said Poppy. "Trust ancestors, trust yourself."

Kai would try.

Chapter 30
THE HAUNTED FOREST

Poppy's memory was sound. They found the trailhead --- a small path leading into the forest along the road. Kai thanked Ruth for the ride and hugged Poppy. Kai hoped he would see Poppy again.

"Good luck!" Poppy said. "You call me, and let me know if you find it. Come back and visit me!" Kai waved. Although he was alone, he had Ruth's cell phone number if he needed it, and also Sue's, David's, and Aunty H's. He had Grandma Lokelani's blessing, and Poppy's directions. He wasn't sure how long this would take, but he was anxious to start.

For a moment, Kai surveyed the forest, remembering Poppy's words.

"First," Poppy had told him, "you walk through the forest of ash. Just like in the chant. See, the chant tells you."

Late afternoon light colored the landscape. High feathery clouds were streaked with orange and pink. Strips of light beamed through dusky black canopy, forming a grated ceiling. Kai gazed at the trail that disappeared into an endless world of trunks, a maze.

He entered the forest of ash. The forest was like a giant cage. All the trees looked alike: a single clump of trees reflected in mirrors.

The air smelled strongly of eucalyptus. The trail lay beneath fallen leaves, and as Kai walked, the leaves shuffled, making a soft whispering noise. The forest was dead, silent, hushed. Kai thought about the chant.

> *The sand of fire leads to sand of night*
> *Kihapi'ilani's road leads behind father's house*
> *Hear the echoes of our song*

Above the land of the pineapple and the paniolo
Above the springs in the forest of ash
Hear the echoes of our song

Beyond the cruel sun to the land of the taro
The stream in the northernmost point beyond the mother's auwai
Hear the echoes of our song…

The first heiau had been behind the Hale O Pi'ilani Heiau. Ruth and Poppy had driven him through the land of the pineapple and the paniolo, Makawao. This trail led to the springs. Now he had to look in this jungle of ash trees for a family heiau older than the one found in Hana.

Kai heard his Poppy's voice. *Trust. Trust yourself. Up the trail, two miles. The clearing. It is there.*

The trail suddenly turned sharply to the left. Kai paused for a minute. On the left side of the path was a short steep hill. On the right side, a narrow trickle with muddy banks wound through reeds and torch ginger. Light reflected off the slow-moving water.

A loud rustling noise came from the brush about fifty feet behind Kai. He whipped around. He couldn't see around the bend in the trail. He heard a scrambling noise as something large ran across the path and splashed into the mud. Kai sprinted and then peeked back around the corner. There was nothing but deafening silence. What was out there?

His heart pounding, Kai slinked forward. The forest seemed to be watching him. The forest was alive, waiting for him.

For a long time, Kai walked alone in silence. *What was that thing that crossed the path? It sounded big.*

When would he find the heiau? How far had he gone? The forest lacked landmarks. The landscape was repetitive: tree after tree after tree after tree. The trail narrowed into a thin strip of dirt between two green walls of bushes. Leaves and branches scraped against his legs and shoulders, and when he looked up, he could see the canopy silhouetted against the indigo sky of the oncoming night. Why hadn't he brought a flashlight? Kai was groping through a shadowy world. He had the unnerving feeling that he was walking into a giant throat.

He stopped. To the left of the path was a hillside of crumbly red dirt: the clay embankment. He scurried up to the top, footsteps dampened by the soft earth. He had arrived.

The heiau lay in the middle of a small treeless patch. About a hundred feet across, the clearing was filled waist-high with ferns. To Kai's surprise, the clearing was brightly lit with the golden light of sunset. Had the woods been that dark? He turned around. Blackness. Kai took a step forward into the ring of sunlight.

Once he was standing beside the heiau, Kai could tell that it belonged to his family. It looked nearly identical to the heiau in Hana. The heiau was comprised of smallish gray stones heaped into a massive pile. The heiau was boxy, about five feet square and two feet tall. Just like the previous heiau, there was a small mound with two bumps rising from the middle. Why? Had his family intended to keep the stones positioned this way? Was it accidental that both heiaus had this strange small mound?

Kai remembered what Poppy had told him about the mountain-sea axis of the heiau in Hana. Kai looked up through the treetops. He could barely make out the brown outline of Haleakala against the sky, obscured by the leaves of ash and eucalyptus. Kai looked off through the trees to his right. A red jagged half-circle was the sun setting over the ocean.

Kai turned back to the left and aligned his body with Haleakala. Which way was the ocean the closest? East, or West? This forest was along the lower mountainside, slanted downhill towards Makawao. Past Makawao, below Paia, was the ocean. Kai was between the mountain and the sea.

Kai looked down at the heiau, then up at the faint outline of Haleakala, then back down at the heiau. The heiau was misaligned: the sides of the heiau were not aligned parallel and perpendicular to the mountain-to-sea axis. This definitely was his family's heiau.

In 1880 his family had been living here. By the 1900s his family had moved to Hana where they had built the heiau he

visited that morning. What time had his family built *this* heiau?
A sinking feeling swept through Kai as he realized that the heiau
was too new. *Only a hundred and some years old*, Kai thought, trying
to lighten his mood. He'd have to find another heiau to find the
Captain Cook artifact. Unless the family had moved the artifact
here from an older location. *Hard to tell with a pile of rocks.*

He could ask David. Kai reached down into the left
pocket and grabbed out his cell phone and the chant. Kai
flipped open his cell phone with his thumb. The display came
on, and he dialed in David Hudson's cell number. Kai held the
phone up to his ear. Out of service. No coverage.

*Was he meant to do this without David? Were there things that
belonged to him and his family alone?*

Poppy said this heiau would show him the way.

I will listen and let the heiau tell me like Poppy said.

Kai put his hand on the box of ashes in his backpack. He
let his fingers rest on it but he did not yet feel ready to take it out.
For a while, he sat on the ground between the ferns. This must
be the place, right? This was where his dad wanted him to
scatter his ashes, right? Right?

*Hi Dad. I'm here. I made it. I came here, all this way, just for
you. Are you here? Are you with me right now? Can you hear me?
Before I do this, I just wanted to say that I forgive you. I forgive you for
never really knowing me, for just stopping by every once in a while. I
forgive you. I love you, Dad. I hope I found the place you wanted.*

Was this the heiau of the chant? Kai unfolded the chant
and spread it between his hands. He could barely read in the
dimming light, but he could almost recite the words from
memory. He thought again about the chant as a compilation of
distinct parts made by different people over time. He
understood the beginning of the chant: the first stanza had led
to the heiau he had visited in Hana, and the next stanza had led
here. What were the other stanzas? Did they lead to other
heiaus? For how many generations had people in the family
seen owls and built heiaus? The "land of the cruel sun" and the
"land of the taro" were puzzling. They didn't seem to be about
this heiau. They seemed to refer to a different, perhaps even

older heiau. Kai wondered if that was where the Cook artifact would be hidden. This place fulfilled some of the chant, but not all.

A loud squealing noise filled his ears like an alarm. Kai's heart skipped a beat. Right in front of him stood three huge wild boars.

Chapter 31
ESCAPE

For an instant, Kai stood paralyzed. He stared at the beasts before him. Sharp white tusks protruded from their upper and lower jaws. They had flattened snouts. Thick black hair. About the length and height of a Great Dane plus its tail. Five hundred pound bulldozers.

The next instant, Kai grabbed his backpack and scrambled backwards. The boars moved forward in unison. Kai ran. Which way was the trail that led out of the clearing? He ran toward the edge of the forest. The boars lowered their snouts down to the ground and charged.

The next few minutes were a blur. Kai took off into the brush. He could hear the boars behind him, crashing through the brush, but he didn't dare look back. He became disoriented. In his escape he only thought of two directions: danger, and away from danger. The woods were dark. The sun was gone. The only discernable objects in the gloom were the whitish tree trunks, hovering between the black canopy and the black underbrush like ghosts. Kai dodged around the trees. Raspberry thorns scraped at his legs, arms and face. He couldn't stop. He could only run.

Kai stepped into mud. Ahead, a swishing noise came through the underbrush. Was it another boar? Then a metallic jingling noise. Kai turned to the left and ran into a barbed wire fence. He stopped and slowly backed away. For a second, he was stunned. Then he realized that the forest was silent. He'd lost them.

A rush of fatigue came into Kai's body. The adrenaline was leaving him. His whole body ached. Where were the boars? How long had he run? How much time had passed? Where was he?

Deep growling noises came from the bushes about sixty feet away. He heard loud snorts. Then a chaotic rustling as bodies tumbled through the brush. Yelping, barking, snorting. Dogs. Dogs were attacking the boars. Kai got to his feet and limped along the fence.

Someone else was out here. "Hey! Don't shoot!" yelled Kai. Even screaming, Kai could barely hear his voice.

"Where the heck are you!?" A gravelly male voice. The scramble and barking and snorting continued. "We're going to do the kill Hawaiian style, with a knife!"

"I'm here!" said Kai.

"You're right next to the boars. Move!" said gravel voice.

Kai hopped back up on his feet. The noise was coming closer. He saw a flash of a dog's bright collar through the bushes. The fight was coming towards him.

Kai jostled along the fence. A silky coat rubbed against him. A growling dog. Dog's teeth. The fight was closing in, pressing Kai up against the fence. "Stop!" Kai could barely speak; his mouth was parched. He swallowed, but no spit came into his mouth.

"What's your problem? Get out of here! I flew all the way from New York for this experience! If I can't do it Hawaiian style with a knife, I'm using my rifle! It's almost dark -- we're running out of time! So get out of the way!" The man was standing on the other side of the fighting mass of animals, about thirty feet from Kai.

Kai was knocked to the ground. A boar had run into him. Dogs followed. Hooves and paws clawed at the mud. Biting, kicking, yowling, snarling. Blood splattered. Kai scooted away. He looked down. He was clutching his backpack. He heard the click of a rifle. The hunter slashed and stabbed with his knife. The boar screamed. Noise and blood filled the clearing. Kai scrambled out of the fray.

Time slowed down. The man, dogs, and three boars were still. Kai was in an empty pocket amid a circle of violence, the eye of the storm. Kai jumped down and sprinted away from the fence. He tripped in muddy water. He had run into the creek he had seen earlier from the trail. Quickly, Kai got back onto his feet. He ran through the creek, wading through thick reeds, and came out on the opposite bank. He held the ashes against his chest.

He heard a distant gunshot. The yelping died down and became softer and softer as he left the hunting party behind. Kai kept on running.

His clothes were muddy, blood stained, and soaked. With every step, his shoes made a sloshing noise. His legs stung from scrapes. At least the dogs weren't following him. They were busy now with the remains of the boars...His whole body ached. After a few minutes, Kai stopped and sat down to rest.

Kai realized that he was miserably lost. He hadn't passed a trail since he had seen the boars. *I should have followed the barbed wire fence.* How was he going to find his way out of the woods? Kai checked his cell phone. No service. What luck.

He could walk downhill. It would lead somewhere.

In a few minutes, Kai was back in the creek. *I guess I couldn't be any wetter than I already am.* Kai followed the current, wading through sludge. His shoes occasionally got stuck in the muddy bottom, and Kai had to slither out of the shoes, extract them from the mud, and put them back on his feet. The water, although dirty, felt refreshing. *It's lucky I'm on Maui, where it's seventy degrees at midnight.* The creek led down into a gulch. It began to meander. Right, then left, then right, then left, right, left…

The creek came out of the woods in a large grassy field. The creek water went into a two-foot-wide pipe. At the edge of the field was a tall electric fence. This was a pasture, maybe for cattle. Kai walked along the edge of the fence where there was a thin strip of grass on the edge of the forest. The night air was filled with the calls of grasshoppers. The moon was hidden behind a translucent veil of clouds. A rainbow-colored corona encircled the moon.

After crossing several barbed-wire fences and passing through several pastures, Kai came to a six-foot-tall chain-link fence marking the outer boundary of a neighborhood of houses.

Kai climbed the fence and walked out onto a dirt road. All of the houses had their lights turned off. The buildings cast silent gray shadows in the light from the obscured moon.

A man walked down the road towards Kai. He was tall, heavyset and of Tongan descent. He was carrying a flashlight, and he was walking two leashed white pit-bulls. He wore a black t-shirt. As he drew closer, Kai saw that a live anole lizard dangled from his ear. The green lizard writhed and twitched, its jaws locked around the man's earlobe. It was a living, insect-eating earring. Kai wondered if it would change from green to brown, like the ones he'd seen in Aunty H's yard, according to what the man wore.

The man shone his flashlight into Kai's eyes. Kai was blinded. Then he lowered the flashlight until it shone down on the ground in front of Kai.

"Hey... do you know the way to the highway?" The man's reply was an awkward stare. For a few seconds, the two looked at each other. The Tongan man had the piercing gaze of a hawk, his lips pursed, eyes narrowed. Kai slouched down in a display of submission.

"What are you doing here?" asked the man.

"I came out of the forest back there. I was lost. I got lost in the woods, and I just happened to end up here." The weakness of his own voice bothered Kai. He straightened up his shoulders.

The man paused before he spoke. "Kid, you don't come here. You do not belong here. When you get lost in the forest, you stay lost in the forest until you find your way back to where you came from. This is not where you come."

Kai couldn't think of a comeback. "OK, then how do I get back to Makawao?"

The man pointed over Kai's shoulder. "Back where you came from. Back over the fence."

"Then where does this road lead?"

The man lowered his eyebrows. "Go. Get out of here!"

"Thanks." Kai walked away. Actually, he did more of a shuffle, maybe even a jog.

"Don't ever come back!" the man yelled.

An hour later, Kai stood beside the Haleakala highway. He hadn't seen a car pass by in more than fifteen minutes.

A car came down the road. It was going about thirty, at least half the speed of the other cars Kai had seen zoom down the highway. *What is up with this person?* But maybe this driver wasn't in too much of a hurry. Maybe he would be willing to give Kai a lift. Kai did the thumbs-up sign and waved. The car pulled out onto the shoulder and came to a stop. The window rolled down.

"Whoa, what happened to you?" asked the driver.

"Long story," said Kai.

Chapter 32
MONEY DOESN'T ALWAYS TALK

D avid knocked on the door of Aunty H's house.
"I'm David Hudson."
"Hepaula'ole." She opened the door half way and
peered out at him.

"I'm an archeologist. I was wondering if I could talk to
you and your husband. Kai talked about you. Did he talk about
me? I'm helping him find his family heiau. You're Kai's aunt,
right?"

"Yes. Don't think I know you, though. What's your name,
again?"

"David Hudson. We just got together the other day, so I
guess he hasn't told you yet. He brought his chant into my office
the other day. I translated it for him. Really interesting chant.
You mind if I talk to you about it for a few minutes?"

"Yeah, David, no problem. Come in. Friends of Kai,
they're our friends too, you know that? Come in, don't be shy.
Call me Auntie H, that's what Kai calls me."

The house was cramped but cozy. Hesitantly, David
followed Auntie H to a small table. Mano sat there, reading a
newspaper and wearing long shorts and a tank top. Dark purple
tattoos decorated his left bicep.

Mano was a strong man, and something about his eyes
warned David that Mano might be like a spring that could uncoil
suddenly at any time with hidden, immeasurable strength. David
would go carefully.

"Mano, David's come. He's a friend of Kai's."

"David Hudson," said David. "I work right down the
street. I came to talk to you two about Kai."

"Hey," said Mano, glancing up. "Call me Mano. What's up with Kai?" He had a deep voice. Despite his tough appearance, he spoke smoothly and softly. "He in trouble?"

"No, no trouble. I'm here to talk about the chant he showed me. I think his chant might be very important," said David.

Mano was skeptical. "What do you mean?"

"Kai and I translated the chant the other day. I think it might be sort of a map. To something very valuable, at least to Kai," David went on.

"Nahoa never said anything about that," said Auntie H.

"The words 'Lono's treasure' are in the chant. Kai and I think that the chant points to a heiau that may contain an artifact from Captain Cook."

"What did you say your name was? David?" Mano asked. David nodded. "David, I don't know what you've been getting Kai into. You're saying that you're going to go to Nahoa's family heiau and dig it up to check for the original haole's stuff? In case there's this Captain Cook 'artifact' buried inside it?"

"No, you don't understand. If Kai finds it, he will decide what to do. He might want to keep it, or sell it. The artifact could be worth hundreds of thousands of dollars," said David.

"Could you please stop giving us this story?" said Mano.

David paused. "Sorry, I guess I haven't explained myself enough. I was trying to help your nephew find something valuable. Something that belongs to you."

"David, you don't..." Auntie H began.

"What do you want from us, David?" asked Mano.

"I want to ask a question. Have you ever heard of where an old family site is located? An old heiau? That would really help," said David.

"Nahoa always talked about a heiau on the South shore," said Auntie H. "Maybe Kaupo? Maybe he learned that from his dad."

"Anything else?" David asked. "I'll tell you what. You guys have been so kind to talk to me tonight. I can tell you need to talk this over.   Here's my card, if you think of anything else…"

"Leave right now!" Mano said, standing up. "I know what you're trying to do. You're going to go trash heiaus, looking for things! You're trying to get Kai involved. Just because he trusts people, you are taking advantage of him! Get out of here, haole! No, that was an order," he said, pointing his finger. "Leave, right now!"

David awkwardly backed out the door and into the dusk's thick air. As he hopped into his BMW, Mano stood at the doorway. "Leave our family alone!"

Chapter 33
HITCHHIKING WITH THE CRYSTAL GURU'S FRIEND

"Hey, man. What happened to you?" asked the driver, as Kai gratefully climbed into the old, rusty Ford Escort. He looked about thirty years old, with a long blond ponytail. He was skinny and tanned. He wore a ragged, faded t-shirt and a collection of necklaces made from some sort of crocheted fiber.

"I got lost hiking," Kai said.

"You look like it." He looked at Kai's muddy backpack. "You want to put that in the trunk?"

Kai hesitated. He didn't want to lose the ashes and chant.

"Or you want to just put it in the back? I'm Phil." Phil surveyed Kai's torn and mud-streaked clothes, bloody knee, and tired face. "Hey, I got something that will make you feel better. You like weed?" his voice lowered conspiratorially. "You know, pot?" he added when Kai just stared at him. "I just picked some up." He patted a bag between their seats. "Good quality, I mean, really potent. This friend of mine grows the best on the island. You want to smoke a little while I drive, go ahead. I've got plenty. You can have it free. No charge, man. I mean, you look like you could really use it. I have this philosophy about helping people out. It's like, I help you out when you need it, and somebody else will help me out sometime. And I love the smell. I'll just breathe the smell while you try out this crop."

"Thanks, but I don't smoke pot," Kai said.

"You never tried it?" said Phil. "But that's cool, whatever you want, man. What'd you say your name is?"

"Kai."

"Where you headed, Kai?"

"Kihei."

"The stars align for you, Kai. I'm driving to Kihei tonight. I can give you a lift all the way there."

Kai let himself relax. Wonderful! There was nothing more to worry about. He had made it out of the woods! In a short time, he would be back in the welcoming comfort of Aunty H and Uncle Mano's house. He would sleep well tonight.

"You ever find some days are just like, crazy good and bad? I mean, really good and really bad all slammed together like some weird thing is going on? No matter what you do, it's a wild ride and you've just got to hang on?"

Kai nodded. Exactly. Today had been a wild ride.

"Like, when you're surfing," Phil went on, seeming glad to talk, "and everything is just right. You're catching these perfect waves, and then, out of nowhere, a monster wave rises up and there isn't anything you can do but just dive through this big wall of water that's going to pass over you one way or another. All you can do is save your neck by meeting it head-on. You just dive in and let it take you and your board and toss you around and turn you in summersaults underwater and break your board or whatever it's going to do. Nothing else to do but let it take you and see where you wash up."

Kai wanted to agree. He liked Phil. He seemed open, and generous. "I've never been surfing," he admitted.

"Whoa! Never? What planet are you from?"

"California."

"Cool, man. I used to live in Santa Cruz. It was a pretty happening place back then. Long time ago. But Maui's better. Everybody's friendly. You'll see. I've got a million friends here."

Kai didn't doubt it. Phil was easy to be near. He seemed upbeat and undemanding.

"How long you staying?"

"I'm just visiting," Kai said. "Staying with my aunt and uncle."

"I knew it!" Phil said. "You've got this local vibe. Like you just want to hang loose. I work in landscaping, and local guys, they always have this special vibe."

Suddenly, the air began to stink with the potent smell of some kind of manure.

"Ugh! I hate that smell. My family moved here when I was thirteen, and I went to this school, Kalama Intermediate." He gestured to the side of the road. "There's a chicken farm near here, so the whole school stinks. The smell of intermediate school."

Kai laughed. "Mine was bad, too," he said.

Soon, they'd left the smell behind. To Kai's surprise, his stomach grumbled loudly.

"Hey, if you're hungry, I've got part of a sandwich left from Down to Earth. It's like, tofu and pepper? On sprouted wheat?"

Kai was suddenly ravenous. The half sandwich looked like Phil had been chewing on it but Kai didn't care. He wolfed it down in three bites.

"Easy, man!" Phil said. "Hey, you want to feel around on the floor? Might be something more to eat kicking around. I kind of forget."

Kai groped around. He felt a flashlight.

"Sorry, man. Keep looking. There's probably something rolling around down there."

Kai felt around some more under the seat. He felt items of clothes, and then something hard and crinkly. A candy bar in a wrapper!

"Jackpot!" said Phil. Kai split it with him.

"I feel so much better," he told Phil. "Thanks." Kai was grateful that Phil was so willing to share.

"No problem, man. What'd you see today, anyway?"

The car felt cozy and safe. It was pleasant to speed through the dark. The sound of the engine was soothing. After the stresses of the day, Kai felt so comfortable, almost lulled to sleep. Phil waited, his face expectant with amiable curiosity. He was already a friend.

For some reason, Kai found himself telling Phil everything. He told him about his dad dying and Phil was sympathetic. Then he told him about Aunty H and Uncle Mano, and about his Grandma's heiau. He told about glimpsing a man he thought was his dad at the fruit stand. He told Phil about Poppy in Hana and the wild boars and the man with the live anole hanging off his earlobe. The only thing he didn't tell Phil about was Captain Cook and the possible treasure.

"What a long strange trip it's been!" said Phil. "It reminds me. This one time, I had these weird mushrooms, everything happened. No wonder you look like you do...I'm sorry about your dad, man. Once you see a person go, it's like you've been to another dimension. You're never the same. One of my friends died at a party. He was with us having a good time and he never woke up. It changed everything. He was a great guy."

Kai nodded. They were at the bottom of Haleakala now, near the sugar mill, turning into the fields of dark cane.

Phil pulled a long necklace out from inside his shirt where it had dangled near his heart.

"The strings are hemp," he said. "A friend made them for me. She's like this self-taught crystal guru. She knows all about which crystals give you strength, power, calm. Some help with addictions. Whatever you need. This one gives understanding. You know, of like, how the universe is?" He slipped it over his head, and passed it to Kai. Phil's hand was rough and stained brown from his work. "You keep it," he said. "You got more of your strange trip ahead. You might need this. Me, I'm good. I work, surf, party. I don't need it as much as you."

"Thank you," Kai said. He felt...touched. The crystal was still warm as it dangled against his chest. Phil was so full of love. For a moment Kai wondered if Phil would expect anything in return for the gift, but then he felt sorry he'd thought it. Phil just liked to give.

"No problem," said Phil. "Yoga's good, too. For centering yourself. My girlfriend, she's a yoga instructor. I'm not very good, but she makes me do it, and it's powerful stuff. You breathe in one nostril and out the other. Stuff like that."

Kai listened.

"Maui is such a spiritual place," Phil said. "You've come to the right place for a spiritual journey. Hey, you know where you should go?" He turned to Kai. "The North Shore!"

Phil sounded excited.

"The North Shore. That's where the power's the strongest."

Kai felt the hairs on his arms prickle. He suddenly remembered the wake at Aunty H's house. What had Dad's friend said? Something about the North Shore, and how special it was to Dad. A place they explored. Was that where Dad saw the vision?

Kai had been seeking a direction. The last heiau hadn't told him anything. He had been so busy escaping the boars, he had forgotten. Or was it that the heiau had told him something?

There had to be another heiau. There was too much more of the chant that didn't make sense yet. Part of it worked.

Above the land of the pineapple and the paniolo
Above the springs in the forest of ash
Hear the echoes of our song

This chunk of the chant made sense, but there was more of it that clearly didn't fit. He wasn't at the end. He needed to keep looking to find one that fulfilled the rest of his family's song. It would probably be older, maybe even as old as Captain Cook's visit.

How did the next part of the chant go? Kai tried to remember. There was something about the north in it. What was it?

The stream in the northernmost point...

Maybe this referred to the North Shore.

"No place on Maui is more spiritual than the North Shore," Phil was saying. Was the North Shore where he was meant to go? Was this the message from the heiau that Poppy had talked about?

"And the best way to feel it is on a bike...and I don't mean a motorbike. I mean the kind you pedal. No noise. It's so peaceful. The place just swallows you. It's like, you're a part of it. Like, the wind washes over you and you are the wind. Everywhere you look it's like a prayer. There are these little rock piles. I don't know who made them, must be old Hawaiians. I don't mess with them, I just go between them. You can feel the power just walking there. It's like...a spiritual vortex."

"I'll go," Kai said suddenly.

They were silent for a few minutes. Kai felt happy with the knowledge he had found his direction. Somehow, he felt that today's events were meant to happen: he was meant to meet Poppy, to find the heiau, to leave without placing Dad's ashes, and to meet Phil and be reminded of Dad's connection to the North Shore. In a weird way, the scrambled events of the day made sense. He felt stronger. He was strangely confident that he was on the right path.

"I have another friend, he's psychic," Phil continued. "He can tell you whatever you want to know, if you ask him. Like this one time, I was really bummed about a girl. He told me I'd find a girlfriend from Alaska who would stay with me for years. And he was right. He's really gifted."

Phil paused.

Kai listened.

"Anyway, he told me that sometimes people are meant to meet each other. Like it's part of the plan of the universe. You know?"

Kai smiled.

"I think we were meant to meet, so I could tell you about the North Shore. Like, it's part of your quest," said Phil.

Kai nodded.

He was glad he'd met Phil. He would listen to the voice of the universe.

Chapter 34
RESPECT

Kai rubbed his eyes as he hopped out of the car and thanked Phil. As Phil drove away, Kai felt secure with the necklace around his neck.

He knocked a few times on Aunty H's front door. No one answered. Was it too late at night? Kai had lost track of time. He knocked again and again. Insects buzzed in front of the light over the door. Finally, the door creaked open. Auntie H and Uncle Mano were both there, looking serious.

"Kai, we need to talk to you," Uncle Mano said. "Come in."

Kai followed them into the kitchen. Aunty H made him a sandwich and he ate ravenously.

"Did you have a good visit with Great-Grandpa?" she asked.

Kai nodded and smiled with his mouth full of food.

Mano spoke slowly, and gently. "Kai, we had a visitor today. I'm sure you know. We need to talk to you about your friend. This haole named David came," Mano continued. "He comes into our house, tells us he is going to go dig up Nahoa's heiau. Says 'Kai's probably told you about me,' he says. Tells us you gave him Nahoa's chant. Wants us to help him destroy our family's tradition. Look at me, Kai. He wants to destroy us. He hopes to make money off us, to destroy what belongs to our family!"

"Uncle, you're wrong," Kai said softly. "David is trying to help me, not…"

"Kai…"

"Really, Uncle Mano, David is trying to help us. Look, my Dad's chant, you know it's not a regular chant. It's a sort of…map. It might lead me to something Dad wanted me to find.

151

David thinks it could be an artifact worth a lot of money. And David has offered to help me find it. If there's anything there, he could sell it for us if we want."

Mano swore under his breath. "David sold you the biggest lie I have ever heard. Kai, me and your aunt trusted you. We took you in. Like our own child. Because we respect your father, see. Deep respect. Deep respect for Nahoa. Now you can't respect us enough to trust us over this haole? You trusted a haole with your chant, your gift from your dad. You trust David for advice? If he tells you to, will you dig up your own family heiau, the most sacred spot of your ancestors? Because you're chasing after this magical fantasy this haole convinced you of?"

"Uncle Mano, David asked me if I wanted his help, and I do. His employee, Sue, has already helped me. I don't think I can find the heiau without them. I don't have to sell what I find."

"Get rid of David, never see him again! He's got no business near our heiau. He's poison, Kai, against everything our family values. You think he's not going to pressure you if he thinks he can make some money? Stay home for a few days, stay with us. Then we'll help you find the place for the ashes."

"Kai," said Auntie H. "Your uncle is right. You've got yourself into bad company."

Kai knew his aunt and uncle would help as much as they could, but they just didn't know enough. Kai needed the expertise of David and Sue. He tried to explain. "They know things," he said. "You have to let me do this my own way. My dad wanted me to find it. I believe he left me something he wanted me to find!"

"Nahoa is gone. You are part of our family, and the heiau belongs to all of us," said Aunty H.

"Dad left it to me!" Kai said. "That's the whole reason I came. He wanted me to do this! You can't stop me. I don't see what this has to do with you!"

"You are our nephew and we love you and that's what we have to do with it. Don't make a big mistake. You got to think about who really cares about you. These haoles, what do you really know about them? Why you trust them so much? All they want is maybe to take something that's yours!"

"That's not true! You don't even know them!" Kai felt anger rising inside him. Why were they making this so difficult? He had to do this for Dad. Wasn't it obvious that Kai would do it right? Didn't they respect his judgment?

"I'm doing this!" Kai said. "Leave me alone!"

"We're trying to help you," said Aunty H.

"I've done everything my dad would have wanted!" Kai said. "Don't stand in my way!" Kai stood.

Mano raised his voice suddenly. "You don't understand anything, do you? You don't have any idea who your dad was! What he loved. What he respected! You're working against everything he cared about, man!"

"That's not true!" Kai yelled. "I'm leaving! If you don't want to help me, I'll do this alone!" Kai turned and took a few steps back. Mano took a step forward, and Kai reached the door. He broke into a jog and then a run. As Kai sprinted away, Mano yelled to him.

"Kai, come back!"

Kai ran as hard as he could.

"Kai, the door is open for you!" Mano yelled.

At a safe distance, Kai sat down beside the road to collect his breath. The humidity of the night was stifling.

I've done everything my dad would have wanted. It was true, right? They were wrong. How could they say such hurtful things? Of course he was doing this out of memory for his Dad.

Then Kai's heartbeat slowed and the reality of the situation kicked in. *If I don't go back to them, I don't have anywhere to go.* Should he go back and try again? *I can't take it. I don't want to hear any more about how I'm doing everything wrong. I'm trying so hard. They don't understand. This is the only way to see what Dad wanted me to find. They won't let me finish this. They don't respect my judgment. They don't think I can do it right. But I can! I won't go back!*

Kai stood and walked farther away from the house. Would Mano come looking for him? Kai staggered away into the darkness.

Chapter 35
THE ROOSTER LADY

For the first time in his life, Kai didn't know where he was going.

The darkness engulfed him. Was telling David about the chant really so evil? *No*, he told himself. *It's my chant. I saw the owl. I have the right to do what I want with my family's heiau. I can't be distracted by an uncle and aunt I hardly even know.*

His cell phone rang. It was Aunty H. Kai ignored it.

But there *was* something uncomfortably true to what Uncle Mano said. David and Sue didn't care about the family site, only about the possible artifact. But if he abandoned Sue and David, who would help?

Ahead, he heard voices. He turned off the sidewalk by the main road and walked across a lawn. A group of about twenty people sat in the middle of the lawn under a light, taking turns speaking. The words were incoherent to Kai, a jumbled mess. He heard swearing and the word "haole." Once in a while, everyone would laugh. The crowd was drinking beer.

As he passed the circle, an old local man with wrinkled skin and a silver tooth asked, "You want to talk-story?" Kai kept on walking. He wanted to be alone.

He reached gated tennis courts. A single light lit the area. For the first time, he realized how tired he was. He needed some time to think. Maybe if he just found a place to sleep… Everything would be better in the morning.

He walked near the court. There wouldn't be many insects on the tennis court, and no one could sneak up from behind him because of the fence. It was a hard surface, which would be uncomfortable, but at least he wouldn't wake up, for instance, with a dog licking his face. Probably.

"What do you want?" A small woman with wiry black hair lay on a sleeping bag on the court. Behind her was a black garbage bag.

A large, colorful jungle fowl rooster with a beautiful tail and mean looking spurs paced beside her, staring with its orange eyes.

"I'm looking for a place to sleep," said Kai.

"Get off my court! They call me the Rooster Lady for a reason! Bet you don't want to mess with my rooster, eh?"

Kai walked to the nearby beach and lay down in the cold sand. But he couldn't sleep. Tears filled his eyes, blocking out the bright stars.

Dad, am I doing the right thing? Don't you want me to find your heiau? Isn't that why you gave me the chant?

Kai thought of his girlfriend at home who had recently broken up with him. Suddenly, he wished very much that he could hold her in his arms. But she had made it clear she didn't want to see him again.

Kai's loneliness grew like a bubble. *Why I am here? What am I doing so far from home?* He thought of his mom. *Home.* Where was his life headed? *I don't belong anywhere.*

He picked up his phone to text his best friend, who worked the night shift at a convenience store. They'd become friends playing rough pick-up basketball at the YMCA, and stayed friends for years. He thought about what he should text. "I'm on Maui. I miss Dad. Wild boars almost trampled me, and this guy with a knife and a rifle..." No, it was too much. His friend was at work, in a different world. There was no way to explain.

Kai typed "Hey man" and sent it.

After three minutes his friend sent the response for which Kai was waiting: "Hey." Kai studied the word, looking for the friendship behind the three-letter retort, searching for proof in them that he wasn't really alone, just a thousand miles from home.

The waves on the dark beach made a soothing sound, like tears. A billion stars filled the vast sky. Kai made an insignificant sound in the darkness. No one knew where he was. No one would know.

He had lost so much recently: his dad, his girlfriend, his feeling of belonging in Mom's apartment. There was little left.

His phone rang. It was Aunty H. Kai let it ring. When she had left a message, he listened to it.

"Kai," said Aunty H. "Please come home. We are only trying to help."

But you're not helping!

Kai had to believe that what he was doing here on Maui was right. He was meant to seek. Dad was leading him. Kai wiped his face on his shirt. It was late. He was cold, and tired. It hurt him more than he cared to admit that Aunty H and Uncle Mano didn't trust his judgment. *I'm not going back!*

Kai tried David's number. The phone rang a few times and then went to his answering machine.

Beneath a billion stars, he was utterly alone.

Chapter 36
THE PRINCESS HIDES THE OBJECT FROM THE MISSIONARIES

Year 1836
Maui

King Kamehameha's daughter, Princess Nahi'ena'ena, lay near death. Her baby had died several weeks ago after living only several hours. The man she loved since childhood --- her brother, Kamehameha III, the father of her child --- was forbidden to her. The Hawaiian priests and religious leaders who taught her all she knew about her bloodlines and responsibilities had raised her to marry him. She and her brother had married. Then, the missionaries Queen Ka'ahumanu supported had decreed their marriage illegal. It was no longer a marriage of love and appropriate bloodlines; it was evil incest. Her brother-lover had become an alcoholic. Her heart was broken. Her body never recovered from childbirth. She was bleeding. Soon, she would join her child.

But there was something she must do first. There was something she must protect. She had so little left. It was important the missionaries not take everything. Summoning her strength, she called her most trusted companion.

The young woman came quickly. She had been waiting to be called. Her familiar face was streaked with tears. The two women had never ceased to mourn since the death of the baby.

"My friend," the princess said, stroking her smooth cheek, "I want you to have this."

The young woman's face crumbled. "Don't leave me," she said. "Where will I go? Who respects the old ways anymore? There won't be any place for me..." Both women pictured the wild, lawless streets of Lahaina, where foreign men arrived daily in hordes to grab and molest any women they could find, willing or no. Their royal town had become a brothel for hundreds of drunken strangers. Many, many Hawaiians had died from disease. More than half the population had died since their mothers' day. And many of the Hawaiian men who were left had become addicted to alcohol. Few people remembered the old ways. There was no place in this new, strange and ugly world for an ali'i companion with sacred bloodlines and knowledge of ancient things. The kapuna were no longer as powerful as the missionaries; their position was as uncertain as hers. The Hawaiian priests would not be able to protect her.

Gathering her strength, Princess Nahi'ena'ena soothed her friend as much as she could. "You have served me so well," she said. "I will miss you." The two women wept on each other's shoulders.

Remembering her task, the princess found the red cloth bundle beside her bed. The sacred object, with its special history, had been her special talisman since childhood, given to her by her father's head priest to protect her. With a shaking hand, she held it out to her friend. This, after all, was all she had to give. She, who should have been the mother of the next king of a thriving kingdom.

"I will find a safe place," promised her companion. She took the object carefully, cradling it like the child who had died. She understood the significance of the object, and the responsibilities that went with it. She recognized the honor bestowed upon her. What she could not imagine was the future.

Chapter 37
A TRIP WITH SUE

The present
Kihei

The beach was cold.
Alone in the dark, Kai thought about tomorrow, or was it today? He had the chant. He needed to finish what he had started. He would fulfill the promise he'd made to Dad and then go home and figure out the rest of everything.

He called Sue. After a few rings, she picked up. "Hello?" she said sleepily, her speech slower than normal.

"It's Kai. Sorry to call you this late. Do you have anywhere I could sleep? Sorry, I know it's a lot to ask…"

"You can sleep on my couch. But only for a few days, okay? I'm not a hotel. Are you at your aunt and uncle's place?"

"No, I left. They want me to stop looking for the heiau. But I won't." Kai felt his anger rise again.

"Where are you?" Sue asked.

"I'm at Kalama Park. There are tennis courts here. Near the ocean?"

She didn't ask any more questions. "I'll be there in a few minutes."

Aunty H called again. Kai didn't listen to her message. *Leave me alone!* He decided to text her so she'd stop calling.

Kai texted: "Don't call me. I'm with a friend."

*   *   *

The next morning, a loud motorcycle roared down a road somewhere in Kihei. Kai half opened his eyes. Gray morning light filtered through white curtains and into the room. It was very early.

Where was he?

His knees felt raw, and his neck was cold and clammy. His brain slowly started to think. He thought back to everything that had happened last night: Uncle Mano yelling at him, visiting the tennis courts, meeting the homeless crowd, calling Sue, going to her house, falling asleep on the couch.

Kai stretched out his arms. He rolled over into a sitting position. His skin itched everywhere.

He glanced at his phone. There were messages from Aunty H. He didn't want to read them.

Kai felt a clenching pain in his stomach. When had he last eaten? Kai walked over to the table and sat down.

Sue walked into the room. He wondered if she always got up this early. "Good morning," she said.

Kai tried to perk up, but he felt awful. "Thanks for picking me up. I'm glad I didn't have to spend the night on the beach."

"Oh, you're welcome. No problem. Are you hungry?" Sue asked.

"Yes." Immediately, Kai was embarrassed by the gusto in his reply. He couldn't help it; his gut was bunched into a tight ball of hurt.

Sue laughed. "All right. There's cereal in that cabinet. Help yourself...We need to get going to Lahaina."

Kai swallowed a big mouthful of cereal. "Lahaina?"

"Yes. I'm thinking cruel sun is a reference to Lahaina."

"You mean… Lahaina's really hot?"

"That too. I guess you wouldn't know this, but the name 'Lahaina' means 'cruel sun' in Hawaiian."

"Oh." *I must sound like an idiot.* "So you think the heiau is in Lahaina?"

"If I'm right, it's *above* Lahaina. Possibly just above the city, in the foothills of the West Maui Mountains."

But I need to go to the North Shore.

Kai wasn't sure how to explain. "I want to try the North Shore. I hitchhiked with this guy, back from Makawao. He told me that there are a lot of heiaus along the highway on the north

160

side of Maui. And I heard this story about my dad, he used to go up there all the time. I think we should look there." Kai paused for a second. Then he continued. "Anyway, this guy was telling me how remote and spiritual the area is... It seems that my family always built the heiaus in the most remote areas of the island, so I'm wondering if they would've built a heiau on the north side. And the chant says *northernmost point*." He thought of something. "What's at the northernmost point of the island?"

"A blowhole. A minor tourist attraction."

"Okay...that's where we should go. It's probably where the heiau is. 'Northernmost point' in the chant must mean the northernmost point of Maui. And maybe 'beyond the cruel sun,' maybe that means if you just keep going north of Lahaina."

Sue paused to think. Then she looked down at the chant on the table. "Land of the taro probably isn't the blowhole. In fact, I don't know if Hawaiians ever grew taro that far north."

"Yeah, but there could be, right? I mean, maybe a long time ago?"

"No," she said flatly.

He thought of Poppy's words. *Trust your instincts...* "Sue... I don't know how to explain...I have a feeling. Can't we drive to the blowhole, just to check?"

"Kai, it's at least two hours out of the way along a narrow road...I'm not going unless we have a good reason."

Kai interrupted her. "Please. I think I can find the heiau."

Sue sighed, and stretched.

"I really feel this is important," Kai said. *I feel like the last heiau directed me to go to the North Shore.*

"Look, this has nothing to do with the chant, as far as I can see, but if you want to go, just to see it...I have a little extra time this morning. A few hours. I'd planned to hang out here for a bit and then drive to Lahaina. Actually, I'd planned to sleep late. But I'm up, and it's early. If you really, really want to go on a tour of the North Shore, we can leave now, and still get to Lahaina by afternoon. So, okay, I'll take you. Consider it a personal favor. But then it's straight to Lahaina, kid."

I'll find the heiau. Northernmost point. It had to be.

"And Sue, can I borrow your bike? I mean, just for part of it? I want to ride. Just a few miles." *I want to be part of the place.*

Sue looked at him. "You're kidding, right?" she said. "I thought we were in a hurry?"

"It would mean a lot to me," Kai said softly. *It's part of my quest. The last heiau told me to do this.*

Sue looked away. She hesitated. *What's the big deal?* Then she shrugged. "Okay, if it's that important to you, and this is your sightseeing morning, I'll bring my bike and you can ride a bit on the way. This morning, I'll be your personal sightseeing guide. But that's it. Then we go where I say."

"Thank you!" said Kai, gulping the last of his cereal and depositing his bowl in the sink. "Let's go."

Chapter 38
BIKING THE NORTH SHORE

W hen they left Kihei, the soft light of dawn was hardening into morning brightness. They drove through Waihe'e.

"This is the last tame part of our drive," Sue said. "It gets wilder from here." She gestured to a windswept hillside far above the ocean. "There's a beautiful hike there. The birds are incredible. I saw some rare ones --- little green honeycreepers with curved bills...Wild orchids and guavas. There's a pine forest, and then you come to a part of the woods that smells exactly like cardamom --- a spice we put in Swedish Christmas bread. There's a view of a large waterfall."

The way Sue described it, Kai wanted to go there with her, now. But they hurried onward, towards the heiau. It was a long drive, and they had many miles to cover.

The two-lane paved highway dipped down into a gulch, Waihe'e Valley. They were in the rainforest. Then the road turned left around a grassy bluff and escaped from the known world.

Kai stared out over the edge of the precipice. Hundreds of feet below him, the white tumbling ocean attacked the rocky shore. This was the end of Maui. Bands of whitecaps streaked the sea, leading off into the horizon. There were only waves for thousands of miles -- no land from here to Alaska.

The road narrowed. On the left side was a mountain, and on the right a cliff. The road was barely large enough for one car to pass.

"So, are you enjoying your tour? Is this what you expected?" Sue asked distractedly. Kai was glad she didn't take her eyes off the road.

"Not exactly." Even with Sue driving thirty miles per hour, Kai still clutched his armrest.

Sue rolled to a stop and pulled off to the left side of the road. Kai's heart almost stopped. They were less than a yard away from the edge of a steep incline. Sue looked over at Kai. "Did I scare you?"

There was a traffic jam. Ten cars going the same way as Kai and Sue had pulled over to the very edge of the road, right up to the cliff. A Hummer coming from the opposite direction was attempting to pass by the string of cars. Somehow, the Hummer managed to squeeze through. The chain of cars started to move again.

The road wound back into another valley. The landscape was changing. It was all fields. Beside the road, in a pocket of trees, a sign advertised an art gallery. Sue slowed to a stop and they got out.

Below them was a wild, windswept garden full of sculptures. The works of art stood around the garden as if they had grown from the landscape. The garden was perched high above the stormy sea. Wind-chimes tinkled. A life-size wooden eagle sprouted from a tree stump. Statues of young children laughed and snatched at carved butterflies. Their eyes had a warmth and depth produced by a trick of their indented pupils. A graceful, life-sized egret made of tarnished metal balanced on one leg.

Sue lifted her bike down from the roof rack. She looked serious. "The traffic can be bad here. Listen! When in doubt, just pull off and wait. I'll follow as closely as I can. You've got to be really careful. The road is narrow." She handed him a helmet. "Hope it fits," she said.

"Sue?" Kai hesitated. He gestured towards the bike. "Thank you." He knew she was doing this for him, and it felt nice. *If you knew what I knew, you would know how close we are to finding the heiau.*

Kai mounted the bike and took off. There was no way for him to know how his bike ride would end.

Kai loved the ride. The air felt like a warm hair drier as it whipped past him. The scenery was beautiful: waves crashing below, hundred foot cliffs, and a rumpled green carpet of mountains. The pedaling was strenuous since the road was a winding rollercoaster of hills.

Phil was right! This is the place and I am part of it.

He passed fields with long-horned cows. He glimpsed a horse with its head over the fence, begging passing cars for treats. He passed vast, green hillsides. He glanced behind him. There was a line of cars but Sue was nowhere in sight. Kai pedaled hard, oblivious to what was about to happen.

The pedaling had a rhythm. *One, two, three, four, one, two, three, four.* So did the road. Downhill, inland, uphill, seaward. Kai felt the rhythm lock into place. He was no longer straining. He was a follower. He was following the heartbeat of the North Side. He was listening for the chant. He was part of the landscape. Faster, faster! Kai pushed against the limit of his endurance, unaware of the danger he was fast approaching.

Kai flew along. He could faintly hear cars, a murmur. Kai was completely focused and alert, yet distanced from his own world. Other bike riders passed him, intent and focused. Then Kai passed some riders. Nothing prepared him for what came next.

He felt wind whistling through the grass, waves crashing against the cliffs, streams rushing over pebbles. Kai was no longer inside himself; he was outside his own body, part of the world. He savored the feeling of being part of this place, absorbed by it. If he had known what would happen in the next instant, he would have done everything differently.

Loud noise pulled his attention back to the road. A car honked. He zoomed downhill, riding on the edge of a cliff. To the right dropped the green void of a steep drop-off. To his left, a car was coming too close, trying to pass his bike. The car crowded Kai closer and closer to the edge.

Another car approached, from the opposite direction. The first car pulled closer to Kai. Suddenly, there was no road left for him. Kai swerved onto the tiny shoulder. His tire hit a dip in the dust. The bike jerked. Kai flew over the handle bars.

He hit the ground, hard, on his helmeted head and arm. He rolled over the edge of the shoulder. He tumbled, crashing against the bike. He flew. He landed in a clump of grass. He slid down the slope.

With a thud, Kai landed in a level place. Instinctively, he spread out his arms and held onto the ground. He was no longer falling. He didn't dare to move. He could hear the bike crashing down the hillside somewhere below. Then it stopped, too.

Kai lay motionless. How had that happened? One instant, he had been riding his bike like a bird soaring through the sky. The next, he was falling, out of control.

He dared to open his eyes. The wispy clouds were beautiful. He felt immensely grateful to see them floating above.

Kai became aware that he was breathing heavily. His heart was pounding. The thought of how the bike had continued to fall made him feel dizzy. He felt like staying here for as long as possible without moving a single muscle. The clouds above him seemed to spin as if the sky were a whirlpool. Kai watched with fascination. On the other side of the ledge, the slope dropped away into the hazy distance. It could be a long fall if he wasn't careful.

"Son!"

Dad!

Twenty feet up the cliff, Dad was leaning over from the road, offering his strong arm.

"Come on!" Dad commanded. "Climb up!"

Kai closed his eyes. He gathered his strength.

"Be careful!" Dad said.

Kai blinked. Dad was gone. A stranger leaned over the edge, offering his arm.

Kai moved deliberately. Bits of soil tumbled off the ledge and into the air. The key would be to make sure of each handhold and foothold. He must never trust only one. He could pull himself up if he remained focused and didn't look down. Slowly, carefully, Kai made his way up the cliff until he could reach the hand. Kai reached. Strong fingers closed around Kai's and helped pull him up to the road. Kai lay sprawling beside the road, shaking from exertion and fear.

The powerful, brown-skinned man swore profusely to express his gratitude and amazement that Kai was okay. "Man, you are one lucky kid!" he said.

Kai's eyes filled with tears of relief. He was safe. He sat up.

"Thank you," Kai told the man. "I have a friend with me," Kai said. "She's driving." His legs seemed too weak to hold him. He sat where he was, near the edge of the cliff.

"Okay. You want some water? You feel okay?"

"Thanks," Kai said. "I'm alright. My friend will be here in a minute."

"You sure? Man, you be more careful! You only get so many lives! On a road like this, you be careful! Hey, I'll wait until your friend comes." The stranger got back in his car and waited with his window unrolled.

Kai's hands were shaking. He was still wearing Phil's necklace, the one that gave understanding of the universe. He touched it for comfort. Miraculously, his phone was still in his pocket. He dialed Sue's number.

One ring, two rings, three rings, four rings, five rings, no answer. Kai left a short message, and then he hung up. He tried texting. Perhaps her ringer was off. Where was she?

He tried Sue again. No luck. He dialed it a third time. Kai turned around. Sue!

The man waved and drove away. Kai walked on weak legs to Sue's car and opened the door. "You okay?" she asked.

"I fell." He hopped into the car.

Sue's eyes grew wide. "You're hurt," she said, pointing to his knee.

"I flew over the handlebars. I went off the road."

Sue's mouth dropped open. She tried to speak but failed. Her mouth opened and closed. "Where?" she said, finally. She handed him her first aid kit. "Where's the bike?" she asked suddenly.

"I lost it," said Kai. Suddenly, he felt terrible. He hadn't thought about Sue's bike until now.

For an instant, Sue's face paled. They got out of the car and stood looking over the precipice. Kai could see where he'd landed, but there was no sign of the bike.

"I'll pay for it," said Kai.

He could see her struggling. "It's insured," she said. She stood looking over the side for a long time. "I'm so glad you're okay, Kai," she said softly.

They got back into the car. Sue moved slowly.

They drove in silence. They passed a pasture of cattle, then a white church with a steeple in a village of four houses down in a valley. The terrain became more bleak and remote.

I'm lucky to be alive. Why wasn't I paying attention to traffic?

Kai got the chant out. He wanted to hold it in his hands. It reassured him, somehow. He'd left the ashes and the chant in Sue's car while he'd been on the bike. If anything had happened to him, what would Sue have done?

Would she have continued to follow the chant without me?

Sue was quiet. Sue wore a grim expression. Kai couldn't tell what she was thinking. She had turned inside herself, and shut him out.

"I'm sorry," he said. "Let's go back and try to get the bike. Maybe we can hike around the bottom..."

Sue shook her head. "I don't think we'll find it," she said. "There's no way to get down, anyway, and even if we could, we couldn't get what's left of it back up."

"I have a little money. I've been saving for college," Kai said. "I'll pay for it."

"It's not the money," Sue said. Kai noticed there were tears in her eyes. *Had she loved the bike that much?* Kai felt awful.

The road widened slightly. Sue pulled the car to the side and parked. A small footpath led away from the road, through dust and grass. Why were they stopping? Was this a special place?

Sue was looking away, out the window at the desolate landscape.

What was wrong?

Sue wiped her eyes roughly with the back of her hand. She turned toward him. There was so much pain in her face Kai was shocked. "I'm sorry," she said quickly. Without any more explanation, she left the car. She didn't seem to care where she was going.

Kai sat stunned. Sue's receding form looked stubborn and hurt. The wind pulled at her hair. She looked strangely as if she were fighting against a strong wind that only she could feel. *Should I follow her? Or does she need to be alone?*

Sue disappeared into the wilderness. Kai felt empty. He felt drained by his recent brush with death, and from the mistaken glimpse of Dad.

After a few minutes, he left the car to make sure she was okay.

There was no sign of Sue. The hillside had many small dips and rises, and rock outcroppings. Perhaps she was hidden in a hollow. She couldn't have gone far. He'd seen her go this way.

He felt lost and raw. Was this really the place Phil had told him to come? He felt swallowed by the North Side. This hillside was all loneliness. This was Maui stripped of its lush vegetation, reduced to its soul: wind, a bit of soil, and lava rock.

"Sue?" His call died in the wind. He could imagine how the old Hawaiians had felt humbled by this place, and by other places on the island.

Perhaps Sue didn't want to be found. Perhaps he should give her more time. She was such a strong person. She probably didn't need help, just a moment of privacy. Kai sat on a rock and scanned the hillside.

I could have died if I had fallen a different way. I am nothing but a combination of elements, held together somehow. My life is a precarious balance of energy that will eventually be released, like when Dad died. He picked up a stone. He remembered his grandma's words: *All of life is a prayer.* He added: *The rocks themselves are a prayer.*

Were rocks a prayer for Grandma? What had she said? The old Hawaiians thought Pele, the volcano goddess, owned the rocks. Or was Pele actually in the rocks? Pele of the sacred land, Pele the eater of the land, Pele the spirit of the redness of fire...Pele was the creator and the destroyer, a beautiful young woman and a powerful old one. Kai fingered the stone.

He thought again of Sue's face, so full of unaccountable anguish. She had to be here somewhere. He hoped she was okay. It was weird, how hard she was taking the bike. He cupped his hands and yelled.

"Sue?"

Then he saw her. She was sitting by a boulder, her hands over her face. Kai crossed the rocky field and sat beside her.

Sue looked vulnerable, totally different from the competent expert she was. Tears were running down her face. Instinctively, Kai moved closer. He thought of Grandma's hand on his back when he'd been startled by the owl. He wondered if he should put his arm around her.

"Are you okay?" he asked.

"Thank you," she said, wiping her face. "Kai, you remind me so much of my kid brother. He's just like this. He'll come up and give me a hug, just when I need it."

"You've helped me a lot of ways," Kai said.

Sue shrugged. "It's my job," she said. She closed her eyes. A few tears escaped. "I'm sorry. I don't usually get so emotional." Sue blew her nose and took a deep breath. "Today, when you told me you fell over the handlebars, it made me remember," she said. She opened her eyes. They looked clear, and hard, despite the redness. "I had this friend," she said. "A really close friend. The one who introduced me to Hawaii. I came here because of him. He showed me Oahu. On the weekends, we'd go biking and have all these adventures...About a year ago, he didn't come. He'd had this terrible accident on his bike. I knew the spot. There were potholes, and he flew over the handlebars. He died."

Kai listened.

"I thought I was over it, but I guess not quite," Sue said.

"I was riding his bike?"

Sue nodded.

You let me ride his bike?

"I'm sorry," Kai said.

"I miss him," she said. "Thank you for letting me tell you."

"I don't mind," Kai said seriously.

Sue regained her composure. She stood, and they began walking back to the car. "Kai, I hope you're not disappointed if you don't find what you're looking for."

"I've already found some of it," Kai said, thinking of Grandma and Poppy. For a moment, Aunty H and Uncle Mano flitted through his consciousness with an ache, but he was too tired to dwell on what he couldn't resolve.

They drove along the ocean toward the blowhole, through the open landscape. Sue seemed strong again, as if she had been washed clean. Her sadness had passed. Kai knew it was still there, beneath the surface, but she had tucked it away wherever it usually rested and she was once again professional.

As Kai looked out the window, he remembered something Phil had told him. "Sue?" Kai asked. "What about the prayer towers on the North Shore? A guy I met told me about them. The rock piles. Where are they? I wondered if they might have something to do with my heiau."

"They don't. They've been removed."

"What do you mean, removed?" Kai asked.

"They were a desecration. Tourists built them. Some kind of New-Age thing. Starting in about 1970. People thinking they were honoring old Hawaii in some way. But really, it bothered locals who still have a feeling of respect for the rocks. Recently, someone cared enough to come here and disassemble all the piles."

Kai was surprised. How had Phil been so mistaken about the meaning of the rock piles? Phil was so caring, and seemed so in-touch with the island. How could a person who meant well, and carried understanding and respect in his heart, have such a misunderstanding of the old ways? Phil must not know any better, but why hadn't he taken the time to find out? *I hope I'm not mistaken like that. I hope when I'm trying to understand my family and do the right thing I don't totally misunderstand.*

Kai thought of Aunty H and Uncle Mano. They were probably waiting. He chased the thought from his mind. He had nothing to say to them. He needed to be free. He didn't want the pressure of the way they wanted things done.

"It happens all the time," Sue was saying. "People come to Maui, they love the place, and they want to be a part of it, own a spiritual piece of it --- so they invent some kind of pseudo-ancient-Hawaiian mythology of their own, that has nothing to do with history or local beliefs. There's so much misinformation out there. Self-help mixed with "Hawaiian Paganism" --- really just uneducated guesses about the past. People make up whatever they want. It's deeply, deeply offensive to people who care about the past."

"That's too bad," Kai said. "I mean, I kind of understand why visitors would want to show they've felt the power of the place, maybe to become part of it. But I see how that would irritate people who feel the rock is sacred."

"It's complicated, isn't it?" Sue said. "You're lucky you're part Hawaiian. It's easier for you to claim the past as your own." Kai heard a wistful tone in Sue's voice. Did she long to be Hawaiian, to be more intimately connected to the history?

"You really love Hawaiian history, don't you?" Kai said.

"I love all kinds of history," Sue said.

"That's what we share, isn't it?" Kai said. "I mean, that's one of the things I've liked about your help," Kai went on. "You're so interested in the meaning of the artifact, not just its value," Kai said. "It's not the money. You care about what it means to me and my family."

"I care about protecting history," Sue said carefully. "I'm glad my job has included this. I think we're going to wrap this up soon --- after we get to Lahaina." She smiled. "We're here. That's your blowhole."

Chapter 39
LOOKING FOR SOMETHING WHERE THERE'S NOTHING

Kaupo

There was nothing in between the searing sun and David's car.

The heat sizzled off red rock. Heat waves blurred his vision of the narrow paved road ahead.

There was no life left here. White skeletons of cattle beautified the desert. How had the deceased cattle found anything here to eat? Occasionally, David spotted a clump of yellow weeds. They were withered, thirsty, near death.

The Piilani Highway was a name for two separated stretches of road. One was the expressway that skirts the outside of Kihei and Wailea. The other was here: a narrow one-lane trail, bewitched with potholes, leading around the south side of Haleakala from Kula to Kaupo. The far end of the road, between Kaupo and Hana, was rough. Recently, while it had remained bone-dry here, heavy rainfall had flooded the portion of the road closer to Hana, disconnecting the Pi'ilani Highway from the Hana Highway. Thus, Kaupo had become a dead end. This was the only road in, and the only road out. David had no choice but to drive this way and return the way he came if he was going to find the heiau.

David passed a gate that spanned the road, the entrance to a cattle ranch. The air conditioning was on high. The car felt cool, spacious.

The road gradually cut out towards the sea. The top of Haleakala seemed so close. The road was part of the mountainside. The grasses became more and more frequent, until both sides of the road were lined with yellow fields. The colors were beautiful: the blue of the ocean, whitecaps, black rock, yellow lowlands, red Haleakala, and blue sky.

The world was so open. The view asked one to stretch oneself, spread out into the limitless horizon.

After driving through a lava field, the landscape became greener. There was water here. David was nearing the edge of the jungle. Ahead lay Kaupo, and beyond, the rainforests of Hana.

On the right side of the road lay an old stone wall bordering a scruffy field. The view of the ocean, half a mile away, was unobstructed. There were few trees, just large bushes and some fluttering palms down by the water.

The ocean horizon was so long that David could see it curve. In the middle of the horizon, David saw a faint grayish lump: the Big Island, Hawaii.

On the other side of the road lay the tiny outpost of Kaupo. Beyond another low stone barricade, a line of coconut trees waved in the wind. A worn down, splintery brown building with a deck out in front was the Kaupo General Store. A few houses were hidden behind flowering trees. There weren't many mailboxes.

In the distance, the road went around a bend. A steep green hillside rose from the water, forming the eastern horizon. David's eyes followed the outline of the hillside, up, up, up. Haleakala rose like a chunk of Mars, looming above Kaupo. Haleakala spanned the entire horizon between the land and the sky. In the west, the reddish-brown mountain sloped back down through a desert and into the sea.

Kaupo was one of the archeological secrets of Maui. Despite its setting in the desert and its desolate appearance, Kaupo's original name, Wahipana, meant "special place" to Hawaiians. There was once a sizeable population. Now only stone remnants of ancient Kaupo remained. When David had heard Kai's aunt mention Kaupo, his hopes of finding the heiau had risen. Modern Kaupo was less than a village, more like a ranching station, and rich in archeological ruins.

Where should he ask about the heiau? Who would know where to find it?

Chapter 40
BLOWHOLE

They pulled off the road into a parking lot of red soil. On the other side of the road, a barbed wire fence hemmed in a herd of long-horned cattle.

"The northernmost point of the island is there." Sue pointed out into an alien landscape. Between the road and the sea lay a bowl of black knobby cooled lava. Every few seconds, a monstrous swell crashed into the rock coastline. The lower reaches of the bowl were glistening wet. In the upper part of the bowl, the ground was speckled with round stones, breakaway pieces of lava smashed and smoothed by the ocean. *This would be a great place for constructing heiaus*, Kai thought. *Plenty of building material.*

"It's around the corner. There is a footpath that does switchbacks down to the water. A short walk. Come. But listen, Kai? Be careful by the blowhole, okay? It looks totally harmless, but people have died here." To his relief, she seemed to be herself again: competent, tough, and quick-thinking director. The window into the sadness inside her had closed, and she was back to normal. Kai felt his own mood lighten.

The path was dusty and winding. Every fifty feet it did a switchback. The distance between the parking lot and the shore looked so close, yet it took at least ten minutes for Sue and Kai to switch back and forth to the bottom of the bowl.

There were many loose rocks. Were any of these rocks once heiaus? Was this a place where anything built by man could last?

At the base of the hill, by the shoreline, the lava flattened into a basin. Spray from the crashing waves filled dents in the surface, creating stagnant pools. Over a hill of rock, Kai saw a fountain of spray thrust into the air.

"Is the blowhole a cave?" Kai asked. If there were caves here, the heiau could be inside one.

Sue was staring off into the boisterous ocean. "A cave? You mean underwater? I guess. The waves probably ate away at the bottom of this lava shelf."

Maybe Dad searched for the family's heiau when he was a teen up here on the North Shore. A cave would keep it safe.

"So are there caves around here that aren't underwater?" Kai asked.

Sue shrugged. "I don't know. I mean, there are probably lava tubes all over Maui."

Kai looked blank.

"You know how Maui was formed, right?"

"It's volcanic, right?" said Kai.

I feel like a part of this place, but I know so little.

Kai heard his Dad's voice answer. *That's why I sent you. To learn.*

Sue was studying him.

"This is hard for you, isn't it?" she said gently. "You were thinking of your dad, weren't you?"

Kai nodded.

She knows me pretty well.

"I'm okay. I feel like he'd have wanted me to be here. Tell me what you were going to, about the islands."

Dad wants me to know.

Sue told him about the hot spot below the Hawaiian islands, down in the earth's crust, where molten rock squeezes out from inside of the earth. When the molten rock cooled, it formed the islands of Hawaii.

Kai listened. He remembered how Grandma Lokelani told the myth of the islands' creation: *Maui pulled the islands up from the sea with a fishhook.*

"So how are there so many islands created from the hotspot? Are there different passages of lava?"

She explained the movement of the Pacific plate over the hotspots. As the plate moved, new islands formed. Niihau was the first of the major islands to be born, then Kauai, then Oahu, then Molokai, then Maui, Kahoolawe and Lanai all at once, and finally the Big Island of Hawaii.

"The Big Island is still being created. Lava is still flowing out of the volcanoes there. And in a few million years there will be another island that will poke up out of the ocean near the Big Island. Geologists have already given it a name, Loihi, even though it's still underwater."

"So Maui is just a big volcano sticking up out of the water?" A big cone with little cones…Something reminded him of part of the chant, he wasn't sure what.

"Actually, it's two main volcanoes, Haleakala and the West Maui Mountains. Maui used to be two islands. Then so much lava flowed out of the two volcanoes that they joined into one island. Basically, Maui is just a huge mound of lava. From the sea floor to its summit, Haleakala rises 30,000 feet."

"That's higher than Mt. Everest!" said Kai. "So, does Maui still erupt?"

"Not since the late 1700s, when the lava field formed down by Makena."

The last eruption was when my family hid its secret and started the chant. What had his family thought of Pele, the volcano goddess, when the volcano was active?

They reached the blowhole. It was surprisingly unimpressive. Every few seconds, a gurgling noise would echo up through a dark tunnel and water would slurp out of the hole in the rock. Every few waves, a wave came that was larger than the rest, and the blowhole would spray droplets into the air.

"Okay, I'm tired. Do what you need to do. I'm going to wait in the car," said Sue. "When you're ready, we'll go." She began to walk back along the trail, retracing her steps. He could see she had no hope of finding the chant's answers here, but she was trying to let him come to that on his own. He appreciated that she had come all this way. It had been a personal favor. She wasn't rushing him, even though she didn't think he'd find anything.

But the last heiau told me to come here! My ancestors are here. I feel them.

Kai scanned the hillside surrounding the blowhole. It was a rocky slope. There was not a single heiau in sight. *Am I not far enough north? Is the heiau at the true northernmost part of Maui?* About a quarter mile off in the distance, the bluff descended into the sea. *Which way is north?*

Kai began searching the ground, looking for rocks that were loose and piled. He looked carefully, examining the slope bit by bit. There were many rocks here, but no piles that seemed to be the remains of heiaus. How would he know? The ocean was at work here, washing over this place sometimes, moving things, disturbing them and taking them out to sea...For some reason, he glanced up. What he saw made him freeze.

A monster wave was coming to shore. It towered above the other waves. It was at least twenty feet tall! A curling wall of water...Kai was paralyzed. He stared into the mouth of the beast. The wave was seconds away from the shore, seconds away from soaking the rock around the blowhole and retreating back into the sea with its prey.

Where do I go? Will I be washed away? Kai ran. The wave thundered behind him. Ocean smacked on rock. Sea water swished through his legs, knocking him off his feet. The blowhole roared. It spewed in all directions. Salt water rained.

Water flooded back down the hillside, into the ocean. Kai was pulled. Water swirled around him. He knocked against rock. The wave receded. Another big wave! Water sprayed. Another wave. More spray.

When he opened his eyes, Kai looked into the dark tunnel of the blowhole.

He struggled away.

The spiritual vortex.

The raw power of the ocean took him. He was utterly powerless. It would destroy him or let him go. God and the water would choose. His life was not his own. Kai was in the water's grasp. Kai and the water were one. He fought to get free. The water sucked and swirled, pulling him down. Into the hole. No!

180

He fought to breathe. He must get air. Air! He was dying. His lungs would burst. He was going to breathe water. His whole consciousness became a single prayer to survive.

Kai's foot struck rock. He pushed up, hard, grabbing frantically. He struggled to his feet, coughing, gasping. *Hurry, before the next wave!* Kai scrambled madly. He was free!

When he reached the high dry hillside, Kai stopped. He dropped down on the smooth warm rocks. He lay panting, unable to comprehend how close he had come to death.

Two near-death experiences in one day? What am I doing wrong?

Kai lay on the rocks. The answer came to him immediately in Dad's voice. *Be more careful! You haven't been paying attention.*

Kai felt dizzy from effort, spent. Careful of what? Cliffs? Ocean? Nature?

The answer surprised him: *Be careful that you are seeking the heiau for the right reasons. Be careful that you are truly respectful. Be careful with the heiau.*

Kai thought again of his fight with Aunty H and Uncle Mano. They were wrong about Kai and those who were helping him. They thought Kai didn't understand how to respect the family and the past, but he did. *Didn't he?*

Kai's whole journey was following Dad's wishes, right? There was something Dad wanted him to discover. He wasn't sure what Dad meant for him to find. It was probably something that would have meaning only to his family. Perhaps it was merely a place. Other than talking to Sue about it, Kai had tried not to think much about the object or what it might be, so he wouldn't be disappointed. Whatever it was, Dad had wanted him to find it. Yet of course Kai hoped it would be something more…something worth a lot of money.

Was that wrong?

It was David and Sue, Kai realized, who had suggested that there might be something valuable. Was he wrong to listen to them? He had certainly been infected by their excitement. Had he been infected by greed?

Kai dug deep in his heart, searching as honestly as he could for truth. He tried to face the tangled feelings had been bothering him since his fight with Aunty H and Uncle Mano. Really, he'd been struggling to understand the purpose in his own heart since meeting David and Sue, and Great-Grandpa. *Am I following the chant for the right reasons? Have I forgotten why I came here?*

He'd received two warnings today: a fall, and a wave. Kai had made two mistakes through bad judgment. Twice he'd been careless and sloppy, failing to stay focused on what he should have been watching. He must be more tired than he realized to make so many bad judgments. Was that why he was meant to come to the North Shore? To think about bad judgments? To realize that to follow the chant, he would have to slow down, and stay focused on what was really important?

Was it wrong, as Aunty H and Uncle Mano thought, to take anything from a heiau --- even though Dad had given him the directions? What was more important, Dad's dying wish, or protecting the ancient family's things? What would Dad have wanted? If Kai found anything, would it really be okay to sell something precious to the family --- something his ancestors had protected for generations? Was it okay to take something from a sacred site?

The answers did not come. Although Kai waited, he was left with a nagging sense of uncertainty.

Suddenly, he wanted to talk to Grandma. Kai trusted her. She would know. He wondered if she had heard that he had left Aunty H's house. Of course, she would have heard.

He pulled his phone out of his wet pocket. The cover was drenched. He wiped it off with his finger, and opened the case slowly. Amazingly, the phone inside was dry. It still worked!

Grandma answered with joy. "Kai! Where are you?"

"I'm on the North Shore, Grandma. I'm okay, but I'm confused. Did Aunty H tell you I have some people helping me with the chant?"

"Yes, she told me." Grandma sounded reserved. She had indeed heard about the fight. Was she on Kai's side?

"I want your advice," said Kai.

"I will try," said Grandma.

182

"I'm not sure what Dad wanted me to do. When I came here, I felt like I knew. But now I'm not sure."

Grandma paused. "I don't know, Kai. He never told me what he wanted. But he loved your aunty." Grandma's last words were a reprimand. Kai had caused Aunty H some worry and pain.

"Do you think I should keep trying to find the heiau?" Kai asked.

"What do you mean? Nothing wrong in a heiau. Heiau is good."

"What if there is something there?" Kai asked carefully, trying to extract the heart of his dilemma. "What if I find something I want to keep. Can I take it?"

"I don't know what you mean," said Grandma. "Heiau is like church. You get prayers there. Guidance. You don't take anything."

Perhaps Aunty H hadn't told Grandma everything.

Kai stumbled over his words. It was hard to explain. He felt embarrassed, but he needed to know. "But if there is something there, where Dad wanted me to go, can I take it?" he said. "Is it meant for me?"

"You don't go to heiau for taking, but for giving. You will find out what you need to give. Like at church. You go there to learn what you can give. You are a good boy, a smart boy. I know you will figure it out! But you call your Aunty H now. She worries about you. Call her right now, you promise?"

"She's mad at me, Grandma."

"No, she loves you. Just like me," said Grandma.

Kai put away his phone. He didn't feel like calling Aunty H and Uncle Mano. Grandma would tell them he was fine.

I just need to find the heiau and then I'll know what to do.

Kai felt the solidity of the sun-warmed rocks beneath him. What a lot of work it was to figure everything out! There was so much to decipher: not only the clues in the chant, but also what Dad had really wanted him to do, Sue's moods, Aunty H and Uncle Mano...

As long as he lay here on the lava rock, he could rest. He lay still, regaining his sense of balance. The ocean roared below him. The wind washed over him, smelling of salt. A ripple in the lava rock comfortably cradled his back.

When Kai stood, he felt wobbly and exhausted. He began to shiver in the wind in his wet clothes. He started up the hill.

When Sue saw him, she found a towel from the trunk. She raised her eyebrows but didn't ask him what had happened, and Kai was grateful. Neither did she ask him what he had found here. Kai was glad for the privacy. He had certainly found something here, but he could not explain it to Sue.

"You ready?" Sue said. "Okay. Let's try Lahaina."

Chapter 41
FINDING THE WAY IN KAUPO

D avid pulled into the first Kaupo driveway he found. He got out of the car and swung aside the metal fence. It burned his hand. He got back in his car and drove through the gate. Then he got back out and kicked the gate back into place. It clanked shut.

A gravel driveway led up to a green house shaded by a dwarf banana tree with huge sheets of leaves. The clumps of bananas were disproportionately large. Bunches of miniature bananas lined ropy stalks that hung down from the branches and nearly touched the ground.

David parked his four-wheel-drive GMC Sierra in the shade of a Kiawe tree. He walked up to the house and looked for a doorbell. There was none. Before he had time to knock, a man came and opened the door. The man was about six foot two with thick black eyebrows and hair. He looked young, maybe thirty years old, and he was Asian-American. He was wearing a University of Hawaii Warriors T-shirt and black basketball shorts.

"What do you want?"

"I'm David, and I'm from Kihei. I'm trying to find a heiau near here. Do you know of anywhere I could look?"

"Heiau? What's that?" The man looked puzzled. "Why'd you come here?"

David smiled. "Oh, I should have explained that. A heiau is an ancient Hawaiian altar, a pile of stones where people who followed the Hawaiian religion prayed and sacrificed. Some people still pray there.   My grandpa was Hawaiian, so I'm part Hawaiian, and I'm trying to find the heiau where he used to pray so I can pray there. You see, he just recently died, so… it would mean a lot to me."

"Well, I think you came to the right place." The man looked over his shoulder. "Alexis?"

A tall woman walked up to the doorway. She looked like she might be part Hawaiian. She had braided black hair and was wearing long golden chain earrings.

"This is my wife Alexis. Oh, and I'm Matthew. She's been living here in Maui for most of her life. I just moved here a few years ago. She's the one who would know what you're talking about."

"What? Does he want to know where to go hiking?" asked Alexis.

"He just asked me about this thing called a heiau, ancient Hawaiian religious site. Do you know about those?"

Alexis looked over at David. "Heiau? No, I don't know about any of that Hawaiian stuff. You should go talk to Jim. He's been living here for all his life, seventy years. He's part Hawaiian. He lives down by the river. Just drive, oh, maybe half a mile farther down the road. You'll cross the river, and then go about a quarter mile farther. His driveway is about a hundred feet before the church, on the left. Look for the white mailbox. Good luck!"

Chapter 42
CLUES

Kai was glad to be back in the car. The bike accident and freak wave encounter had taxed him. He felt weary, but as he rested, he began to get his energy again. Sue handed him a bag of trail mix, and he ate.

The road wound past cliffs of red-orange rock the color of sunset. They entered a new microclimate. This valley was wooded, dark green. These were the first trees in miles.

What an effort this journey has been!

They passed around a scallop-shaped bay filled with whitecaps.

"We're at Honolua Bay. I went snorkeling here once, but the reef was rather dangerous because the waves are so rough. Some people go surfing here."

The road cut back into the hillside, skirting a dense jungle of trees.

"Banyan trees," Sue said. "They were probably planted many years ago by the missionaries who came here."

The trees were a tangled mess of limbs. A limb from one tree would loop down into the ground, and come up again a few feet away as a new tree. They looked like strawberry plants with runners. The forest floor was barren. Vines hung down from the tree limbs like ropes. Through the trees, Kai could see several children swinging on the vines, pretending to be Tarzan.

On the left side of the road, several cars were parked at a pull-off. One of the cars had a yellow surfboard strapped to the top. Two young men were sitting inside, listening to blasting music.

The road left the banyan forest and climbed back up the hillside. From the top of the hill, Kai could see far out across the water. On the horizon were two large silhouetted bulges. Two islands. Kai remembered that back in Kihei he had seen only one island, Lanai. Now he saw both Lanai and a new island, to the right.

"What's that?" Kai asked. He wanted to learn whatever he could. After all, the heiau had brought him here to the North Shore. Perhaps, as well as warnings, this place would offer clues that would help solve the chant.

"That's Molokai. It used to be a leper colony. Now, tourists go there. A few thousand people live on Molokai."

"What about the other island?"

"Lanai. The whole island was once a gigantic pineapple plantation, but now the land has been bought out and there is a fancy resort on the island where a few tourists go every year. You can escape the crowds that you find here on Maui, and be isolated from the rest of the world. Not very many people live on Lanai. If you want to see the two islands, there are ferries that go from Lahaina to both Molokai and Lanai."

"So there are two other islands near Maui?"

Sue paused. "Three. There's another island that you can see from the beach in Kihei, called Kahoolawe. It used to be a bombing test site. People call it the target isle. But now the government is cleaning up the bombs and is going to give the land over to people of Hawaiian ancestry as a reservation. Hawaiians fought hard to get rights to it. But the land is terrible. There's no water for irrigation. Maybe someday in a few hundred years there will be resorts on Kahoolawe, but as of now, it is an uninhabited wasteland. Oh, and there's also Molokini, a tiny volcanic crater that barely pokes halfway out of the water between Kahoolawe and Maui. It's a famous snorkeling area. Tourists go by boat."

Resorts. Land ownership. Plantation. Irrigation. The lava birth of the islands...Be careful!

Somewhere in all this is the answer to my chant. Kai read the whole chant quietly to himself again.

The sand of fire leads to sand of night
Kihapi'ilani's road leads behind the father's house

Hear the echoes of our song

Above the land of the pineapple and the paniolo
Above the springs in the forest of ash
Hear the echoes of our song

Beyond the cruel sun to the land of the taro
The stream in the northernmost point beyond the mother's auwai
Hear the echoes of our song

Lono's treasure in the small shrine
Near the great shrine
Hear the echoes of our song

He who sees the owl possesses the power
Lono's treasure, power of the ancestors, power to find,
power to protect
Hear the echoes of our song

Why can't I figure this out?

"We'll get it," Sue said, reading his mind. She flashed him a smile. "We're close. I can feel it."

Kai felt it, too. A wave of excitement energized him. They were nearing the heiau.

Chapter 43
TO LAHAINA, "PLACE OF THE CRUEL SUN"

As Sue and Kai neared Lahaina, the sunlight was rich gold reflecting off the developed landscape of Ka'anapali's golf courses and hi-rise time-share condominiums. They pulled in at the parking garage for Whaler's Village, the upscale mall beside the beach, to find a restaurant. Kai changed into a clean shirt from his backpack. They walked to a restaurant with outdoor seating under umbrellas right on the sand. It was a busy place, with people entering from both the mall and the beach. A beach volleyball tournament was finishing nearby, and swarms of vacationers passed constantly on the sidewalk along the sand. As they walked back toward the garage, they passed a small museum displaying a forty-foot whale skeleton.

"Where do you think we should look for the heiau?" Kai asked. Unlike the places he'd found the other heiaus, this area seemed developed. Where could one possibly find a heiau in the middle of hotels and condos? "Any ideas?" he asked. It seemed to Kai that one or maybe two more heiaus would satisfy the remaining description. They were closing in on the original Cook-era heiau.

They began driving toward Lahaina. He felt close. This would be the place. But where would they look when they got to town?

"I think the stream is a clue," said Kai suddenly. He pulled a detailed map from Sue's collection. "Look, there are three big streams," he said. "Kahoma, Kanaha, and Kauaula. They look like they run out of the mountains down into Lahaina. So, what's this other word in the chant, auwai?"

"Auwai is an irrigation channel, for taro and fishponds," said Sue.

"That's weird," said Kai. "They had irrigation channels built when the chant was written?"

"Lahaina's been irrigated since at least the 14th century," said Sue. "There were thousands of taro and fish ponds in pre-contact Lahaina. The Hawaiians raised fish: moi, mullet, u'u."

"We know the history here as far back as that from chants?" asked Kai. Almost everything known about ancient Hawaii seemed to be from chants.

"Genealogy chants," said Sue. "One auwai was named for Cheifess Wao in the year 1390. Another for King Pi'ilani in 1450."

They talked for a little about old Lahaina, or Lele, as it used to be called. For hundreds of years, the village was crowded. Most people lived near the shore. There were many heiaus for the people. Behind the thickly populated area were wet and dry farms. For centuries, until the era of sugar plantations, the historic auwai were the source of water for all.

They entered modern Lahaina, and drove down Front Street into the center of town. They passed a crowded, funky mix of fine art galleries, t-shirt shops, fancy restaurants, and souvenir shops, all bustling with tourists. Tourists carrying ice cream cones crammed the streets and the boardwalk along the ocean. They passed historic Prison Street, a shady park, a church, and a school.

"I think it was here, but I don't really know how to start looking for this heiau," Sue said. "It seems like we're missing information. We've got the stream, and the auwai. But there are three streams, and they run from mountain to sea. It's going to be too hard to search along them all."

"I wonder if we could look for a street sign with my family name on it?" Kai suggested. "Sometimes when a family lives somewhere, their name ends up on a street sign in the area."

"Check the map, but really, I doubt it. I'll bet most of the streets are newer than the early 1800s, or at least their names are.

The ones that have old names are like Canal Street, where there used to be water."

Kai checked one of Sue's maps, and was disappointed.

"So we don't have any plan?" Kai asked, feeling suddenly desperate.

"Well...I don't know...I'm hoping something will jog your memory of a family story. A name. Anything to help start our search. Can you remember anything that might help? Something your dad, aunt, grandma, or Poppy said?"

"My dad didn't tell me many stories about the past," said Kai.

Sue pulled into a parking spot by an empty playfield. She gestured toward the field. "I wasn't planning to show you this, but since we're parked here, I will. This place was called Moku'ula --- the sacred island."

Kai raised his eyebrows. Everything he could see was dry, parched by the strong sun.

"The center of Hawaii's government used to be right here. Kamehameha III lived here, governing the whole Kingdom of Hawaii until the mid 1800s. Probably for twenty generations before that, too. Maui Loa, the first local ruler to consolidate most of Maui, is one of the more famous early chiefs to have had his court here.

"When Cook arrived, this was a 17-acre freshwater fish pond with the royal palace on a small island in the middle. Only royalty was allowed. This was the umbilical center of all of Hawaii. A powerful water spirit --- a supernatural giant black monitor --- was said to rise up from the water like a dragon to guard the sacred island."

Kai tried to imagine this playfield as the seat of government for all of Hawaii. He pictured a shimmering, peaceful lake. Protected by the calm water, the rulers relaxed in privacy on their island, escaping temporarily from troublesome duties and decisions.

Was his family ever invited onto the island? Probably not. They would have stood respectfully as Kai did now, admiring their king's aura from across the wide waters, perhaps waiting for a glimpse of the mystical guardian lizard.

"The pond was filled in later. Once the sugar industry diverted the flow of water, the pond turned into a stagnant swamp. It became infested with the mosquitoes brought here by a Mexican ship."

Kai sighed. So many bad things had come to his people! So much had been lost.

The playfield was hot, dusty and deserted. A piece of litter fluttered in the hot wind.

"There's a plan now to restore the pond," said Sue.

I wonder if I was meant to see this sacred place and think about the rulers of old Hawaii, Kai thought. *I wonder if I came here for a purpose.*

Was Moku'ula a clue? Was this a place that was important to his family? But Sue had said that commoners never came here.

Had his family members been commoners? Or had they been ali'i, rulers?

He remembered something his father had said once. He had been a small boy. Someone at school had poked him with a pencil. He had come home from kindergarten in tears. His father told him to be strong, and fight back.

"Don't let anyone do that to you, Kai. Never! Your Hawaiian family ruled. Don't forget them. You've got some of their power. They were great, Kai. Like you."

What had Dad meant? Had his ancestors once literally ruled as chiefs?

Chapter 44
DAD SINGS IN THE TONGAN CHOIR

Sue and Kai walked away from the site of the royal pond, toward the center of Lahaina.

"At the time of Cook, most people farmed taro," said Sue.

"That doesn't help us much," said Kai. "They might have farmed down here by the sea, or up on the hillsides. Either place could be near a stream and an auwai."

He envisioned the scene. He could picture the hillsides covered with taro plots and ponds. He could picture old Lahaina as a development of thatched huts spread thickly around the king's sacred complex.

Kai imagined his family. They looked like his father.

A big woman was smiling, joking around. She had full lips and kinky hair. Her children and her husband were with her. The man wore a loin cloth and she wore a skirt, both made from pounded bark. There were two kids, a girl and a boy. Usually, taro planting, tending, and harvesting, and preparing the food were men's jobs. But this was a special moment in the construction of a taro pond. The whole family was there to help.

The family stood together in a muddy field inside a small stone embankment. A little stream flowed along one side, ready to be diverted to give its water to the taro when they needed it. A few Kukui branches stuck out from the mud, half-rotted and partly submerged where they had been buried earlier as fertilizer. A fresher layer of tough leaves from sugar cane and coconut was on the surface like a carpet.

Now the whole family stomped the leaves into the mud to prepare the ground for planting. The woman began telling an old, familiar story about how humans are the younger siblings of taro plants who grew out of a little twisted root in the ground just like the taro. They stomped together in rhythm like a song. The two children stayed near to hear her words over the squishing sounds of the warm, murky water and mud oozing between their toes. The scene reminded Kai of stomping grapes.

But were these really the family members who could have hidden a treasure? They seemed loving and playful, but to collect and hide anything valuable, they would also need to be cunning.

The big woman looked straight at Kai and laughed. There was mischief in her eyes. She looked very, very much like a twin of his dad. She emanated power.

She said something in Hawaiian to the two children. She pointed and they all stared at Kai as if he were a ghost. The children hid behind their mother's mud-splattered legs. But their mother stared at Kai with intelligent curiosity, as if sizing him up.

"This is what I have," she said, gesturing to her husband, her children, the taro, the mud, the river, and the sky. "I don't have what you seek."

Kai rubbed his eyes. He was back in modern Lahaina, walking with Sue.

"It doesn't make sense," said Kai. "I think my ancestors who hid the artifact --- if there is one --- must have been ali'i. How would taro farmers get anything valuable? I think they'd be afraid to be caught with something so valuable. I mean, ali'i would feel more powerful. A member of the elite would be more likely to take the risks."

"It's possible," said Sue. "Your family certainly wrote a chant and kept it alive, which seems like ali'i. Ali'i were accustomed to keeping genealogy chants alive for many generations." She was beginning to get excited. "The only strange thing is why your family wouldn't know it. Why wouldn't your great-grandpa know you were once ali'i? People keep careful track of bloodlines like that. Being ali'i is like being related to Charlemagne, or the Queen of Sweden."

"It will be easier to trace my lineage if that's true, won't it?" said Kai.

"If you're really ali'i," said Sue, sounding unconvinced.

"Maybe I had a relative that was ali'i but married a commoner. You know, after Hawaiian religion ended? I mean, maybe I'm just a little bit ali'i."

"It still seems like your family would have kept track of a famous relative like that. Unless..."

"What?" asked Kai.

"Unless the relative was infamous for something. Maybe the relative did something bad? Maybe he or she was a traitor, or married a social outcast or did something else your family really couldn't be proud of...You know, it's just as likely to have been a woman as a man. Old Hawaii had a lot of chiefesses. A lot of female leaders. Women could own land, when land ownership started. And they traced their blood lines through both men and women."

Ahead of them was a little church with open doors.

"In ancient Hawaii, religion ruled everything," said Sue, looking at the church. "And then afterward, most Hawaiians converted to Christianity and followed a new set of rules. Maybe you had a high-born relative who was an embarrassing rule breaker," she said.

"A rule breaker would be willing to steal from Cook and touch a heiau," Kai said.

"I think we're getting somewhere," said Sue.

"Maybe," said Kai.

"I just remembered something I learned about heiaus. I don't know if it will help, but...Did you know the heiaus and rituals led to huge taxes?"

"Taxes?" said Kai. "I thought each family just built their own heiau," Kai said. "Like my grandma and great-grandpa did. With stones they found."

"Sure, there were little ones like that. But big, official heiaus of the elite required more work. And priests had to be supported. Offerings had to be made. In the 16th and 17th centuries, as kings and ali'i gained more power, more big heiaus were built. More rituals developed. All that had to come from taxes on the commoners.

"Archeologists have carbon dated the coral used in some heiaus. They found many were built around 1600. It had to do with chiefs solidifying their power. Hawaiian chiefs built more heiaus and made their hierarchical social system stricter. Kings and priests started claiming the gods as their personal ancestors. And commoners had to do more and more religious rituals, and follow more rules.

"There were rules about marriage, death, building, war, farming, fishing….At the same time, the rulers gained power. All land became the king's. The commoners were forced to grow taro more intensively to pay their taxes."

"You're totally wrecking my image of heiaus," said Kai. "For me, they are personal places for meditation and gratitude…What you're talking about sounds like the feudal system, like slave farmers supporting a bad habit of the rich. I don't like it. I wish you'd stop talking like that. It's like you don't understand how heiaus are sacred," said Kai defensively.

"Okay," said Sue carefully. "I didn't know you felt that way."

"I didn't when I started…but meeting my family and finding out all this stuff about my family…It's different now. I feel connected," said Kai.

"I thought you just wanted some history, to help you figure things out," Sue said slowly. "So we could maybe find the treasure. I didn't know you had…feelings…about heiaus."

"Well of course I have a feeling for heiaus," Kai said. "Why else would I leave my dad's ashes there? Have you forgotten that I'm part Hawaiian?"

"Not for an instant," said Sue. "I'm sorry I said that. It's just that we're wasting time. I'm anxious to figure this out, and we're close."

Kai sighed.

"Look," said Sue. "This is going to be a hard one. I'd like to help. Are we looking for the chant heiau, or not? The goal is to find the heiau now, before dark, and deliver your dad's ashes. Right? And see if anything else is there. It would be stupid to have driven all over the island and come this far and then not find the heiau." She paused. "I respect you deeply," she said, "and it's been a pleasure helping you. I think I know some things about Lahaina's history that might help you figure this out."

"Of course," he said. "You're right."

They were standing still now, in front of the little church. "What are you thinking?" she asked.

"I think the one we're looking for here will be exactly like the other two in Hana and Makawao," Kai said slowly.

Sue listened.

"It will be built in a place that was hidden at the time, by someone in my family, in the special shape of a pyramid and on a particular axis compared to the makai-mauka line. Just like the others. It will be older than the one in Makawao. It will be obvious when we find it. And it won't have anything to do with...taxes, or forcing people to follow rules. But I feel...frustrated. That we don't have more to go on. At the other heiaus, I had my great-grandpa to lead me."

"Look, why don't we try a different tactic?" asked Sue. "What if I tell you all I know. Everything. Maybe it will spark something. Shall we try it? I'll just try to download everything I know about Hawaiian history right into your brain, starting with Hawaiian land history. I keep coming back to the fact that we need to locate the farm site to find your heiau. Most people built their altars near their own farms."

Sue explained how before 1850 all land belonged to the king. Commoners could use it, but there was no land ownership. The king demanded taxes, but a law guaranteed commoners the right to the water they needed to grow taro. Every fifth day they could take all the water they needed. Under the king, small farmers were protected. "Unlike later, when the foreign-owned sugar plantations diverted water without thought to the Hawaiian family farms that would dry up," Sue finished.

"So it was better for my relatives before private ownership of land?" said Kai.

"It was better for many Hawaiians, for many reasons," said Sue.

From the open doors of the little church flowed a haunting, beautiful note by a lone singer. The sound wafted into the street, washing over them, beckoning to them. The note was lonely and lovely, full of ache and promise. Without thinking, they both turned toward the music.

Kai looked inside. The Methodist church was packed. The congregation was Tongan. The crowd wore flowered dresses and dress shirts. Fans whirled. The walls were white with dark brown beams. There was beautiful stained glass.

"They must be practicing for the Tongan service on Sunday," said Sue.

Deep, throaty singing in Tongan language rose from the congregation. One voice started, and then others joined. Soon, sixty voices mingled in perfect harmony. Two melodies seemed to overlap and separate. The tones harmonized flawlessly into one human voice rising up to God. The music was all pure voice, only voice.

Kai caught his breath. It was more beautiful than any singing he had ever heard. It was as if all the members of the church were producing a single tone.

Everyone in the church clapped once, together, and then the singing continued. Suddenly, a high voice rose above the rest, dipping and soaring, and then subsiding into the single sound. They seemed to be improvising harmony on top of harmony.

"They sing for hours," Sue said. "It's beautiful, isn't it?"

The music was like distilled joy and sadness. The one voice of many singers swelled, evoking the ocean, mountains, and a wide, perfect sky. Somehow, Kai found himself thinking of the taro farmers, and their obvious love for one another.

The music changed. There were words rising out of it, deep and powerful.

It was his dad's voice.

Kai's heart pounded.

Follow the signs. You're close. Be careful.

"You don't look good," said Sue, examining Kai. "Come on. Let's get you in the shade."

They left the Tongan church and walked to the park, the harmonies of the hymns following them like a blessing on a hot breath of wind.

"I'm still thinking about the ali'i thing," Kai said suddenly. "Doesn't the whole thing seem like it was done by ali'i?"

"Yes," said Sue.

"Won't there be records of my family if we have some ali'i blood?"

"Definitely," said Sue.

The park was composed of a single giant banyan tree that stretched 200 feet across a plaza, and its pool of welcome shade.

From here, the Tongan singing was just a part of the wind rustling the leaves. Kai listened intently until the music died into a whisper of song.

Kai turned to Sue.

"I have an idea," he said.

Chapter 45
DAVID'S "GRANDPA"

David knocked on the door to the Kaupo house where he had been directed.

"Aloha! How's life?" Jim was shortish, thin and had deep smile lines across his face.

David explained how Jim's neighbors had directed David here because they thought Jim might know where to find the heiau.

Jim thought about it. "Many heiaus here in Kaupo. What kind of heiau are you looking for?"

"I'm not exactly sure. I think it might have belonged to a family of ali'i, and it probably is rather large, but it's not a heiau that was used for sacrifice. A heiau for prayer," said David.

"Why do you want to know about this heiau?" asked Jim.

"I want to find the heiau my grandpa used to pray at. He just died, you see," lied David. Sometimes, he found, it was necessary to lie in order to get information.

"Oh, okay, okay. Okay. What was his family name?" asked Jim.

David's mind went blank. Then he thought fast. "Maka. But he was a *hanai*, adopted, so his name may have changed."

"Oh, okay. I don't know that name. But I think I know the heiau you are looking for. You know Kaupo Gap? Kaupo Gap Trail?" asked Jim.

"Uh, is that the trail that leads up Haleakala from here?" asked David.

"Yah, yah. That's the one. Go, say, three miles, up the trail. Great heiau, not many people know about it. The family that built it moved to Hana, but they used to be a rich, powerful family here in Kaupo. That's probably the one. The others are all far away from the road. None are like the one you describe, just small piles of rocks. So, do you need directions to the trail?" asked Jim.

"Please," said David.

"Okay. Go back into Kaupo. Turn right, before the store. Go up the road... you'll find it. Send a prayer from me!" Jim waved before David drove away.

Chapter 46
WHALERS FISTFIGHT THE MISSIONARIES

Sue led Kai toward a bench in Lahaina's banyan park. Giant branches spread protectively over sidewalks and benches. The huge branches that so strangely found their way back into the ground as roots seemed like the legs of a giant still animal. It was dim and cool under the banyan's belly.

Sue's cell phone rang.

"Just a minute," she said, and walked away.

Sue walked to a place far enough from Kai that he would not hear.

She glanced behind her. Kai had not followed.

"This is Sue."

"Hey, Sue," said David on the other end. "Just wanted to check in. How's everything going? You find anything yet?"

"Yes, actually we're in Lahaina right now. Maybe there's a heiau here. Right now, we're just trying to sort everything out."

"Sue? We're still a team, right? You sure you haven't found anything?"

"Yes, what do you mean?"

"Oh, nothing. Just making sure you're still on board. We've got to work as a team—you, me, and Kai. If there is an artifact, you're not going to find it by yourself."

"Yes, David, I understand."

"Good. I'll call you again if anything comes up."

While Sue answered her phone, Kai waited. A middle-aged couple wearing matching dressy white pants and aloha shirts sat on the benches resting in the relative coolness, sipping Starbucks iced coffees. A down-and-out looking self-proclaimed

minister waved a Holy Bible and preached to whoever was too
comfortable to move away. His eyes looked crazed, and his
clothes were old, but the words he proclaimed were peaceful.
Nearby, his blond, barefoot children played in the dust. A small,
dirt-stained box in front of him begged for donations. Mynah
birds fought noisily on the ground and in the branches.

Sue found Kai reading a plaque. The tree had been
planted in the 1870s to celebrate the arrival of missionaries early
in the 1800s.

Kai wondered about that. Was the arrival of missionaries
an event worthy of celebration?

"So what's your idea?" asked Sue. "We need more than
what we've got. I think you've got the clue we need inside your
head."

"My ideas is, I thought it might help if I try to think like
my ancestors," said Kai.

"That's all?" asked Sue. She seemed disappointed.

Kai nodded. "I mean, try to enter the mind of my family.
Really understand them. Could you tell me some stuff about
Hawaiian history? I need to know more."

*I think they'll tell me, if I let them lead me to their secret sacred
site,* Kai thought.

"I don't think so," said Sue, sounding a little exasperated.
"Kai, I don't think the history will help us find the heiau."

"No. Please. Tell me something."

"All right," Sue said impatiently. "If you insist." She led
him across the park. She seemed to relax more as they walked.
"Actually, the history is all around us right now. That's a little
piece of a fortress. Rebuilt, of course. From the 1830s," said Sue,
pointing.

"Why did Lahaina need a fort?" asked Kai. This whole
journey, he had felt himself moving closer and closer to his
ancestors. Here in Lahaina, where so much had happened, their
presence was intense. He wanted to find out how his ancestors
had lived. What had they cared about? He wanted to get to
know them.

A fort sounded like war. *Had there been wars here?* Kai wondered.

Sue moved closer. "The fort had a 20-foot wall with mounted canons. Stretching all around there," she said, pointing. "Now it's just one little rebuilt corner."

Kai tried to think like his ancestors. "So there were foreign attackers?" Kai guessed.

Sue shook her head. "Good guess, but no."

She led him across the park and a street, to the harbor. She stopped when they were facing a reddish plaza near the ocean. Sue pointed at the plaza, maybe some kind of old volleyball court. "This is the Brick Palace of King Kamehameha I, built in 1802," said Sue. "When he united the Hawaiian islands, he made Maui's capital into the capital of his new large kingdom. It was the first western style house in Hawaii. He set it here by the harbor so he could greet ship's captains.

After 1802, things changed greatly on Maui. It was the end of the golden age for the Hawaiians."

Sue led him toward an old tall ship with masts and rigging.

"First, organized Hawaiian religion died in 1820. King Kamehameha II decreed the kapu system of religious taboos to be illegal. Statues of gods were burned. Heiaus destroyed. There was a battle between two parts of the royal family. One part of the royal family defended the Hawaiian religion, and its temples and priests. They lost."

"With so much fighting over religion, my family would have kept their heiau secret from everyone outside the family," said Kai. "To keep it safe. Hopefully, it's not hidden from view, and hard to spot."

Sue nodded.

"Shortly after the Hawaiian religion was defeated, missionaries arrived. Churches were built, and schools. Lahainaluna School, up on the hill above Lahaina, is the oldest school west of the Mississippi River. The Bailey House Museum is a missionary house you can still visit. There's a replica of the original printing press at Lahainaluna School, like the one the was used to put the Hawaiian language into print."

Sue led Kai into the shade. She seemed excited as she racked her brain for history.

Somewhere in here is the clue.

"The missionaries gave the Hawaiian language 12 letters. Having a written language helped keep Hawaiian history and culture alive. Missionaries helped preserve memories. But mostly, the missionaries taught the Hawaiians new ways. Bibles were printed. Missionaries taught Hawaiians to read."

They sat on a low wall. Kai listened intently. Somewhere in this history was something that would lead them to his family's hiding place.

"Next came the era of whaling. It lasted from maybe 1820 to the 1850s. Lahaina was totally transformed into a pit-stop for sailors. It was a rowdy, lawless time in Lahaina.

"Whaling really took off when an offshore hunting ground was discovered west of Peru and then sperm whale grounds were found off of Japan.   At first, about 150 ships came per season. By the 1850s, 400 ships came per year. 100 at a time would stop in Lahaina. The ships stayed for weeks.

"The whales were valuable because the oil from their blubber could be burned in lamps. Once petroleum refining processes were discovered and kerosene replaced whale oil, the whaling industry slowed to a trickle.

"A lot of people who visit Maui assume it was all local hunting of humpback whales, because you can still see the humpbacks here today, but it wasn't. It was whalers traveling the whole Pacific and stopping here to rest. They wanted to stock up, and do a little trading. They came for alcohol, and women."

Women in my family? Kai felt something dark growing in him.

"The humpbacks still migrate here for the winter to give birth," Sue continued. "A pod of several hundred whales still does. The whole time they're here they don't eat. The water here is like a desert without food. They fast, growing thinner and thinner, while their newborn calves grow strong enough for the long journey back to Alaska where they feast on krill.

"You want me to keep going?"

Kai nodded.

They turned up a street back toward the banyan park. They had walked a small loop, and were back at the banyan tree's rebuilt fort.

Sue stopped in front of the small, tumbled-down looking fortress wall. "Soon, Lahaina was a war zone."

"Between Hawaiians and whalers?" Kai asked.

Sue shook her head sadly. "The Hawaiians had died, mostly."

In thirty years? Kai's brow furrowed.

"The leaders who were left were weakened."

How quickly his people had lost everything! After countless generations, how quickly everything about them disappeared.

"The war in Lahaina was between the two groups who had power. The missionaries and the whalers," she said slowly.

In as short a time as thirty years, the Hawaiians weren't even much of the equation?

No wonder my relatives hid whatever treasure they had! Kai thought. It was such a time of turmoil. They had to hide it to keep it safe. They had to hide it to keep hope alive. They had to believe that someday in the future, there would be a better time when a future descendant could safely retrieve what they valued most.

Kai swallowed. In a strange way, the chant represented hope. Hope had helped his family get through the loss of everything. In a short time, they had lost so many people to disease, lost their religion, seen the power of their kings diminished, lost use of land and resources to foreigners, and witnessed a loss of respect for their women and for their whole culture. They had survived, in part, by creating a new chant and placing hope in the future. Whatever they had hidden, they had hidden with the hope that a future descendant would survive to find it.

"Are you thinking like your ancestors?" Sue asked.

"Yes," Kai said quietly.

"Any ideas?"

"Not yet."

Family, you can show me now, he thought. You can trust me. I'm ready to hold the family's hope in my hand. I won't misuse what you give.

Kai listened intently, but the only answer he heard was his own breathing and the beating of his heart.

Chapter 47
KAUPO GAP

T he trail was a dirt road, wide enough for a jeep to pass through. The Kaupo Trail ran up through a wooded valley, the Kaupo Gap, one of the largest valleys on Haleakala. For three miles, David had hiked through private property, alongside cattle ranches with large tanks of water for the cows. At first, the trail had meandered through a forest of guava trees and red Christmas berries. Then the trail had led up to a fence, the edge of a ranch, and then skirted ranches for a couple of miles.

Back at the trailhead, down by the road, there had been a brown and white National Park mileage table with directions on it: 3.5 miles to the park entrance, where he now stood. He must be getting close to the heiau.

The trail rode up the side of the valley. Across the valley, over a jungle of trees, he could see a face of lava that had rolled down from the Haleakala Crater. The trail was narrow, covered in fallen leaves from the tunnel of branches hovering above the trail.

A worn footpath cut away from the trail. David decided to take it. The path snuggled through a tall grassy thicket. Fifty feet in, he found it.

The heiau was mossy. It was a neglected heap. Stones had tumbled down and lay scattered on the sides of the big stack. It was about twenty feet long. The angle of the heiau to the mountain-sea axis was indeterminable.

This wasn't the right heiau. Was this where Jim had directed him? It seemed to be the one Jim had described; it was definitely a large heiau, and it appeared that not many people had come here to maintain the heiau.

This heiau didn't belong to Kai's family. Their heiaus were strictly rectangular and had the little peculiar mound on the top in the shape of an owl's head. Neither of the standards had been met here.

David lay down on the ground. He let out a sigh.

Had Kai's aunt and uncle lied to him?

Was he even on the right side of Maui?

Chapter 48
LAHAINA'S FORT

"Okay. Here's the rest of the fortress story," said Sue. They stood together in the banyan park, in front of the unimpressive wall. "It was built when Queen Kaahumanu protested the selling of a young, unwilling girl as a sex slave."

So my relatives were bought and sold?

"She was purchased by an English Sea Captain. There's some debate…Nothing is ever quite as straight forward in history as it seems. Leoiki was high-born, and she went on to have children with the captain. None of those details seem to fit with our contemporary idea of slavery. But the way the newspaper of the time wrote it up, she was purchased for sex, and she was an unwilling slave."

Sue paused. "Of course, Hawaiian women from the time of Cook were famous for giving themselves to foreigners. They swam out to Cook's boat just to offer themselves freely. The chiefess of Kauai supposedly offered her own daughter to Cook.

Leoiki was a pivotal case, however. She was symbolic of all the prostitution that had developed in Lahaina. Because the missionaries wanted to fight prostitution and sexual slavery, they talked to the Queen. Queen Kaahumanu took a stand. The Queen had already outlawed fighting, murder, and theft.

The sailors didn't like the Queen messing with their affairs. A whaling crew came as a riot mob and attacked the missionary William Richards' home. He had started a Christian mission in Lahaina.

"They didn't bother Queen Kaahumanu," Sue finished.

Kai looked down. The whole history was making him sad. It was more painful than he had imagined to think like his ancestors.

"They didn't attack the Queen, because she wasn't really the one setting the rules anymore," Sue said. "The missionaries had taken control."

Kai felt a heaviness growing inside him.

"The missionaries complained to the Queen about the attack, and she had this fort built," Sue said.

Suddenly, his sadness turned to anger. Kai began to boil. Sue looked away.

"I know," Sue said. "You're right. And we haven't even talked about the worst of it: small pox, measles, whooping cough, flu, gonorrhea."

"How many survived?" Kai demanded.

"There were 100,000 Hawaiians on Maui when Cook arrived. By 1920 there were about 20,000 people who called themselves Hawaiian. And they were probably exaggerating their bloodlines...People want to be Hawaiian, like the kings. Now people are proud to be part-Hawaiian, like you. People have family trees that date back centuries."

"Sue, that's it!" Kai's eyes lit up. He suddenly knew what they needed to do. "I can't believe I didn't remember this before. My dad, he told me once that somebody was making a family tree. I just never looked it up because I didn't feel connected enough. If we look online maybe--"

"Bingo!" said Sue. Her whole face lit up in a smile. "I'll run back to the car and get my laptop and let's see what we can find. If someone's bothered to make a family tree, maybe you really do have an important ancestor."

Chapter 49
RETHINKING THE CLUES

It was late afternoon before David gave up searching in Kaupo. He had visited ten different heiaus. Ten different rock piles of various ages around the area…His legs were tired from hiking, and scratched from walking through brush. He was exhausted. Sweat and dried dust stuck to his skin. So much effort…A whole day's work for nothing! Not one of the sites had corresponded with Kai's description of the pattern of his family's altars: the distinctive owl's head or possibly pyramid pile on the top, with the base built askew to the makai-mauka axis. What a waste of time the search had been!

David started the car to head for home. He would have to give the treasure heiau more thought. He finished drinking the last drop of his last water bottle. He had a long drive ahead of him, so there would be plenty of time to think.

Chapter 50
THE VOICE OF THE DEAD

S ue and Kai found a comfortable spot near the Pioneer Inn
with its whaling harpoons on the wall. Their wi-fi
connection was good.

"Let's start with your great-grandpa's name, okay?" asked
Sue, as she typed quickly. "We might have to sign up for a
genealogy search site membership, but it won't take long. Here's
something good," she said. She clicked on a Hawaiian genealogy
site. "Because genealogy has always been so important to
Hawaiians, there are some wonderful, accessible collections of
online documentation available to help people trace their
Hawaiian roots. A lot of Hawaiians lost track of their family lines
and want to reconstruct them now." Sue browsed the site menu
and chose "find your family."

Kai spelled his great-grandpa's name, "K-u-'-u-a-k-i-a H-
o-k-o-a-n-a."

Nothing came up.

Sue frowned.

"Hmm, are you sure you spelled it right?"

Kai nodded.

"I was just thinking about what could have made your
family, if they were ali'i, keep the chant going in the family and
yet lose track of their family lineage." She tried alternate
spellings of Hokoana, without luck.

"Maybe there was a hanai --- an adoption. Hanai
relationships were common. People gave their children to
relatives to strengthen family ties, or so the children could learn
a special skill. Sometimes a child was hanaied because the
adoptive parents were childless…Hanais can really complicate
genealogy searches.   Sometimes the hanaied child would lose
complete knowledge of blood family. Once a few generations

pass, it gets harder and harder to uncover. If the hanai took place before the Circuit Courts took over the records, you have to resort to the Bureau of Conveyance --- sometimes a family gave a child with a piece of land to another family...But it's kind of hit or miss."

They both stared with disappointment at the lack of results on the screen.

"So do you think there was a hanai?" Sue went on.

"I don't know," said Kai. "Why would the child keep the chant alive, but not know who blood family was?"

Sue sighed. "You're right. The hanai scenario doesn't hold up because of the chant. People in the family had to keep the chant going and keep passing it on. Maybe what we were talking about earlier makes more sense: someone in your family did something shameful. It would have had to have been after people started having last names, say by 1880. So the family decided as a group to take a new last name to forget the old one, to leave that person and the shame behind. But they kept the chant going."

What kind of thing could bring that much shame to the family? Kai wondered. A marriage to someone of the wrong class? Birthing a sailor's illegitimate child? Practicing the ancient healing arts of a kapuna after Christian missionaries declared it was illegal sorcery? Building a heiau after practice of Hawaiian religion was declared illegal?

"We need another name to work with," said Sue.

"Try my dad's and mine."

Sue tried. "Nothing."

Kai bit his lip. Another name...Hawaiians went by many names. Dream names. Spiritual names. Place names. Event names. Legal names. The same person might have many names, but probably would use the same one always on legal documents. Maybe Ku'ukia was his middle name, or his informal name.

"Sometimes if a child got sick, the family changed his name, to give him mana, and then if he got better he might keep the new name," Sue said.

If Poppy had another name, what would it be? What had he said?

"You are the seeker, and I am the guide."

"I've got it! Look up 'guide' in Hawaiian," Kai said.

"Alaka'i ho'ike," Sue read.

"Try that as great-grandpa's first name."

Sue typed. Almost immediately, the screen changed.

Like magic, his family tree appeared. Grandma Lokelani's name jumped out at him, and Aunty H's. Kai found he couldn't speak. Here were all the answers he had been seeking!

"I don't see any hanai," Sue said. "Look, it goes back to 1820!"

Kai gasped. "Who put this together? Does it say? This has been here the whole time and I didn't know about it?"

Sue scanned the page. "It looks like maybe your dad's oldest cousin's grandchild. Somebody name Ruth Johnson in Honolulu."

"Wow! I've never heard of her." Kai studied the page greedily. The oldest generation listed was a woman, Ulumaheiheiokalani from Lahaina in 1820. A Hawaiian phrase followed her name. For each person on the page, it showed sex, date and place of birth, and for most, date of death. Kai studied the unfamiliar names. The most recent generation included on the chart and directly related to Kai was Aunty H's mom, Grandma Lokelani, the Iao Valley nursery owner. Grandma Lokelani was born in Hana in 1946, where Poppy lived now. The parents of Poppy's wife, Meli, were David Ahupuaa Kaleipaihala, and Mary Meli Hinau Hokoana. They were born in Hana in 1890 and 1888. Mary Hinau's parents, John Hokoana and Edith Nanahapa, were born in Makawoa in 1869 and 1865. Edith's parents, Kealoha and Leialoha, were born in Lahaina in 1840 and 1846.

Who built the Makawoa heiau where I saw the boars, and added that stanza to the chant?

"The last names don't make any sense," Kai said. "My great-grandpa's mom had the last name Hokoana, like me, but her dad has a different last name."

"If the woman was higher ranking, the man took her name and that was the one passed on to the descendants," said Sue.

"I don't understand the pattern of last names before that," said Kai. "Wait! Those Hawaiian names aren't last names, are they?"

Sue shrugged. "The English names, they were required by the King. In 1860, a lot of Hawaiians didn't have last names yet. Only a few people, who had converted to Christianity and had taken new Christian names and then used their old names as surnames. King Kamehameha IV signed an act requiring that all children have Christian names and a surname based on their father's name. Hawaiian names became middle names. But some Hawaiians didn't have last names until even 1900."

Kai felt dizzy with happiness. Here was his whole family, spread out before him. Here were the names he sought. Here was hard information to go with his search based on interviews with living family, intuition, and listening to signs and voices. Here was proof of his group, his people. He belonged.

Why hadn't he thought of looking for this earlier?

The answer that came surprised him.

Because you didn't care about this until now.

But he did care now, suddenly, very much. These names linked him to the past, and to Dad.

Suddenly, Sue whistled.

"Double bingo," she said. "The oldest ancestor's name? You know what it means?"

"No, what?" asked Kai.

"Here," said Sue. "Let's do it like this. Then we can be sure." She typed in the web address for a Hawaiian history site through the University of Hawaii archives. She typed in the name.

"It's the last bit I recognize," said Sue, "o-ka-lani," They waited two seconds. The meaning appeared.

"...Meaning of the heavens," Kai read. "found usually at the end of a long Hawaiian name, indicating connection to royalty." She was ali'i! "What about the phrase in Hawaiian that follows her name?"

"Oia kekahi kauwa wahine a Nahienaena. It says it means..." They waited for the online translation. "One of the serving women of Nahienaena," Sue read. "I've read about her. Nahienaena was King Kamehameha I's daughter. I know her story, but let's get it so we don't miss anything. Let's look her up." Sue typed for a moment. They read together.

Nahienaena was a princess, famous for how she was torn between following the old ways and the new Christian religion. She was prepared from birth by Hawaiian advisors to marry her brother to keep her Hawaiian bloodlines pure, and then told by missionaries that such a marriage would be illegal because of incest. She loved her brother, but was compelled to marry someone else. She gave birth to a child that may have been her brother's. The baby died after a few days, and then a few weeks later, she died.

"And my family served her," Kai said. What a sad era in history to serve Hawaiian royalty, as their ancient, protected bloodlines were broken! The Princess must have wrestled for years with her destiny and purpose. What was it, his great, great, great, great great-grandma? Ulumaheiheiokalani, must have had the job of comforter in the midst of a court filled with immense sorrow. The sadness would have been stifling, overpowering even before Princess Nahienaena lost her baby. Could people die of sadness?

"Princess Nahienaena's lover and brother was Kamehameha III," Sue said.

"The one who instigated property ownership in 1850?" Kai remembered. He had paid careful attention to Sue's rendition of Hawaiian history. Suddenly, he had an idea. "How did property ownership start? Are there records of it?"

"You're right! Of course!" Sue exclaimed with excitement. "Now that we have the name of your family member from 1850, we can find her land claim and trace it to the site! That's brilliant, Kai!"

Kai beamed.

Sue typed hurriedly, talking at the same time. "There's so much interest in Hawaiian genealogy, history, archeology--- the land claims touch on all that. Plus land developers are interested. Some modern Hawaiians have made money by finding ancestral lands that other people claimed under questionable circumstances. The original Hawaiian families have then claimed the land as their own in court. Sometimes, they get paid off by developers or others who are currently using the land.

"I'll bet the land claim documents are digitalized...Yes! They are! What a fabulous website! There's a fee but it's modest." She turned to Kai. Her eyes shone with anticipation. "The Great Mahele worked like this: every person in all of Hawaii who wanted to claim land had to appear before a committee and testify about his property, its location, description, and say why he or she had a right to it. The committee then ruled as to whether or not the person should get the land. Then the person who wanted the land had to pay a fee and apply for a Royal Patent before their ownership was established. You can imagine what a herculean task it was to survey every single family's plot on all the islands...Surveyors were needed, so some got hired that didn't know what they were doing. They were supposed to document which land was being used by whom. But some outsiders didn't know the most basic things, like the fact that taro plots lie fallow for three years and might be resting but were still used by the families...There were countless disputes, and many mistakes. Some people couldn't appear before the committee. Others couldn't pay the fees. Land that went unclaimed was put in a special category and eventually much of it was sold to foreigners. Hawaiians ended up losing the right to use much of their islands."

"It's Ulumaheiheiokalani's claim," Kai said softly.

There it was. His ancestor's own words, recorded in court in 1850, describing her land.

On the island of Maui, in the Ahupua'a of Lahaina, in the 'ili of Moehanui, is my claim for land, which was received in the time of Kamehameha I. Before that, the family lived in Makena until the time of the lava flow. Concerning the dimensions: 40 is the length on the north, 232 is the length on the east, 40 is the length on the south, 232 is the length on the west. The description of the land is: a milo tree and 'ohia tree are on the north, Waioholinei's claim is on the east, on the west is an auwai, and a land named Kulihaku on the south....The description of the house lot is: with the taro and breadfruit before your eyes, and the bananas hanging, on the east is a grove of trees, on the north is a rock, and on the west the water bringing life, and on the south the trees full of O'u birds chirping and the white-flowered food for the bird.

This claim for this land is made by Ulumaheiheiokalani.

Kai's heart was beating quickly. Ulumaheiheiokalani had spoken to him directly. Her words, carried through time, had reached him. Her own voice. As if she had spoken to him.

"It gives us latitude and longitude," said Kai.

They hurried back to the car.

Chapter 51
LAHAINA HEIAU

They drove up the hillside towards Lahainaluna High School. Kai was bursting with excitement. They were going to find his family's farm. They were going to find the heiau! He could hardly sit still. He needed to talk.

"I bet the way Lahaina grew as a town was from the sea up the hillside," Kai said. "The water always runs down to the sea. Hawaiians would have settled first. Down by the royal pond. Then, when it got too crowded, they had to move up the river. They kept spreading along the river, up and up, until they were way up here, on the hill, along the water --- the auwai in my chant."

They drove through a steep neighborhood with beautiful views.

"But when the settlers up here took water from the river, they'd have to think about people living downstream who were using it and still needed it. They couldn't divert too much water, or change the course. They had to share," Kai went on. "So when it says 'auwai' in the chant, it's not just a ditch, a landmark…It's a way of living, a reminder of how Hawaiians shared and managed their most important resource---water --- for the good of the whole community. The chant is a poem. Auwai means the actual ancient ditch, but it also means how people took care to leave enough for other Hawaiians downstream."

Kai glanced at Sue. Unlike Kai, who was flying high with anticipation, Sue seemed subdued.

"Uh-huh," Sue said. She seemed worried. What was wrong? She glanced at the car's digital clock.

Kai was sure he was right.

We are going to find it! I am beginning to understand the past.

221

The chant was meant to lead him not only to specific locations, but to remind him of the way his ancestors had lived and their attitude toward community.

They reached Lahainaluna High School. A sign said "Lahainaluna High School 1831." As they pulled in, Kai finished his thought. "The 'northernmost point' in the chant probably means way up the hillside, in a place so far up that others would never develop the spot into taro ponds, no matter how big Lahaina grew. We probably have a big hike," Kai went on. He was proud of himself: he was interpreting the chant himself now, and it felt right. "If we just find the family plot, find the nearest auwai, follow the path of the old auwai to a northern point, I bet it will lead us to the right coordinates. I think that will be the best way, to follow the auwai, the old source of life."

Sue was hurriedly checking her text messages. She held her phone away from him, protecting it from his view. "Look," Sue snapped, "I need to get going. It sounds like this hike is going to take a long time."

Kai was shocked. What was wrong with Sue? Why wasn't she as overjoyed as he was?

"We can hike fast," Kai said.

"Look, I can't spend the rest of the day," Sue said, putting her phone away. "I need to get back to Kihei." Kai waited for more of an explanation.

Did she just get an important message? Didn't she want to find the heiau?

"But we have to find it!" Kai said. Wasn't each and every heiau in the chant part of the journey?

"I've been thinking," Sue said, "about the land claim. I think we should go straight to Makena," Sue said. "Remember how it said in the land use documents that the family used to live in Makena? If you look at the chant, you'll see there are two stanzas left. One is probably about this heiau. The next will have to be about somewhere in Makena, on the south side of the island."

"Every heiau is important," Kai insisted. Poppy had told him to let the heiaus lead him. How could Sue have helped him

222

find the coordinates of his family plot and then not even want to visit it? It was the actual site where his relatives had farmed. Having come this far, how could he not see it?

"I think we should skip it," Sue said. She put the keys back in the ignition.

"No!" Kai said. "I have to see it. It's part of the chant! The chant is…it's like a process. It's something my dad made me promise to *do.*"

Sue glanced at him like he was crazy. "Are you searching for the right heiau…or are you on a pilgrimage?" she said.

"Both," Kai answered evenly.

"Have you forgotten what you're searching for?" Sue said.

No, Kai had not forgotten. Soon, he would be able to fulfill his promise and receive his inheritance…But it was strange, the possible artifact didn't seem like the most important thing anymore. Following the chant and delivering the ashes seemed most important. But that didn't seem to be the way Sue was thinking about things.

"Sue, this might be the right heiau," Kai said persuasively. "Maybe the whole chant ends here. Maybe the artifact is here."

Sue sighed. "Maybe." She waivered. She checked the clock again. "We should probably at least check it out. Okay, but we have to hurry. I have my GPS." She dug around in her purse and pulled it out. "Let's make this quick."

Kai felt light, buoyant. Maybe it was the nearness of the heiau, and the end of the chant. He was actually close to finding the place to leave his dad's ashes! He had always hoped he would find it, but it had seemed so difficult that he hadn't been sure he could actually find the right heiau. Now, he felt confident.

"Soon, I'll be able to deliver the ashes," Kai said softly.

Sue didn't answer. She got out of the car.

Didn't she care about his delivery of the ashes? Was her only concern the historical object? Wasn't she in this to help Kai as well?

"Remember, we're going to make this quick," Sue said. They walked to the end of a sidewalk and crossed out of the

223

landscaped development. An overgrown path led in
approximately the right direction through the dry, brushy land.
A no trespassing sign guarded the path's entrance. Sue led him
around the sign. They passed a small stream and continued
uphill.

"This must have been so different when it was irrigated,
before haole companies took the water," said Kai.

Sue nodded. "You're right," she said. "It was shared
through an elaborate system prior to the Pioneer Mill
Company." She wiped the sweat off her brow.

In the distance, up even higher, was what looked like a
small ravine.

"That must be Auwaiowao," said Sue. "The irrigation
ditch named after Chiefess Wao from 1390. What's left of it."
She studied her GPS. "I think you're family's land was there."

"The mother's auwai," breathed Kai. "Chiefess Wao must
be the symbolic mother."

The hike was hard. When they reached the family plot,
Kai was drenched in sweat, scratched and thirsty. They rested
for a moment, enjoying the view. Below them, a patchwork of
irrigated, landscaped greenery and development spread to the
blue sparkling sea. Some of the houses were designed in Spanish
style with beautiful tiled roofs. Where patches of dirt showed, it
was a deep, rich rust color. This place seemed far above Lahaina,
as if it were part of the sky.

Kai opened his mouth and gave a long, elated whoop.

The sound died. It was quiet here.

I am here, finally!

It was cooler than down in the low land. The ocean was
intensely blue. Across the channel, the island of Lanai rose like
the back of a giant whale. His family had found peace here, he
was sure.

"Come on," Sue said, starting out again. She pointed to
the nearby dried auwai.

"Can't we pace off where the boundaries of the farm
were?" Kai asked.

But Sue had already started away from the family plot in search of the heiau which must be nearby.

The auwai was a deep, dry riverbed. On its floor, trees grew. They made their way along the ridge above the ravine.

"We need to cross," Kai said. "The chant says northern."

A little while later, on the opposite ridge, they found the heiau. It was on a high spot with a rocky outcropping that looked down into the dry auwai. It was definitely Kai's family's heiau: it had the familiar protruding cone and the slightly skewed axis.

Kai circled it, entranced.

Sue recited from memory:

"The stream in the northernmost point beyond the mother's
auwai

Hear the echoes of our song.
Lono's treasure in the small shrine
Near the great shrine
Hear the echoes of our song."

Sue stopped, and they both looked. There didn't seem to be any small shrine and great shrine here. There was only one heiau. Sue glanced at Kai.

"Looks like we've got another heiau to find," she said.

"I want to look around," Kai said.

"Fine." Sue held out the topographical map she was holding. "Just don't take too long, okay?" She turned back toward the car.

Kai watched her go. Kai needed to look at the heiau, and think. He needed time for the heiau to give him directions to the next one. He would look at the heiau and then catch up with Sue.

He turned his phone on to check the time. He'd had it turned off for a while. Eight missed calls from Aunty H! To his surprise, he no longer felt angry, merely irritated that he had been so misunderstood. The missed calls nagged at him. If Aunty H was done trying to control Kai, he wanted to tell her about the family tree. But this wasn't the time. He needed to hurry, Sue was waiting.

Kai walked around the stone altar. It was just like the others…except, what was that little line of lighter colored rocks right there? The line led away from the base of the cone. Kai pulled out his phone and took a quick picture. It was a curving line, meandering away…

His eye fell on a single light rock embedded by itself in the surface of the heiau, a little apart from the cone. Kai drew closer to it. He reached out and touched the rock. He felt a tiny cone-shaped bump on the special rock. He took another photo.

Then he bounded down the hill.

Chapter 52
DAVID FIGURES IT OUT

Keawakapu Beach

David drove out of the desert, through Maui Upcountry, back down through the sugarcane fields and into Kihei. He kept driving toward Wailea. It was late in the afternoon. The sunlight was golden, and the breeze was light.

David was frustrated. His mind was tired; he had no idea which direction to head next. Maybe he should go back to the site in Makena.

I need a break. David turned off the Pi'ilani Highway at Kilohana drive. In a minute, his car was parked underneath the shade of a grove of coral bean trees. David walked down the sidewalk to the corner of South Kihei Road and Kilohana Drive. Brown banana-shaped pods that had fallen from the coral bean trees crunched under his sandals.

David looked down South Kihei Road. There were no cars. About fifty feet away, a white sign read "Wailea." He was at the undefined border between Wailea and Kihei.

David jogged across the street. A pair of green dumpsters sat behind a chain link fence. The stink of the trash was stifled by a wonderful fresh smell of salt water. David walked along a sidewalk that led away from South Kihei Road, beneath the fronds of tall coconut trees. On either side of the paved path, privacy walls blocked the view of hidden multi-million-dollar villas.

Several beachgoers were washing sand off their feet in the public showers supplied with recycled city water. Pools of sandy water spread across the sidewalk. On the right side of the showers, thirty feet up in the coconut trees, a man with a machete was cutting down coconuts. He had an area roped off below the trees where the coconuts were landing hard on the

227

sandy ground. *Thud. Thud.* Several tourists watched from
below. David remembered the time when a man had attempted
to steal a coconut from a cutter. A coconut had landed on his
arm and fractured it. He had to be taken to a local hospital.
David knew to be careful when they were cutting. At the base of
the trees, there were smooth metal bands to keep rats from
climbing the trees to eat the coconuts.

David walked farther down the sidewalk. The sidewalk
turned to sand and led between green leafy bushes. David could
hear the sound of a thundering wave. *Boom.* Then he heard the
sucking sound of the water drawing back into the sea. Then
another wave struck the shore. Through the narrow aisle
between the green bushes he saw the sky, the water with lines of
waves, and the yellow sand beach. This was Keawakapu.

He stepped out of the trail and onto the beach. Boogie
boarders bobbed up and down, waiting to catch perfect waves.
Because Maui's southwestern shore had so many miles and miles
of beaches, no one beach was too crowded. The beaches along
this stretch of Maui from Sugar Beach through Keawakapu and
on through Wailea were clean, and the water usually had only
small waves and no undertow.

David lay down on the beach and relaxed every muscle in
his body. He felt the hot sand roll under him. He looked out at
the small lava rock formation jutting out from the beach into the
waves. He remembered the time when a big storm had washed
away most of the sand from Keawakapu beach, transforming it
into a land of gnarly lava bedrock. It had surprised him how
thin the layer of sand was on this beach. There couldn't have
been more than ten feet of sand that had been washed away.
Lava lay underneath all of Maui, covered by less than a foot of
soil.

A pack of tourists strolled into his field of vision. Judging
from their swimsuit styles, they were international. What
language were they speaking? Was it French? All David could
understand were the occasional fits of laughter. A group of
friends having a good time.

David closed his eyes. *Heiau.* He could find it. Not right now. Later. It would come to him. If he just gave it some time, it would come to him.

Down the beach, someone was softly strumming a ukulele. It was gentle, like the sound of the palm fronds and the waves that were now becoming smaller and smaller as the breeze died down. The chords were bittersweet, entrancing. They evoked an image of the Hawaiian hula, slow, serene movements full of meaning. A story kept alive. Secrets. Treasure. The heiau.

David opened his eyes. The brightness burned in his eyes. He rolled on to his side and looked down the beach to the north. In the distance, the eight-story white Mana Kai loomed above the beach. Below the resort hotel, tourists walked out into the water. They were visiting the tide pools, an area where lava rock was submerged at high tide, and at low tide water was retained in the low pits in the rock, trapping sea creatures. Fish, eels, crabs and others often left their offspring here. Their young lived in a safe environment protected from the churning waves and potential predators, and when the time came, they could escape from the tide pools at high tide.

David hoped the tourists knew not to remove or touch any of the sea life, such as periwinkle shells, urchins, cowries, and sea cucumbers. He also hoped the visitors knew about the dangers of the tide pools. Cone shells could send stinging darts through the water. Wauna -- black, sharp poisonous sea urchins – could sting. Moray eels could bite. Corals could slice bare feet. The tide pools were such a beautiful ecosystem. He hoped all its visitors respected its inhabitants.

David still remembered the Kihei of twenty years ago, when he had just moved here. Makena and Wailea didn't even exist yet. Kihei had but a handful of hotels. The commercial district was made up of one store, Azeka's market. Kihei-Wailea used to be a desert, unlike the new green irrigated golf course and resort community that upscale Wailea had become. The beaches in Kihei had also changed. In the past, sea turtles had laid their nests of eggs on these beaches. David could remember seeing baby turtles the size of quarters crawling up through the sand and scurrying down the beach towards the brightness of the sea to disappear in the foam. Sea turtles still were thriving in the water around Maui; snorkelers found them all the time in the reefs. But where did they hide their eggs now? David hoped the turtles had moved to more remote beaches to give birth, beaches where the eggs could lay undisturbed in the sand until the turtles were ready to hatch.

The sun was setting. Time was slipping away. He didn't care. He had no particular plans for where he would go next. He was worn out from the day's journey.

David rolled over. He looked down the beach a couple hundred feet, where a green bushy embankment pressed toward the water and the beach narrowed and turned a corner.

David half-closed his eyes. He shouldn't fall asleep here. He should get up. No, it didn't really matter did it? He could take a short nap, couldn't he? It wouldn't hurt.

Squinting, David looked off into the distance. There was the end of this stretch of the beach. Some swimmers, standing up in the water. Behind them, in the distance a few miles south of here, stood a black hump of rock, a kind of pyramid, with the top chopped off. It was the cinder cone in Makena. Red Hill. Puu Olai. "Mound of pumice" in Hawaiian. A tiny volcano, a detached vent of Haleakala. A powerful upstart that spewed the inside of the earth out onto the surface, building Maui. A dome of rock... a dome of rock... stone... a massive stone feature, a cone...

David opened his eyes wider. He could see the two small humps in the top of the outline of the hill. The rock stuck out from the shore, jutting up out of the flat gray-blue sea.

Lono's treasure in the small shrine
Near the great shrine
Hear the echoes of our song
The echo, the echo, the echo...
The small shrine, the heiau.

The echo! The mound that adorned each of the heiaus Kai had described was a small stack of rocks that appeared to be a two-peaked pyramid or cone from the side, or a portrait of

Pueo, the owl, the guardian, the protector. Would the Makena cinder cone look like an owl from the top?

Near the great shrine David would find the heiau.

Puu Olai.

Could the cinder cone be the great shrine, the big heiau? Then all he'd have to do is find the small shrine, the little heiau, near it.

David got up. Next stop: Makena. He was near the end of the hunt.

Chapter 53
SNORKELING AT OLOWALU

Sue and Kai drove quickly down the hillside and turned south toward Kihei and Makena.

Kai thought about the photograph in his digital camera of the strange little line he had found in the rocks at the Lahaina heiau. Should he tell Sue? She seemed preoccupied. She had not bothered to look at the heiau. Perhaps it was a message from his ancestors meant for Kai only.

They neared the ocean. Sue pulled off the highway. The car bumped from the sudden stop. It was late in the day, but the water was unusually calm here. They were at a narrow beach lined with palm trees. Cars zoomed by behind them.

"I need to make some important phone calls," Sue said. "Why don't you go for a swim? This is Olowalu, a great snorkeling area, and I have my gear in the trunk. I think it will fit you."

Kai was surprised, but a swim sounded good. He had never used a snorkel mask, but Sue showed him how to place the goggles over his eyes and nose.

"If you need to clear the water out of your snorkel tube, breathe hard, like a whale spouting out of its blowhole, to push the water out so you can breathe again. Keep a little air in your lungs at all times in case you need to clear the tube," Sue explained.

"Will I see whales?" Kai asked.

"You might," Sue said. She glanced at her watch. "Okay, I'm going to be busy for a while. You have about an hour. Watch out for the coral. It's sharp. And don't touch the black wauna --- sea urchins. Look, but leave things alone."

Kai hesitated. Sue climbed back into the car.

"Hey, Kai," she called. "Don't worry about anything, okay?"

What was she talking about? He wasn't worried.

As soon as Kai was gone, Sue dialed David's number.

Kai left his shoes, shirt, and phone under a tree and walked across the short, rough beach. At each beach on Maui, he had noticed that the sand had its own color and texture. Here, the beach was gray and covered with bits of rock and coral.

He studied the water. There were two other snorkelers far up the beach. Otherwise, the shore was deserted.

What was going on with Sue? She was in such a hurry. Kai suspected that the phone calls had something to do with the heiau. She knew the final heiau would be in Makena. She didn't want him to listen to her calls. But why was she in such a rush? The heiau had sat there for at least two hundred years. What was the hurry now?

The ocean temperature was cool but pleasant. Sue seemed worried, and uptight. He was glad to leave her behind for a while. He let his body fall into a pattern of strong, steady strokes, propelling him farther and farther from shore. In the water, all was calm and comfortable. Sunlight made patterns of ripples on the underwater sand. With the mask on, he could see clearly. Underwater was a green, undulating world. He heard nothing but water and his own breathing through the tube. He was alone, a visitor in a strange world.

Yet he wasn't really alone. How good it was to have found written proof of his ancestors. The family tree was etched in his consciousness. He would never be alone again. Not only his living relatives --- he imagined Mom, relaxing after work with her shoes off, Grandma watering her plants, Poppy strumming his ukulele --- but also those who had died would accompany him now, giving him strength. He felt as if he had been claimed. He belonged. He was the end of a long chain. He felt a pang of guilt about Aunty H and Uncle Mano. Maybe time would heal what had gone wrong.

The sea floor was a three-dimensional maze of corals. Coral shaped like brains and cauliflowers and six-foot tall mushrooms sprouted from the sand. Some seemed to cling to rocks. Kai wound his way between coral antlers and coral leaves.

The mounds were pale white, greenish, reddish, and brown. A few were darker, dead.

Green algae covered some of the mounds like sea moss. Other growths looked like fungus. Shadowed cracks in the coral were places to hide. Pencil sea urchins were like thick-fingered flowers, bright orange. He was in a green tunnel, navigating narrow passageways of water between underwater canyons and ravines. He swerved to avoid sharp, black wauna, and held his body still, gliding without kicking, to pass above a coral shelf without scraping his bare legs against the prongs.

Fish appeared. A large, dark, teal and purple parrotfish nibbled near the bottom. Convict tangs, striped like jail suits, swam nearby. He chased a big unicornfish with a stub dangling out of its head. A triggerfish, the famous Humuhumunukunukuapua'a, darted beside him, its colors as distinctive and vibrant as the feathers of a wood duck. Kai swam farther and farther from shore. Black and yellow Moorish Idols hung in the current, their long dangling dorsal fins undulating like ribbons. He looked up at the surface and was shocked to find a thin fish as long as his forearm hovering horizontally in ripples by his face: a trumpetfish. Fish as tiny as his thumb colored purple and yellow slipped into invisible caves. Suddenly, Kai felt surrounded. This was their world, not his. The fish were flashes of darting vivid colors, a mosaic of suspicious strangers. Kai felt overwhelmed, immersed. He was a trespasser in a varied, complex, foreign universe.

Underwater, Kai heard a screeching noise in his ears. The screech fell in pitch. It cascaded down to a low moaning noise, and back up again into a high screech. The noise sounded like it was coming from close by. He tried to pinpoint the direction. It was impossible.

He looked around him. He was swimming about six feet above the platform of coral, and ten feet above the sand bottom that lay beneath the coral. There was a corridor of bare sand nearby. It appeared to be moving. There was a school of blue-gray fish swimming right above the sand. The fish had yellow tails and stringy forks underneath their mouths that looked like beards. The whole group of hundreds of fish was synchronized, darting around underwater together. What had made the noise?

Kai popped his head up out of the water and treaded for a few seconds. He looked back into shore. How far away was the beach? A hundred yards? He wasn't afraid. He could float if he got tired, and he wasn't yet tired. But he felt disconnected from shore.

There was a giant snorting noise behind him. He looked out to sea. Drops of spray hung in the air, not more than two hundred feet away.

A huge black flipper came out of the water and waved. It was a humpback whale. The whale rolled over and slinked underwater. Kai stared in awe. A few seconds later, another whale slumped above the water and rolled back under.

Kai put his snorkel back into his mouth and stuck his head back underwater. He could hear them again. The whales were singing. They were howling like dogs, whining, groaning.

He swam towards the whales. He felt drawn to them. He held his breath and swam down a few feet into the water. He swam hard and fast.

The ocean bottom dropped off down to about thirty feet of depth. The floor became a desert of rippled sand. He could see them. There were eight whales, suspended in the water less than forty yards away. They were gigantic. He was so close that he felt like he could almost reach out and touch their smooth backs.

Pink clouds of blood hung in the water, obscuring his view. Was one of the whales bleeding?

Kai returned to the surface for a breath of air. He blew the water out of his snorkel. Two whales, no, three whales, had their noses poking out of the water. Two adults and one baby, a calf. Kai realized that the blood in the water was left over from the calf's birth. The adult whales were holding the newborn out of the water so it could take its first breaths.

He put his head back underwater. An invisible force was pulling him towards the pack of whales. The whales seemed so gentle, slow-moving, loving. He wanted to be part of their family. His whale family.

He lifted his head out of the water. Kai thought back to the internet research. He felt warm inside. The heiaus he had visited had been built by documented ancestors. He had been on the right track the whole time. And he knew where to go next. His family had originally lived in Makena. The heiau must be there. His quest was coming to a close. Kai wished he could talk to his ancestors, thank them for helping him on his journey.

Suddenly, he saw a dark shadow on the ocean bottom. The shadow was moving towards him. It was his dream, the dream he had on the airplane!

Fins. He spun around in a circle. They surrounded him. Short, triangular, pointed gray fins, about twenty of them, a circle of fins shrinking towards him.

Not really...Sharks? !!!!

Kai looked back at the shore. He was half a mile away. Too far to scream for help. Those on shore might hear him but they would never be able to help. He was alone.

He dipped his head below the surface. Pudgy snout, eyes on the sides, white belly, gray back. Ten feet long. Tiger sharks!

Slowly! Sharks attack if you move fast.

Blood. It must have been the blood. Sharks smell blood. Don't swim in blood. He was too easy to catch. Too soft. Slow. They were coming closer.

Kick the snout. But twenty sharks coming in from all directions? They were ten feet away on all sides, coming.

The sharks halted, an arm's distance away. Kai was paralyzed. The underwater world was eerily silent. Twenty pairs of eyes, staring into his eyes. Teeth.

There was no way out. If he moved, the sharks might decide to attack him. He must remain motionless. Maybe they would leave him and go for the whale calf.

One shark began to move again. The leader? It swam towards him, its tail flicking right and left like a snake charmer. Kai stiffened. The shark's snout was two feet from his head. Kai began to swim frantically away. He struggled through the water, churning, making bubbles.

He looked behind him. Another shark, two feet away. A ring of death. No escape!

Suddenly, a strange calmness flowed through his body. His whole body went limp.

Was he about to die?

The shark closed in. Kai stared. Grim expression. Mouth closed. The shark was a foot away. Its eye studied him. Kai jerked backwards. It turned and swam under him. Kai froze.

Hadn't his ancestors believed sharks were deceased family members?

I am one of your own! Kai thought.

He closed his eyes.

When he opened them, the sharks were gone! They were swimming off into the distance, a cluster of fins. Kai didn't wait. He dived into a mad crawl stroke, frothing up the water. He knew the way to shore. He didn't look to see where he was going. He swam. He looked behind him. No sharks. A dark shape passed beneath him under the water. A black diamond, five feet across, with a long skewer-like tail: a stingray.

Kai almost laughed out loud. Wow. What luck.

The coral was close, five feet below him. The stingray was hovering above the coral, flapping and rippling its wings, gliding. It circled beneath him.

Kai knew that the stingray's barb contained dangerous venom. If it punctured his chest or his stomach, he could die.

Kai swam a breast stroke. He was careful not to kick his feet down into the water. The stingray was floating three feet underwater. Its beady eyes on the top of its body watched Kai swim away.

Coral rose up around him. He made his way through a forest of coral. He was tired now. He needed to keep going. Soon he would be safe. The shore came suddenly. Kai waded through the shallow water, stepping down on sand. There was not a single wave. This beach was surprisingly protected.

A group of sunbathers floated nearby on green plastic couches. They looked over towards him. A woman yelled at him. "Watch out! There's a cone shell over there!"

"There's a what?"

"Cone shell! It can sting you! Don't move! Watch where you're walking!"

Kai looked down through the water. He saw it. A few inches long, spiral shaped. White and brown spots. It looked so harmless.

Kai laughed. "Are you kidding me?"

"No! It can send out darts of poison through the water! Get away from it!"

Kai shuffled through the surf. When he was ten feet away, he shook his head. "Sharks! Don't swim out there."

The tourists yelled back at him. "Thanks!" It was a group of men and women, maybe in their late thirties. Kai could hear a man mumbling behind his back. "I bet he's pulling our leg because he saw the shark signs along the beach."

Shark signs?

Kai stumbled out of the water. He did a flop, face-first, into the sand.

After a few minutes, he looked up. Sue was nowhere in sight. He looked for the car. It was gone. He stood dripping. Where had she gone? He looked around for a note. Nothing. She had left him here with nothing but his wet swimsuit and a snorkel mask! He had Phil's necklace. Where was his backpack? He'd left it in Sue's car! Kai felt sick. She'd driven away with Dad's ashes.

He found his shoes, shirt, and his phone. At least he had his phone. No new messages from Sue, just from Aunty H. He felt a pang of remorse. His anger over their controlling advice had fully cooled, and he regretted what had happened. He wished he could do last night over again.

Sue didn't answer her phone. He texted.

Kai waited. After ten minutes that felt like an hour, he stood and stretched. Had there been some emergency? But she hadn't even left him a text.

He would have to call David for a ride. It would be a favor. But Kai had no one else.

A very young boy ran up to Kai out of the scrubby forest along the road. He was brown and totally naked. In his hand he held an elaborate wooden fishing spear.

"I have a message for you," he said.

"What?" Kai asked. Had Sue left a message for him with someone on the beach? Was she okay?

"Be careful which haole you trust," said the boy, looking him in the eye. Then he turned and ran back down the beach. *Did some local family see me get left here by a haole?* Kai watched the little boy run away and disappear into the bushy trees like a ghost.

Chapter 54
THE CINDER CONE BY MAKENA

D avid opened the door of his car. He changed out of his sandals and put on socks and hiking boots. He was at the foot of the hill. It rose up 360 feet into the sky. The sides were steep. There was only one way to see if the cone looked like Kai's heiaus from above: he needed to get to the top. It would be a quick, tough scramble.

David stepped out of his car and into the Makena State Park Big Beach parking lot. He walked across the parking lot, past dusty cars. Tourists were walking back from the Big Beach, a white strip of sand a hundred feet away down a sandy trail. David came to the far end of the pavement. Then he whacked straight into the brush of Kiawe trees, bushes and shrubs.

The climb was strenuous. He took a shortcut, not a path. David pushed his way through the pili pili grass and short scrubby shrubs. Soon he was scrambling up a steep slope of red volcanic rock.

In about ten minutes, he had reached the top of the cinder cone.

David was standing at the rim of the crater, a bowl four hundred feet across. Below him, he could see tiny people swarming along Big Beach, watching the sunset. On the near end of the beach was a rock barrier with a trail running over the top. On the other side was Little Beach, Maui's nude beach. To the north, David could see the entire sprawl of Makena, Wailea and Kihei, a strip of city along the beach. Inland was the desert of cactus and Kiawe. The desert led up the slopes of Haleakala to the road he had just taken to Kaupo.

Lono's treasure in the small shrine
Near the great shrine
Hear the echoes of our song

If this cone was the great shrine, then he needed to find a shrine, a heiau, near where he was standing right now.

Could it be in the crater of the cinder cone? David looked down into the dip. There was nothing but bushes.

David walked along a trail that led around the rim of the cinder cone. As he walked, David glanced back and forth, looking down the slopes of the hill, and then back into the crater. There were no heiaus here.

The small shrine... near the great shrine. Did that mean the heiau was on top of Puu Olai? On its side? In the general vicinity? Somewhere in Makena?

He looked back down the Haleakala side of the cinder cone. He saw the parking lot far below him, his car parked off to one side. Most of the cars had left by now. There wasn't much light left in the day. He should be going back to his villa soon.

David looked beyond the parking lot. Down Makena Road, over Makena Golf Course...

Many heiaus now lay buried beneath the grass turfs of the golf courses and resorts. A few stood like little islands in the midst of the development. Had the heiau he was seeking already been disassembled, bulldozed or covered before it could be documented and protected? Did the heiau still exist?

Past the end of Big Beach, there was an immense lava field. La Perouse. La Perouse Bay was around the corner, past the end of the beach. In between the lava field and Makena Golf Course, along Makena Road, he saw the gravel pull-off, the familiar parked cars, the site... How close was he to the site for which he'd been hired to do the archeological survey? It couldn't be more than a few miles.

The hardest thing to find is the one sitting right before your eyes.

Could the heiau be in that direction? Could it be near the site where he was doing the archeological survey for the gargantuan new luxury resort --- including the undocumented work tonight? His thoughts drifted to his project in the area. The extra work after dark would virtually guarantee that the permit process would be quick and smooth...there would be no extra time-consuming excavations and expensive protective procedures. It was no secret that zoning regulations were about to change. If that happened before David got things in order, the resort might no longer be allowed on that site.

He had, of course, already done a thorough survey of the resort site to identify anything of real historical value and also anything that might slow down the permit. He'd found a heiau, as he often did. In the past, people would have simply recycled the stones. They would have taken the heiau apart in daylight, and dispersed it. Heiau rocks had become church walls, and property markers. Now, of course, everything was so much more complicated.

But what if the heiau on the resort site was important? What if it was Kai's heiau? David brushed off the thought.

The whole island is covered with heiaus, and I'm searching for only one.

David suddenly felt surrounded by heiaus. There were so many in this southern tip of the island. The artifact was probably near. But where was the small shrine? Where should he look next?

His cell phone rang from inside his pocket. It was Kai.

*   *   *

As Sue drove through Kihei, her phone vibrated.

"Hey Sue," said a high-pitched woman's voice. "How's everything going?"

"Hey, boss. Everything is excellent. Coming together. Tonight, actually."

"Nice. Call me if you need anything."

"Thanks. Look, I'm driving right now. I'll call you in the morning, though. Everything will be finished by then, hopefully."

Chapter 55
BETRAYED

K ai immediately knew it was David's car. Its shiny black
paint reflected the yellow sun that was sinking in the sky.
"Thanks, David!" Kai said with enthusiasm. Exhausted,
he entered the air-conditioned vehicle, hoping that David didn't
mind his salty shorts on the leather seats. *David must be rich*, he
thought.

"No problem," said David. "Go for a swim?"

"I saw sharks."

"Olowalu means 'place of the shark,'" said David. "A
woman was killed here, oh, about ten years ago. And there were
several other attacks. But it's a great place to snorkel."

So why had Sue encouraged him to swim at the place of
the sharks?

"I'm sorry about Sue. I didn't think she'd leave you,"
said David, "but I guess she saw her opportunity and took it."

What? Why had Sue left him? She had sent him on a
swim with the sharks…Why had she wanted to go on alone,
without Kai? Why was she in such a hurry? Had she really
ditched him?

Kai thought of Sue picking him up last night and
bringing him to her apartment. He thought of sitting beside her
by the boulder at the North Shore, and of the frenzied
excitement of their discussion of history in Lahaina. No, it was
impossible that she would have deliberately left him to get the
artifact on her own. Wasn't it? But then where was she? Why
hadn't she texted or called?

It didn't make any sense. She had helped him so much.
She had forgiven him for losing her bike. She had helped him
ceaselessly. Yet she had driven off. Had he been wrong about
her this whole time? Had she deliberately planned to leave him,

without caring how he'd feel? Now that she had enough information, she didn't need him anymore...She wanted to get there first on her own. Was David right? Or was he just jumping to conclusions?

She had been his helper and constant companion for so many hours. How could she just drive off, after all they had done together? They were friends. At least, he had felt they were friends until now. Kai felt a cold emptiness spread inside his chest.

Forget Sue! I need to think about the heiau.

David drove as quickly as possible on the curving road near the ocean. A short tunnel blocked Kai's view of the ocean for a moment. To his left, a tall net blocked the fall of rocks down a steep cliff. To his right, the sun was sinking before his eyes. Soon, it would be dark.

All the strengths that Kai admired about Sue would be problems now if she was working against him. She was determined. She was a fast driver. She might be at the heiau already.

"I should never have had her work with you," David went on. "I told her to stick with you no matter what. She obviously didn't listen to me."

"You think she's going to the heiau?" Kai said, fearing he already knew the answer.

"I'm afraid she's close. We can stop her though. We'll have to get to the artifact first," said David.

"Doesn't she work for you though? Can't you just call her up and tell her to wait?" Kai suggested.

David sighed. "That's what I thought, too. I guess not. Looks like she's out for herself." He pressed on the gas a little harder, now driving dangerously close to the car in front.

Sue must have realized that she had a chance to get rich, Kai thought. Maybe she needed money, or was more interested in money than he had realized. "David, we've got to stop her," he said. "We have to make sure she doesn't dig up the heiau."

"You're right, we're going to get there first. Now tell me...what did you find at the heiau in Lahaina? You said you think you know where the heiau is?"

Kai explained about how Sue was headed for Makena. Then he described the design on top of the Lahaina heiau. "I don't know what it means, though. Maybe you can help me with that."

"Is there that owl shape on top of it?"

"Yes. Just like all the others."

"Is there another small figure on top?"

"Yes, there is. How'd you guess?"

David paused a moment and shook his head, perhaps trying to figure out how to explain something. "That owl shape, I figured out what it means. It's a miniature replica of the cinder cone down by Makena."

Kai unfolded a modern map and studied it. If Makena's cinder cone was the great shrine...He thought of the photo on his phone. The shoreline looked very much like the line of rocks...Of course!

The cone shape on top of the heiaus represented the Makena cinder cone. The small white rock, with the little conical bump on it --- it must be the small shrine that might contain the artifact! The pattern in the rocks was a map leading from the cinder cone to the heiau. "The line of rock leading to the white rock ---it's the coastline down by Makena. The white rock, it's the location of the heiau."

David smiled. "Kai, did Sue see this?"

"I didn't show her," said Kai.

"Good. As long as we get down there quickly, we'll have the upper hand. Keep the map out. I want to look carefully at your photo when I'm not driving. I might know the place," he said. "I know that part of the island well."

They entered Kihei and stopped at a traffic light on Pi'ilani Highway. "Is it undeveloped? I don't know the area south of Makena," Kai said.

"South of Makena isn't developed yet, but it will be soon," said David.

"So development is gradually spreading south? It says on the map here the area our heiau is in is north of La Perouse Bay. It looks like there's nothing there."

"There's not much down there. Actually, back in 1950, hardly any of the land from Kihei south was developed --- Kihei was tiny, and there was no Wailea. Makena was very, very small...Maui hasn't always been such a busy tourist destination. Before World War II, it was agricultural. After the War, Maui actually lost a good chunk of its population as they left to find jobs other than agriculture."

"So then the island started promoting tourism?" Kai asked.

"Yes. Ever since then, new developments have gradually been spreading south. First Kihei, then Wailea, then Makena. Now south of Makena. The population of the Kihei region was less than two thousand in 1970. Now it's almost thirty thousand. I've seen all that happen. Huge change. Too bad I didn't invest even more heavily in south shore land back when it was cheap. Even in 1985, you could still find beach front lots on the best beaches for $400,000 or so. Now those are all worth multi-millions."

"So are we going to find the heiau under a resort, or on undeveloped land?"

"Undeveloped land, is my guess. When we get a little closer I need to take a closer look at your photo to be sure. There's a lava field south of Makena from Haleakala's most recent eruption. Scientists used to always date the flow to 1790, but now there's a lot of debate. The precise year is based on stories from the great-great-grandparents of locals about when their families lived on the site before the flow. Also on maps made by explorers just after Cook. La Perouse came in 1786, and Vancouver in 1793. Their two maps of the coastline are different, maybe because the eruption happened between the two voyages.

"But geologists recently have thought the flow is much older," he went on. "There are minerals in lava that align to the magnetic pole when it forms. I guess the pole is always shifting, so lava that's older is aligned differently…Anyway, they studied it, and now people are thinking the lava is about 400 years old instead of 200.

"The heiau we'll find in the area you're describing might have been built on top of fresh flow," David went on. "The lava field is huge, though. We'll need to pin it down…maybe your family built the heiau right on top of where the family farm used to be. Or, if the magnetic pole theory is right, and the lava is older, maybe your family had a farm near the edge of the older lava, and built the heiau on top of it. They might have been living in the area forever, and have had a farm that was buried in lava in about the year 1600, and built an original heiau on the lava to mark the old farmstead way back then. I'm betting that the heiau is on lava."

He paused to think.

"This area of the south shore is full of archeological ruins," David said. "At least thirty four on record. Ancient burial grounds, maybe a thousand years old. And foundations from houses. The early explorers described some little villages down by the shore. There are also more than a hundred adze sharpening pits in the bedrock. Probably the biggest sharpening area on all the islands. So it's an old area, used by Hawaiians for a long, long time, and pretty well documented. But the lava fields are so big, and so difficult to explore, and the heiaus are made of the same lava rock as the fields. The lava looks like chunks of black dirt. Then you get close to it, it's sharp pieces. What I'm saying is, a heiau is hard to spot in all that lava. Harder than out of the lava field. So I'm guessing --- since I've never heard of a heiau the shape of yours, with that weird cone on top --- that your heiau isn't yet documented. It's one of the undiscovered ones. And it's more likely to be hidden in the lava field than in the remote ranchland above it…It's really not an area that gets as much use as most of Maui, which is good for us. It's probably undisturbed."

"So the big lava field runs all the way down to the shore," Kai asked, "and you think the heiau is on the mauka edge of the field?"

"I'm just guessing until I study your photo, but I'll bet it's somewhere up there on the hillside at the upper edge of the lava flow. I hope we can locate it quickly."

"You think someone's going to build a hotel near there soon?"

"Very soon," David said. "The largest, most extravagant high-end resort in the islands."

They traveled in silence once again. David seemed different than when they had first met. Previously, he had been relaxed, and excited. He was still excited, but in a different way now. He seemed a bit anxious, as if something had just occurred to him. He looked nervous as he furrowed his brows while passing cars on the highway. "We're almost there," said David. "I can't wait to get my hands on the artifact. All this supposition...Soon we'll know if we guessed right, and if this whole search was worthwhile. It's always like that for me when I ---" David hesitated, searching for words. "When something really special from the past like this comes my way," he finished.

Something about David's voice was unsettling to Kai. David sounded almost loving when he said "really special." He sounded...hungry. He was ravenous with anticipation. Why was he so excited? Wasn't this whole search for Kai? Why was David taking such a personal interest?

"David," Kai said. "I've realized something important. I don't want to dig up the heiau."

David raised his eyebrows but said nothing.

"I don't want anyone to even touch it. Do you understand? This heiau was built by my family. It's sacred. It would be totally wrong to receive the chant like I did and get help from my family and then find the ancestral site and wreck it."

David stared at him in silence.

"I'm sorry I didn't tell you this earlier. I know I've probably wasted your time, since you're so interested in finding an artifact. But I didn't know I'd feel this way when I started. It just kind of grew in me. I'm totally sure, though. Once we find the heiau, the right thing to do is say a prayer, and then do everything we can to protect the site from development forever. That's what my ancestors would have wanted. My dad would have wanted that, too. It's what I want. I'll do everything I can to protect it."

"What about Sue?" David said.

"I'll stop Sue!" Kai said with conviction. *It's my destiny as the seeker also to protect.*

David was speechless.

Now everything darkened as the sun sank behind the horizon. They turned down toward the luxurious upscale mall, The Shops at Wailea, turning left toward the south near a Tiffany's jewelers and an Armani store. They passed the Grand Wailea, and the Four Seasons. Soon, the road became a dark snake winding along shadowed golf courses. David sped down the dark lonely road to Makena. After a bend in the road, lights from cars and flashlights interrupted the darkness. All the traffic was heading the opposite way, back toward town. Only David and Kai drove toward deeper darkness.

Suddenly, David slowed the car. He pulled off to the side.

"Give me your phone," he said. David sounded serious.

Kai handed him the phone. David stared at it, looking closely. The car idled.

David swore under his breath. He seemed to be bursting with excitement.

Does he know where it is? Kai wondered.

"Unbelievable!" David breathed. "Absolutely incredible! What are the chances? The same site?" He seemed to have forgotten Kai. He was lost in amazement over the photo of the Lahaina heiau's stone map. Could it be possible?

"What?" Kai asked.

David didn't answer.

"David?" Kai said.

David would need to act fast. The machinery was scheduled to work on the site tonight! It had seemed like a good thing to have the developer taking care of that end…it was hard to find people who were willing to work at night, who weren't superstitious --- especially about this part of the island. But now it looked like he was going to have to stop the work, or get there before the dozer.

"Get out!" David said.

Kai looked around. Outside the car, the headlights revealed a forest of twelve-foot-tall cactus plants beyond the dirt pull-off. David still had his phone. Why were they getting out? Was this the heiau site? But they weren't quite to the cinder cone. Kai could see the cinder cone down the road on the left.

In one swift motion, David reached across Kai, opened the door, and with surprising sudden strength, shoved Kai out onto the dirt.

Kai landed with a painful crash. He'd been totally taken by surprise. He struggled out of the path of the car. David! His eyes filled with hot tears of pain, shock, and betrayal.

The car sped away. Kai brushed the dirt of his legs. His arm was scraped, but not badly.

Anger flared inside him like a rush of adrenaline. He started to run after the car. He needed to get to the heiau first! He had led Sue and David to it. It was his fault! He couldn't let himself be too late!

He slowed to a walk as frustration and the darkness surrounded him. What should he do next? He reached in his pocket for his phone. It wasn't there. David had taken it! But it had the map. Without his phone, how would he find the heiau?

A car pulled up alongside him. A tan teenage girl wearing a string bikini unrolled her window.

"You want a ride? Looks like you're in a hurry. We can give you a lift."

Kai was breathing hard. He nodded his thanks and hopped in the crowded car. The three girls in the backseat scooted together and then one sat on the lap of another to make room for him.

"How'd you hear about the party at Little Beach tonight?" a girl asked. "We're trying to keep it low profile, you know? The cops will come if we make it too big. Like, no one's supposed to be here after dark, you know? We're going to have to hide the car someplace and hike in with the beer. We were thinking we'd like, unload, and then find a place for the car..."

Kai studied the road. Ahead was the turn-off for Big Beach Parking. The silhouette of the cinder cone rose against the sky like a solid, unshakeable guardian.

"I'm meeting someone here," he said. "Can I get out?"

Alone on the dark street, he tried to remember the photo on his phone. He could picture it. Which way to the heiau? He oriented himself. Sea, Makai. Cinder cone. Ocean shoreline. Heiau should be...up there. How far? There was no sign of David's car or Sue's.

A police car with two officers pulled into the parking lot of Big Beach behind him.

Kai jogged quickly down the road. He wanted to sprint but he needed to pace himself. His eyes had adjusted to the dark. The road was paved. He let his body fall into a rhythm. He might have a long way to go and there was no time to waste.

Chapter 56
MAKENA HEIAU

After a few turns, the road became straight. Now there was no light but the moon and the stars. How long had he been going? Forty minutes? An hour? There was nothing but darkness ahead.

Kai was in the lava fields. Lighted by moonlight, the lava looked eerily like the shadowed surface of Mars. As far as he could see toward the sea, there was no vegetation. The road had turned to rough gravel and brought him inland. He studied the field where it receded into the distance up the foot of Haleakala.

He made out two cars parked along the side of the road now. Was David parked here?

As he drew nearer, he realized he did not recognize either car. Suddenly, a beam of light. A flashlight came from down the road. Instinctively, Kai moved into the shadows on the side of the road. His feet crunched over pumice as he ducked down and tried to stifle his breathing.

He heard a man speaking. He sounded local.

"Okay, boss. Won't take long with the bulldozer. Good thing you came. Never would've found it."

A sliver of moon came from behind a cloud. Now Kai could see the two men. The boss was a giant. He said something Kai didn't catch.

"I got it," said the bulldozer guy. "No daylight work. Nothing left behind."

The giant's voice rose. He had an unusually deep voice. "Everything gone by morning! You understand? Everything! Not a rock pile, not an adze pit, just a level field. I can't afford a delay."

The moon disappeared behind another cloud and the night seemed darker than ever. Keys jingled as the deep-voiced man opened his car door. Two pairs of headlights lit up the

252

night. For a moment, Kai was scared that they would turn towards him, but instead they turned in the other direction, away from Makena beach, into the empty, undeveloped lava fields. *What were they doing here?*

Kai broke into a run down the road again. The red lights of the cars far ahead shrunk smaller and smaller. Who were those men?

Then he lost sight of the lights. The cars must have parked up ahead. He pushed forward with renewed effort. He ran until he thought he'd reach the cars but he did not see them. He ran farther. Dizzy and gasping for breath, he finally slowed to a walk.

He stopped. Ahead, there was a large shape beside the road. Was it a rock? It was lighter in color than the lava rock…

It was a giant vehicle. The monster towered over him, a strange dormant beast of the night. A metal blade like a wall on the front: the bulldozer. Was the guy inside? Kai gave the dozer a wide berth. Other than the two cars, it was the first sign of humans he had seen in this landscape. The darkness and the bizarre landscape concealed it, welcomed it.

He backed cautiously away from the vehicle. As he did so, something shimmered in the distance. The moon had appeared again, and moonlight caught a shiny surface for an instant. He walked closer and strained to see in the darkness. Beyond the bulldozer, up the road and mostly hidden behind a rock outcropping, was another vehicle, a vehicle that barely protruded from its hiding place like a black beetle. Shiny black paint against black lava. Black metal in black night: David's car.

Kai stood near the car for a while, searching the horizons for any sign. Was anyone there? Sue? David? The bulldozer guy or his boss?

Finally, he saw it. A quick spark at first, up in the lava fields across the road, away from the ocean. Then it shone brighter, a lasting light, bobbing up and down, meandering around. A flashlight! Someone was searching for the heiau!

Kai didn't hesitate. He moved towards the light.

A rough road led through the lava. Kai followed it. It led generally toward the light. He didn't want to start out over the lava field: what looked like piles of plowed dirt in the dark were sharp and hard. He hurried silently up the road. His view of the light came and went. The lava seemed like a flat, even surface from a distance, but up close, it was full of small pits, canyons, and pinnacles.

Aunty H had said this place --- this exact place --- was the territory of the Night Wanderers, the restless spirits who roamed and caused trouble. Dark little clouds by day that swirled black and low. Omens. Bad luck.

The light flashed again, and then disappeared. The light must have moved around behind a rock. Was someone already at the heiau?

The light stopped moving. He could see across the lava field. Kai pretended it was a star guiding him in the right direction. He was tired, but he was excited. He was close to the end. He had more energy than he ever had before. He moved as quickly as he could over the rough road.

Now he squatted behind a small hillock of lava. The light was behind it, spreading light over the desolate landscape. Kai crept out from his hiding spot, inching closer. A heiau!

No one else was there. A platform was in front of him, and a flashlight rested near it, spreading beams of light on the scene. Lava rocks lay strewn randomly beside the platform. Kai walked closer, fascinated. He peered at the rock shape. Was this the right heiau? It had a rectangular base....an owl cone shape on top. Kai smiled. It was just like every other heiau he had found. It was so mysterious, half-illuminated by the flashlight. Yet it was so much the same...But one end was crumbled and irregular. Someone had started taking it apart!

Without thinking, blinded by anger, Kai roared with rage.

Suddenly a strong force hit him from behind. Kai fell. Strong hands clamped onto his neck. "You're not getting in my way!" David said. David was middle-aged and skinny, but he fought like one possessed. He flipped Kai and tried to pin him to the ground.

I can take this guy! Kai thought. *I will not let you do this!* They landed on the flashlight and it went out.

"You think you're going to stop me?" David yelled. "You stupid little ---! You never would have even found this without my help!" With one big hand, he tightly gripped Kai's neck. The noose tightened. He raised his other fist and tried to punch Kai. Kai twisted away and punched back. He jabbed David's groin with his knee. But David continued to fight.

"This is my site, my artifact!" David yelled. "For my private collection! I've worked for years!" He hit Kai again, hard. Hot blood spurted from Kai's nose. "You think a punk like you is going to stop me?" He punched Kai's right eye, and dug his knee into Kai's stomach. "Think again, punk!"

Kai fought back. He hadn't ever been in a real fight before, but now a strange energy rose inside of him, showing him what to do. He was mad. He aimed a fist at David's face, slowing David.

Then a light turned on behind them. A woman's voice. "This is FBI Agent Sue Olafson. Put your hands up!" David stopped hitting him. "Now get off him!" Sue yelled. "Move away!"

Chapter 57
SUE

Kai stared through a haze of darkness, blood, and swollen pain. Sue had a gun, and she was pointing it at David. "Get your hands up, I said!" she yelled. David raised his hands.

"Sue?" David said. "You're not going to shoot me, are you, honey?"

A bullet whizzed by, narrowly missing David and the heiau.

Kai winced.

"You have the right to remain silent. Anything you say can and will be used against you in a court of law..." Sue said. She approached cautiously, gun steady in front of her. She moved swiftly, handcuffing David. She kept the gun on his back. "Kai, get to the road."

A sudden noise startled them. It was some kind of big vehicle. The bulldozer! Loud, crunching over the lava. Driving this way. Suddenly, it appeared around a distant hill of rock.

"What?" Sue said.

"The developers," David muttered. He laughed. "Cleaning up. Before the inspection tomorrow." He sounded strangely giddy, as if he didn't care what he said.

Suddenly Kai understood: David's firm had recommended they remove the heiau to prevent delays. Wouldn't that be illegal? But wait, Sue was FBI...Kai felt blood rush in his swollen face as he stood.

Sue pushed David ahead of her. They began walking toward the road and the bulldozer.

The driver of the bulldozer stopped a distance away and stared at them across a sea of lava. For a moment, he idled, staring, trying to make sense of what they were.

He thinks we're Night Marchers, Kai thought.

The driver turned off the bulldozer and stepped out, staring.

Kai heard David tear himself out of Sue's grip in the dark.

There was a crunching sound on the lava behind them. Kai whirled around.

"This is the police," an officer yelled, stepping out from behind some rocks. "Stay where you are!"

Chapter 58
EXPLANATIONS

The rest of the night was a confusing flurry.

A policeman took David away.

"We need to ask you some questions," said an officer. Suddenly Kai was surrounded by questions. Questions about David. Questions about the bulldozer. Kai explained everything that had happened since he had arrived on the lava field. He explained how Sue and David had helped him find his ancestral heiau, and how Kai had tried to stop David from destroying the heiau. He talked about how David had hoped to take an artifact from the heiau.

Then Sue talked with the officers. Kai waited along the main road. As his adrenaline wore off, he sat against a rock near the road and closed his eyes. He had nowhere to go, and no way to get there. He was exhausted. Sue had protected him and the heiau. Yet she had never told him she was FBI. Who was she, really?

After a while, Sue pulled up in her station wagon.

"Hop in," Sue said.

"Thanks for helping me out with David. I didn't know you were FBI," said Kai.

"Yes, of course. I couldn't tell you. I'll try to explain on the way. Let's go home and get some sleep. Do you want me to drive you somewhere? Your aunt's and uncle's? Or you can come to my place?"

"Sure, thanks." Sleep sounded good. He had some things *he* needed to explain to his aunt and uncle, soon. But he would need to get some rest first.

Sue drove them away from the lava field. It was the middle of the night. Sue explained that in the next day or two she would book an inter-island flight and return to her apartment on Oahu.

258

"Could you bring me back here before your flight?" Kai asked.

"You're not still hoping to find treasure, I hope," said Sue. "You know, for a while I wasn't sure if we'd find anything. Yesterday, at the Lahaina heiau, I started to realize we probably wouldn't...But I needed to witness David's attempted robbery. David dug the heiau up pretty good, and there's no artifact."

Kai looked down. "Explain it to me."

"Look, I had to encourage David to believe there would be a treasure because I needed to catch him in the act of attempted theft of a valuable artifact," Sue said. "As a government inspector, I had a specific task. Usually, I work at the Bishop Museum. Renaissance art is my specialty. I had to read up a bit before taking this case. Although I'm of Swedish descent and I attended the University of Stockholm for a year, I'm not really Swedish."

Kai waited. *Who are you?* He still couldn't believe she was FBI. Had she carried a gun the whole time?

"It was my cover...I figured that David would never suspect me of working for the FBI if I was foreign."

"And you like it, your job?" he asked.

"Oh, yes. It's great. When the FBI first contacted me for special assignments on the mainland, I just worked for them as an art expert, but I wasn't yet an agent. I would identify stolen art through a national computer database, and sometimes examine pieces in person for authenticity. After a while, I decided to become an agent so I could work out in the field, out of the office, in the action. I took the job with David on Maui about four months ago in order to watch him. Since then, I've been waiting. When you came along with your chant, I knew I had what I needed."

"So people were trying to catch David for a long time?" Kai asked. He was trying to make sense of it all.

"The case against David has been brewing for a while. A lot of people suspected him, but no one had any proof. Now that we can search his place, I believe we'll find quite a few artifacts, maybe stashed somewhere safe in David's home or office. All of them will be illegally acquired. I'll bet David's entire stolen collection will be worth well over ten million dollars. The collection will end up in museums, where everyone can enjoy it and learn about Hawaii's past. I'm hoping if undocumented items and stolen items are found, the second violation combined with his defacing the heiau will lead to a fine of $100,000 plus 5 years imprisonment. If he's got anything stolen worth more than $5,000 and more than 100 years old, it's a federal crime. Between the Archeological Resources Protection Act of 1979 and the Native American Graves Protection and Repatriation Act of 1990, he won't get off easy. Plus, David's archeological inspection firm will go out of business. There will be no more opportunities for him to steal artifacts.

"Local art dealers tipped us off first...They contacted a government watchdog agency to report that David had been secretly collecting artifacts that didn't belong to him. David made a few mistakes. A couple of years ago, he asked a well-known art dealer to appraise a pre-contact war stick that the dealer recognized as having belonged to a well-known local family that had lived on a site David's firm inspected for development. The stick was worth maybe $80,000. Many of the artifacts are valuable...there just aren't that many in circulation. The dealer asked David how he got the stick, and David didn't have a credible answer. The family reported to the police, but of course they couldn't do anything. Then there were some archeological sites he worked on where artifacts were categorized and then later the reports were changed. The artifacts were reported lost or missing by David's firm. But even though people suspected David, there was no proof, and his company pretty much has a corner on the archeological inspection market on Maui. Every piece of land that's going to have any sort of construction has to hire him. He had plenty of opportunities."

She sighed. "I guess that explains what I was doing, and David's crimes. But it doesn't really explain why I let you think you'd find a treasure...I had to encourage you to keep searching, because you would help lead David to where I needed him."

Kai just looked at her. He was still trying to make sense of who she was.

"I had my doubts if we would find anything after all…At the beginning, when he asked me to help you, I could tell David was very interested in your heiau. He didn't need much encouragement. He was already hooked. He was so anxious to find a valuable artifact that he could hardly see straight. In my capacity as FBI agent, I helped you find the heiau so we could share the site location with David. But I had to time it correctly so I could be there at the moment he found the heiau. Once I realized that he knew where it was, I had to hurry to get to Makena and hide my car so I could watch him until he found the heiau. I knew he might be dangerous. That's why I left you at Olowalu.

"Kai, I imagine this must be confusing…You didn't find anything, but at least you learned about your family from this whole thing. I think it's amazing that your family kept the chant all those years, but I'm not surprised there's no treasure. I mean, what family would set it up so that someone would have to wreck a heiau? It goes against everything Hawaiian. It goes against all the religious beliefs. The only reason David didn't see that basic flaw in the treasure theory was that he was so greedy he blinded himself. I guess I blinded myself, too, a little. Sometimes I believed in a treasure, too, because I needed one…I needed to witness David stealing something valuable. And you, you probably blinded yourself because you wanted an inheritance. But we were all deceiving ourselves. You understand you're not going to find anything at the heiau, don't you?" Sue said.

"I'm not going back to look for treasure," Kai said. "I'm going back to repair the heiau and say a prayer."

"I hope you're not disappointed," Sue said. "You did your own part to help."

"I'm not disappointed," Kai said. *You are amazing!*

By the faint light of the dashboard, Kai met her eyes.

"Kai, I was always honest about liking you. I'm glad the job threw us together. You really do remind me of my little brother!"

Kai waited.

"If you're ever in Oahu, visit me," Sue said.

Kai smiled. "I will," he said.

Chapter 59
THE INTERVIEW

Too early the next morning, a car pulled up at Sue's. Hurriedly, they answered the door.

"Hey, I'm Ronald Wayne from The Maui News," said a man with thick hair and glasses. "Could I get a quick interview?"

Kai turned to Sue, and she motioned that she wasn't in a hurry. "Okay."

Ronald followed them into the apartment.

"Kai Hokoana, correct?" he spoke rapidly. "I heard you were a hero last night. Do you mind if I write a short article about how you saved an ancient Hawaiian heiau?"

"A hero? Maybe you should talk to Sue. She saved what's left of the heiau, too." Kai said.

Sue smiled. "You were the one who fought David, Kai," she said.

"Tell me what you did to help protect the site," the reporter said. "We won't worry about the crime until I learn more about the charges. For now, we'll just put in a short piece to celebrate your heroism. Looks like you got a little banged-up."

As he answered questions, Kai remembered first arriving on Maui. *So much had changed.*

"So you fought him in the dark," the reporter said, eyeing Kai's black eyes. "Good for you. Do you have one message for our readers?"

"Yes," said Kai. "I'm hoping that the heiau site becomes a park and that it's protected...I hope the rules protecting Hawaiian archeological sites are enforced. We have to protect our old places, our sacred things."

"And you're part-Hawaiian, right? This is your family heiau?" the reporter asked.

"I am Hawaiian," Kai said. "The place is sacred to me and my family."

The next morning, Sue gave Kai a ride from her place back to the lava fields. She had given him a pair of tough work gloves belonging to David's firm, a small shovel, and three bottles of water.

The lava stretched all the way to the ocean like a black, uneven field ready for planting. The sun cast yellow streams of light over the lava. Everything was gentler now. Some of the rock was a beautiful shade of red-brown. Bright green trees grew beyond the dark lava on the slopes of Haleakala.

Kai felt disoriented.

"That way," Sue unrolled her window and pointed. "See the road leading past that outcropping up there? The big one? That's where I hid. Good luck, Kai," she said. "I really respect what you did." He watched her turn around, and waved goodbye. He would visit her in Oahu, sometime soon.

Chapter 60
TREASURE

The field of lava stretched to the blue ocean. Black sandwiched between blue sky and blue sea. Heat waves rose off the rock. There were no plants. Now that he was out of the car, he could see clearly how barren this place was. It was inhospitable and boiling hot, without life. A few cars drove slowly down the rough road, but the tourists inside didn't stop to hike.

He picked his way over the rocks. This was Pele's territory, Pele the volcano goddess. Pele, the goddess of lightning, fire, dance, volcanoes, violence. Don't mess with the lava rocks... Don't collect them. The lava belongs to Pele. Kai was sweating. He was lost in a black desert. He hiked far from the road, leaving it behind. He was alone.

If his family's farm had been under the heiau before the lava came, how had they felt when Pele took their livelihood? How had they understood a goddess that would destroy all they had? But she was also the goddess who formed the land.

He reached the broken heiau. Beside the heiau, lay scattered rocks. David had worked quickly, without care. Kai put his gloves on. He bent down and carefully chose a rock to replace. He fit it into a spot that felt correct.

Let the heiau lead you.

After several hours, the heiau stood repaired and complete. Kai was tired, thirsty, and wet with sweat. He admired his work, and took a long drink from his water bottle.

It was time for his prayer. He had brought his dad's ashes with him, but now that he thought about it, he was worried about leaving them at this site. What if the development that was coming accidentally hurt this heiau? The resort would be built, after all. Sue had promised that she would help make sure the heiau would now be documented and protected by the State of

Hawaii. The resort would not flatten or cover the heiau. It would have to be designed around the heiau. But the complex might be built very close to the altar. The heiau might end up as a sort of small island in the midst of a development's landscaping. No, he would have to find another place for his dad's ashes. After such a long search to reach this place, it felt wrong.

Kai bowed his head, as he'd learned to do in church.

God, hear my prayer.

Thank you for this journey. Thank you for leading me here.

Thank you for the people I met. For what I learned.

For my time on this beautiful island.

For understanding my dad better.

For the time I had with my dad when he was alive.

Thank you for all of it.

He opened his eyes. He wanted to sit and rest for a minute before hiking back to the road. There was a rock outcropping nearby. It was hard to tell if it was the one Sue had hidden behind. Everything looked so different in daylight. He started walking.

A few yards from the heiau, the lava rocks slipped under him. He looked down. The rocks looked just like everywhere else. But the rocks had actually rolled around and had some give. He jumped up and down on the spot. The rocks tumbled down into a depression. He jumped again. They slipped farther into the earth. He bent down. Where the chunks of lava had settled from his weight, there was a smooth round wall, like a giant wormhole.

It was the mouth of a cave. A lava tube.

Quickly, Kai scooped rocks out of the mouth of the cave. There were many. Layers and layers of rocks. He worked with the shovel, and with his gloved hands. Gradually, more and more of the cave wall revealed itself. He was standing in a pit that went straight down as deep as his waist. Then the tube turned and became more horizontal. A tunnel into Pele's heart.

Kai kept digging. Even with the gloves, his hands were raw. It was getting late. He needed to get in before nightfall. Suddenly, he reached the end of the wall of rocks. The cave let out a breath. Cool, dry air passed by like a ghost.

Inside the dim cave was a smooth round chamber filled with bones. With the bones were piles of smooth polished wooden bowls the size of skulls. Small gods and goddesses intricately carved of wood stood guard over the bones. An ancient wooden rattle hung with shark's teeth like dangling chimes, sat near a drum with a carved stick like a magic wand. There was a sharp adze and a battle weapon like a club with a stone tied firmly to the end. There was a ceremonial mask, stone poi pounders, fishhooks, a shell necklace…A large spider clambered over a container of something formed from wood and a gourd. Kai stared. In the furthest shadows, he glimpsed a faded scarlet bundle.

Everything was well preserved. He was afraid to touch anything. His family's treasure. His ancestors had hidden it to keep it safe. To protect their culture.

What should I do?

Kai thought about David's greedy voice as he described the artifacts. He thought about Sue's objective dedication to her museum. He thought about the hordes of visitors who would soon come here to the new luxury resort. He thought about Aunty H and Uncle Mano. He thought about his mom, waiting in California. He thought about relatives he had never known. He thought about the many generations of the dead. What would his ancestors, the ones who hid this, have wanted him to do?

Kai felt a presence behind him. He turned, startled. He imagined someone was there. He recognized her immediately: it was Ulumaheiheiokalani, the handmaiden to Princess Nahi'ena'ena, the oldest ancestor in his family tree. She stood before him, a beautiful young woman. The vision was so vivid it was as if she were real. She had full lips, and brown skin. Her kinky hair was braided and pinned. She looked hot, dressed like a formal Englishwoman in the midst of the heat waves coming off the sweltering lava field. Her long, light-colored gown had wide, old-fashioned sleeves that reached to her wrists. She smiled at him. When she spoke, her voice was soft yet carried authority.

"The seeker becomes the guardian," she said. The
Hawaiian language was smooth and melodious on her tongue, a
cascade of vowels like water flowing from one deep pool to
another.

Kai blinked. She was gone.

When did I learn that phrase in Hawaiian?

Kai remembered his father's voice: "Kai, you're lucky.
Me, I been looking my whole life and I never see an owl..."

He heard his grandma: "People we miss when they die,
people from long time ago, old gods, old places ---- they don't go
away. They stay. Keep us company..."

What had Poppy said? "The heiau will show you..."

Kai thought about the heiau and about how David had
taken it apart.

If I tell anyone about this, other heiaus will be destroyed.
People would go on treasure hunts and wreck the ancient sites.
What Hawaiians still had left of their past would be taken.
Sacred, ancestral places would be disturbed and harmed.

Kai said one more prayer.

God, please keep this safe.

He backed out of the tube, and replaced the rocks that
blocked the entrance, packing them well. When he was done, he
found several large stones a few yards away, the largest he could
move. He carried them and placed them firmly over the hole.
With great effort, he rolled the largest rocks he could move to
the mouth of the cave.

Kai brushed himself off, and took off his work gloves.
He began walking back to the road to hitchhike to Aunty H's
house.

Chapter 61
THE FINAL HEIAU

Kai walked across the driveway. It was a warm night, just like last time he had been to Aunty H's house. He felt apprehensive, but he needed to do this. He tried to find the strength inside himself to explain.

Aunty H opened her door. To his relief, she gave Kai a wide, toothy grin. "Kai! I'm so glad you're back." She hugged him, and in Aunty H's strong arms, he tried to explain about David, Sue, and the heiau.

Uncle Mano appeared in the doorway. He must have been listening. In his hand he held a newspaper.

"Uncle Mano, I'm sorry…" Kai started.

Uncle Mano interrupted him. "Kai!" He held up the local Maui News. The article about Kai was on the front page of the newspaper, with the headline: California Boy Fights for Heiau. "You're famous! We read what you did! I'm sorry, Kai. Good job, man! We feel so proud."

To Kai's surprise, Aunty H's next words cut straight to his heart. "Your dad would have been so proud of you," she said.

Thank you.

Now Mano hugged him, too. "Now you've found the heiau, you got to take care of it. You're the guardian."

"There's something I need to do," Kai said.

*　　　　　*　　　　　*

The next morning, Kai and his aunt and uncle drove through the sugarcane fields and followed the highway uphill past Pukalani. They had both taken the day off work to help him implement his plan. They took a turnoff to the right, the Haleakala Highway.

The landscape changed drastically. The road zigzagged up the mountainside, first through forest, then into high grassland, then through an area of dry shrubs, and finally out into the rocky mountain desert. They had driven up through the layer of white clouds. Above the cloudbank, the sky was clear, blue. They were headed for the house of the sun. Pele's realm.

Uncle Mano had one hand on the steering wheel. With the other hand, he was tapping softly on the dashboard. The sound of his fingers, the gentle bends in the road, it was all very soothing. Kai was happy. He had succeeded in his quest. The only thing he still needed to do was find a safe place to scatter his dad's ashes. Aunty H and Uncle Mano had agreed with him: the Makena heiau was not the right place. Right now, the site was in a state of unrest. He needed to find a more peaceful and stable place for the remains of his dad.

Aunty H was sitting in the passenger's seat. She turned her head around.

"Can you feel it?

"Feel what?"

"Power of the mountain."

Kai thought for a while. He could feel a force beneath him, something powerful that lay below the turning wheels of the car. "Yeah, I guess so." Then he added, "I'm surprised by how quickly the drive has gone by. I thought it was farther up the mountain."

"Yes, fast, it is. Drive to Haleakala, two hours. Ocean to top of mountain, 10,000 feet up."

Wow. Two hours. They were almost to the top. He should start looking for the place.

"Aunty H, do you know of any really special place at the top of Haleakala? A sacred place?"

Aunty H looked over at Uncle Mano. "Mano? Do you know?"

"Yes. I know of a place. We're almost there. It's in a few miles."

A convoy of bicyclists passed by their car. The bicycle ride looked refreshing. Tourists were gliding downhill, effortlessly, enjoying the view of the bank of clouds and the West Maui Mountains.

The noon sun blasted down on the road, creating mirages of heat. The landscape was shrubs and red rock.

At a sharp bend, Uncle Mano turned off the road and parked the car in a small gravel pull-off.

Uncle Mano spoke. "Here it is. Time to get out."

Kai hopped out of the car. "Thanks!"

"We'll come back in an hour. We'll go to the visitor center. Okay?"

"Yes, that sounds great." Kai looked out onto the rocky mountainside. A narrow footpath led out into the desert, disappearing over a crest a few hundred feet away. "So take the trail? How will I know when I get to the place?"

"I think you'll know."

Kai's aunt and uncle drove off. A cloud of dust hung in the air.

Kai began to walk over the crunchy lava ground. He hiked uphill for about two hundred yards.

He came to a ledge. Overlook. He peered down, down into the Haleakala Crater. He could see for miles. Ant-like people stood a couple miles away, a tour group. Off in the distance, Kai could see some silversword bushes, the only sign of life other than hikers.

Triumph swelled inside him. Kai yelled. "Ow!" His voice echoed back. *Ow!* Again. *Ow!* Again, and again. *Ow, ow, ow, ow.* Kai counted seven echoes. He yelled again. Seven more voices shouting back to him from across the emptiness.

This was the place.

The place of the echoes.

Hear the echo of our song.

Kai felt the wooden box in his backpack. *Dad, I found the right place. Thank you for leading me here.*

An hour later, he stood above a pile of rocks. He collected small stones from the surrounding hillside, carefully piling them into the rectangular block. Atop the heiau, the little owl. *The guardian. The protector. The sign.*

His hands were sore. It had been hot work. A small pile of rocks. A new heiau. A final heiau. The final resting place.

He who sees the owl possesses the power

Lono's treasure, power of the ancestors, power to find, power to protect.

Kai was ready.

He opened the box. The white ashes. All that was left on earth of his dad.

Kai scattered the ashes atop the heiau. A dusting of snow. As he spread the ashes, Kai said a prayer.

"God, bless this place. Help those who come here to think about my dad, remember him. Help me and my family to remember the Hawaiian blood that flows through us. Help us to remember our history. Our Hawaiian past. The Hawaii of now. Our future in Hawaii. Help us to remember.

"Dad, I will not forget."

Kai closed the box.

          *   *   *

Kai was back in the car with his aunt and uncle.

"Aunty H, do you have something I could write with?"

"Is a pen good?"

"Sure. Here."

He took the chant out of his pocket.

He eyed the blank space at the top of the chant above the first line. *The line that led to the most recent heiau in the chant, the one Poppy showed me. No, the second newest heiau. After the one I built.*

Kai put the pen point down upon the top of the page. He wrote:

In the house of the sun
In the place of the echoes
Hear the echoes of our song.

Epilogue

Two years later, the Hokoana family was able to establish a family trust fund with proceeds from the AgriCentral Development Corporation's long-term lease of their ancestral lands near La Perouse Bay. Circuit Courts found the family's ownership of the ancestral parcel to be unchallenged due to irregularities in documented land transactions. The family used a combination of Great Mahele records, early church documents, and recorded oral histories including a family chant to prove the location of their ancestral site. Proceeds from the trust fund are divided equally among all living descendants in the Hokoana family. Kai Hokoana, who spearheaded the lawsuit, is currently a student at University of Hawaii, Manoa, and shares a portion of his benefits with his mother, Carla, who recently also moved to Oahu.

The Hokoana heiau site has become a small park, protected by the State Historic Preservation Division of the Department of Land and Natural Resources. It is included in the State's list of archeologically noteworthy sites. The heiau's unique design and its location near the new luxury Kahana Resort make it a popular tourist destination. The area immediately around the heiau, including several rocky outcroppings and two acres of land, was donated by the Hokoana family to be included in the State Park. While no trails cross through the rocks and entering the rocky preserve is not permitted, visitors are welcome to follow the sidewalk around the perimeter during daylight hours, but must remember the rules which apply to all Hawaiian archeological sites.

Bring only prayers,
Leave with only memories.
Ua mau ke ea o ka 'aina I ka pono.
"The life of the land is preserved in righteousness."

Acknowledgements

Thank you to editors Harold Peterson, Holly Turley, and Teri White, and to the readers who offered encouragement and suggestions, including Lynn Christensen, Michelle Donner, Julie Higgins, Tesa Johnson, Beth Jordan, John and Elin Kjekshus, Maureen Mayo, Joanne McDonald, Kathy McDonald, Christine Michaud, Marta Oneill, Jane Ostericher, Laurie Piacitelli, Diane Sahlin, Andy Sharp, and Carol Wilson.

READING GROUP QUESTIONS AND TOPICS FOR DISCUSSION

1] Kai has some unusual experiences that border on the supernatural. He has a vision of an owl made of moonlight, and two heiau visits are interrupted by real animals --- first by an owl at Grandma's heiau, and then by wild boars in Makawao. In addition, he has several life-threatening experiences --- falling off his bike, fighting a monster wave, and swimming with sharks. What do these experiences teach him? Are these extreme experiences necessary parts of his journey?

2] The book is a coming-of-age story about Kai's journey toward an understanding of his Hawaiian heritage. At what point does Kai begin to think of himself as Hawaiian? How does his emerging sense of ethnic identity change the way he thinks and acts?

3] Sue is a complex character. Should she have shared more information with Kai? At what point? Would she still have been able to do her job? Do you think she has Kai's best interests in mind?

4] In some sense, the island of Maui is the main character of the book. Describe Maui as if the island were a person. What was the island's youth like? How did the island come of age? How have Maui's experiences shaped what the island is now?

5] Aunty H, Uncle Mano, Grandma, and Poppy represent Kai's living relatives in the book. Do you think Kai bonds with each of them deeply? Is he ever unfair to any of them? How does he balance his feelings toward his family with his desire to follow the chant?

6] Is Kai's progress toward self-understanding linear (gradual) or meandering? At what points in the book are his actions selfish? When does he make sacrifices, and for whom or what?

7] The progress of the secret object through successive eras in history is one thread of the plot. What do you think the secret object was? Why isn't the object ever revealed to the reader?

8] What characteristics does Kai share with each of his relatives? Which of their beliefs and attitudes does he adopt? Which does he resist?

9] Why is it important for him not only to meet his family and to hear their history but also to travel around the island to the places where they lived? What does he learn from standing where they once stood?

10] The book begins with Kai's father's dying wish that Kai follow the chant. As the book develops, Kai imagines that his father intended him to discover all that he actually finds. How much do you think Kai's Dad knew and intended? What exactly did Dad hope Kai would discover?   How does Kai's feeling that Dad wanted him to follow a certain path help Kai with the grieving process?

11] Do you feel Kai did the right thing with the artifacts? Should they be in a museum? Why or why not?

Meet the Authors: D.W.M. Beck

Wolfgang   Mimmi   Dirk

Dirk Beck was born on Maui. He visited his grandparents on Maui many times. Dirk was a winner of the Pierce County Teen Writing Contest, and is the author of several novels, including The Mars Project. Besides writing fiction, he composes and performs music for the jazz orchestra he organizes and directs, Arletta Sound (www.arlettasound.com). He plays tennis, basketball, and track. Next year, he will be a student at MIT.

Wolfgang Beck composes jazz for Arletta Sound and was selected to compose for the Seattle Symphony (Young Composers Benaroya Hall performance May 2011). He competed in track at the State level and in cross country including at Nike Nationals where he ran the fastest cross country time in the nation for high school sophomores (2011). He won first place in a regional competition for non-native Chinese language public speaking, and also was the Washington State champion for two consecutive years for the Scholastic Challenge Test (2009 and 2010).

Mimmi Beck is their mom. She studied creative writing at Wellesley College and in Columbia University's M.F.A. program. She is the co-author of an illustrated children's book, <u>The Girl Who Loved to Draw Birds</u>. Mimmi worked on Maui and visited the islands many times while her parents taught in the Maui County public school system for more than twenty-five years. When Dirk was born, Mimmi and her mother buried Dirk's umbilical cord in their Maui garden beneath the lemon tree to connect the next generation of their family to the island they loved.

When Mimmi's mom got cancer, her parents left the island for treatment and were never able to move back. This book was written in memory of countless dreamy trips to Grandma's and Grandpa's island home.

Dirk, Wolf and Mimmi co-wrote the book equally, following a careful outline by Dirk of characters, plot, and places. Though this is a work of fiction, the authors tried to include accurate historical, geographic, cultural, and religious information and depictions of historical events. The chant, David's agency, and all characters are entirely fictional.

ENJOY OUR NOVEL?

Like us on Facebook and check out photos of the places Kai visits.
https://www.facebook.com/TheMauiQuest

PLEASE WRITE US A CUSTOMER REVIEW!
http://www.amazon.com/books

The more reviews we get, the more people who are browsing on amazon.com will find our book. To write a review, search for our book at amazon.com/books, then click on the thumbnail image of the book, and then scroll down and click on "write a customer review." You need not have purchased our book on amazon.com to write a review.

Made in the USA
Charleston, SC
09 June 2012